Forever Driven

Forever Bluegrass Series #4

Kathleen Brooks

All Rights Reserved. No part of this book may be used or reproduced in any manner whatsoever without written permission, except in the case of brief quotations embodied in critical articles and reviews.

This book is a work of fiction. The names, characters, places, and incidents are products of the writer's imagination or have been used fictitiously and are not to be construed as real. Any resemblance to persons living or dead, actual events, locale, or organizations is entirely coincidental.

An original work of Kathleen Brooks.
Forever Driven Copyright © 2016 by Kathleen Brooks

Prologue

"What do you think of Riley Davies?"

The dim yellow glow of parking garage lights kept the faces of the people in shadows as they met in secret for one last time before the November elections.

"I think she's going to lose the election to Skites of Lipston."

"Damn." A hand slammed onto the trunk of the car. It didn't matter if it made a sound. It was two in the morning and the state's small capital city of Frankfort was empty.

"You don't think we can control Skites?"

"No. He's a stubborn prosecutor. We've talked to him, and he's not telling us anything about his plans once he's in office. We can only assume he'll be in favor of the highway since it will help Lipston, but I hate assuming anything."

The snort of amusement echoed in the empty garage. "As if Davies will support it? It's her town we're destroying."

"True, but she's just a hick who works on her daddy's farm. What does she know about how politics are played?"

They looked at each other in the darkness.

"You think you can control her?"

"Everyone has a price. And her price will be significantly less than a righteous prosecutor's."

Their white teeth showed in the shadows as they gave each other knowing grins.

"It's going to be hard. She's an Independent."

"It doesn't matter. The polls show she's only a few points behind Skites. And we don't need to worry about the other candidate since those photos came out showing his secretary taking his *dictation*."

"Then we agree. We will have Riley Davies elected next week. Do whatever it takes to get that win." Heads nodded in agreement in the cool night air.

"And you do whatever it takes to keep her in line once she reaches Frankfort."

"Of course. And if she doesn't, well, we'll just have to find a reason to have a special election. It's always so tragic when someone dies in office. However, they do get to lie in state in the Capitol's rotunda."

They parted silently after their plan was made. In the stillness of the fall night, the cars left the garage and drove off in different directions.

Chapter One

Riley Davies ran into the house she and her twin sister, Reagan, shared at the back of their parents' farm. "Crap, crap, crap!" Riley shouted, kicking off her dirty cowboy boots.

"You were supposed to be here an hour ago!" Reagan yelled as she rushed forward with a wet paper towel in one hand and a pants suit in the other.

"I was helping Wyatt deliver a new foal and lost track of time." Riley kicked off her jeans and ran toward her sister, stripping her dirty clothes as she went.

"You're going to be late to your own fundraiser. It's your last week before the election. The whole town is counting on you to win, and you have your arm up a horse?"

"That was Wyatt. I was just helping," she explained about their cousin who worked with his mother, Katelyn, as the town's veterinarians.

Reagan rolled her matching hazel eyes at Riley. They might be fraternal twins, but since Riley announced she was going to run for the State House of Representatives, Reagan decided they needed to look even more different. Riley didn't really care. She hadn't wanted to wear suits either, but Reagan had made her do it. Riley was far more comfortable with her red hair in a sloppy ponytail while wearing jeans, a flannel shirt, and cowboy boots. But Reagan had taken her to the Fluff and Buff, the new hair and nail salon in downtown Keeneston, to get her hair cut and nails painted. Now Riley's red hair was shoulder length with a little curl to it, while Reagan's was still long and straight.

Riley ran the wet paper towel over her face as Reagan held out the pants for her to step into. "Do you have your speech?" Reagan asked as she took the dirty paper towel and handed Riley a light pink blouse.

"I memorized it last night." Riley buttoned her blouse and stepped into the heels Reagan had set in front of her while her sister ran a brush through her hair as if she were an errant child late for church.

"Good, let's go." Reagan had her keys in hand as she dragged her sister from the house.

Riley ran through the talking points in her head. Contrary to what her sister thought, she wasn't taking this election lightly. She was just trying to do two jobs at once. Her competition, Jamie Skites, had given up his law practice to run full-time. He was a family man in his late thirties. Riley was single and twenty-eight. It had been an uphill battle to prove herself, but even so, she was determined to keep working on the farm as much as she could. Politics was not her first love — horses were. But she wasn't going to sit idly by, waiting for Frankfort to pass a budget allowing for a new highway to cut Keeneston in half. If no one else was willing to stand up for the town, then she would.

Her sister sped out of their farm and down the winding country road toward Ashton Farm. Will and Kenna Ashton, friends of Riley's parents, Cy and Gemma, were holding a fundraiser at their farm for her. It was to start in fifteen minutes. She was supposed to get there early, but Will would understand. After all, he ran a horse-racing farm and understood about untimely foaling. They never had their foals at the time you planned.

They drove past the large farmhouse belonging to Will's parents, Betsy and William Ashton. As they approached the white house with fall decorations outside the front door, Riley counted the cars. There were at least fifty parked in the grass and four news vans. Riley needed a good turnout today to have a chance of raising enough money for a first and final run of commercials that week.

She took a deep breath and closed her eyes. She could do this. It was for her town, her farm, and her friends. And if there was one thing Riley was good at, it was never backing down from a fight. This week would be nonstop from here on out. She had tractor pulls and dirt track races to attend. She had a town hall meeting for the women of her district at the Fluff and Buff and rally speeches all over her district. This election all came down to each candidate's ability to gain votes in the other town. If she could take more votes from Lipston than Skites could take from Keeneston, she could win.

"Miss Davies!" a reporter waved and hurried forward with a cameraman trailing close behind. "If you have a moment, we can go live to the newsroom for the noon show. Would you mind taking a minute to answer some questions?"

"You should never do live television," Reagan whispered.

Riley plastered on the gentle smile she had practiced for a month before announcing her decision to run. "Of course. It would be my pleasure."

Reagan shook her head as she moved to stand behind the cameraman in case she needed to "accidentally" knock the camera from his hand.

"Thank you. We're live in thirty seconds." The woman moved Riley into position and Riley tried not to laugh as the reporter went from bubbly to serious. She'd been practicing her looks in the mirror, too.

"Thanks, Dan. I'm here with Riley Davies at Ashton Farm in Keeneston where the race for the district's House of Representatives seat is coming down to the wire." The reporter turned to face Riley, and Riley worked hard to keep her gentle smile on her face as she waited with dread for the first question.

"Your opponent, Mr. Skites, has been hard pressed to state where he stands on some of the local issues. Are you as tightlipped about what you stand for?"

Riley took the softball. "I do have a reputation for being outspoken on issues close to my heart, and nothing is closer to my heart than this community."

"When asked about the proposed highway from Frankfort to Lexington, Mr. Skites said he would reserve judgment until he was elected and talked to the engineers and the governor. What is your stance on this new highway?"

Riley let the smile slide from her face. Instead of focusing on smiling, she was focusing on not getting angry. "As you can imagine, I'm very concerned about this proposed highway. In fact, it will be the first issue I intend to address when I'm elected. First, there's already an interstate that connects the two cities. Second, this highway would destroy Keeneston's beautiful farmland by cutting many of our famous thoroughbred farms in half. But it's not just those farms that are being hurt. Worse yet, it's the small family farms that work hard with every acre of land to supply corn, soybeans, and hay to the citizens of Kentucky and beyond. Those innocent people would be hurt the most as acres and acres of land would be taken from them through eminent domain. The cost of defending their property in court, since none of them want to sell, will be an economic burden to these hardworking people."

"How would you respond to the citizens of Lipston who want this highway since there are rumors of an exit ramp to their historic downtown?"

Riley shook her head. "At the expense of Keeneston, whose historic downtown is being threatened. The highway will be miles from downtown Lipston, while the shops at the end of Main Street in Keeneston are slated to be destroyed so the highway can be run *through* our downtown—all because of an underground waterway they have to build around to satisfy the environmental surveys. I say to the voters in Lipston—if you support this, what's to stop the redesign of the road to run through your downtown? What's to stop Frankfort from deciding to take some of your land, houses, and businesses to build an unnecessary road? Keeneston has stood by Lipston when they had to rebuild from a tornado, and I intend to stand by Lipston again to make sure no road will ever cut either of our towns in half."

"I guess it will be up to the voters to decide. Thank you for talking with us today, and good luck on the final week of campaigning. Back to you at the studio, Dan." The red light on the camera turned off and the reporter tossed the microphone to the cameraman. "Thanks for the interview, Miss Davies."

"Anytime." Riley placed the smile back on her face and started for the house. A small group of people came up to her to shake hands. "How are you doing?" Riley asked as she saw her sister go inside to announce that Riley had arrived.

"Great interview, Miss Davies." Riley shook the older gentleman's leathered hand. It was obvious by the calluses on his hands that he worked outdoors a lot. He was probably a farmer, maybe even one affected by the proposed highway.

"Thank you—"

"LeeRoy, ma'am. I'm sorry to stop you here, but we have to get back to work. I just wanted to give you some money the other workers and I raised to support your campaign."

Riley took the check without looking at it and shook his hand. The people with him took pictures and looked so excited they could bust. "Thank you so much, LeeRoy. Every penny matters during this last week. I hope I won't let you down."

"You could never do that, ma'am. It was a pleasure meeting you, and I sure hope you win."

LeeRoy stepped back as the people with him hurried forward to pose for pictures with Riley before quickly waving their goodbyes and shouting their best wishes. Neely Grace Rooney stood in all her elegance at the open door, watching. Neely Grace and her husband, Henry, were Keeneston's defense lawyers and served as Riley's counsel for the election. Neely Grace was also her treasurer, and Henry advised her on any potential legal trip-ups in the issues being debated.

"You're late," Neely Grace said in her perfect lawyer voice.

"I was giving an interview and then had some supporters stop with a donation check before going back to work." Riley handed the check to Neely Grace who glanced down at it quickly.

"Jeez, this is $50,000. Who is Hager, Inc.?"

Riley froze. "Seriously, $50,000? That's almost our entire fundraising goal."

"I know, but who is he?"

"I think he's a farmer. He looked like one, and he said he and the rest of the employees raised that for me. I met some of the other employees and they said they were glad to help out."

Neely Grace's brow creased as she thought. "I wonder if this is one of the accounts from the big farming business that was just built in Keeneston near Lipston? You know, the one Miles and Morgan fought against but our mayor gave a tax break to anyway?"

Riley shook her head. "That's Luttrell Food Industries. Although, this could be one of the farms they acquired. Just don't tell my aunt and uncle I took their money. Uncle Miles hates that place and its CEO."

"You would, too, if your job was to help the small

town farmers out, and in comes a corporation that has farms all over the country."

Riley nodded. She understood. Miles and Morgan had vented about it plenty at the family dinners out at her grandparents' farm. The mayor was just happy she brought jobs to the town and didn't really care how she did it. "Well, are they ready for me? It's been a great start so far. Let's hope we can meet our goal today, and then I can worry more about gaining voters instead of asking for money."

Riley walked into the House and was met with cheers. She shook hands, gave her speech, and held a question-and-answer session. By the end of it, she had raised enough money to get her platform out via television ads. She just hoped the people of Lipston liked her more than some of the people of Keeneston liked Skites.

Chapter Two

"Can I buy you a drink, babe?" Matt asked as he tossed back a vodka soda. The woman who had approached him at the bar had fake red hair, a fake black leather dress that barely covered her boobs and ass, and track marks up her arms. She would have been pretty if she weren't so emaciated from prolonged drug abuse.

For two months, Matt had been coming to this small-town bar in Eastern Kentucky four nights a week after getting off work. He was seen as a regular now. He told them he had to drive a lot between their town and Lexington for contracting work. As long as he paid his tab, no one cared what that work was. They all assumed it was on the new highway being built and didn't ask questions. Mostly because they didn't want to answer any questions he had. So he had sat by himself and drank night after night.

"You can buy me a drink to start with and then buy a little more later. What's your name?" she asked in a seductive voice. "A shot of gin. And leave the bottle," she instructed the bartender.

Matt didn't bother raising an eyebrow at the command to leave the bottle. She probably thought he was loaded compared to the men around here with barely two nickels to rub together. Unemployment was high but the highway had hired a lot of the men who could manage to stay clean—which meant none of the men in that room.

"Matt Wilson," Matt told her as he shoved back the hair he'd been growing out the past few months. He'd also opted to dye his hair raven black, getting rid of the normally dark blond locks.

"Are you with the highway?" she asked after downing her first shot.

"Mmm." Matt said before tapping his glass and asking for a refill of his own.

"I bet that's hard work, but it must be nice to have all that cash in your pocket. Or are you just thinking about buying a little sumpin' sumpin' now instead of later?"

Matt's lips tipped up at her hint. It seemed she was using prostitution as a way to pay for her drugs and wasn't approaching him just for his devilish good looks.

"Oh, I'm thinking about it, babe. Let me have a couple of drinks first. I'm so tired from working, and I'm out of my regular pick-me-up."

"Aren't you worried about losing your job?" she asked, picking up on his need of drugs.

"Nah. I have my cousin pissin' in the cup for me."

"Well, then, maybe if you scratch my back, I can scratch yours."

"What's your name, babe?" Matt asked as the bartender handed him another drink.

"Crystal," she winked, and she tossed back another shot.

"Funny, since that is exactly what I'm looking for. I

guess I get two kinds of crystal tonight. If you can scratch my back, that is."

"I can scratch your back and more. My dealer is out back. If you buy me a little ice, we can get high together and screw each other's brains out."

Matt took his time looking her over with appreciation. "I may want a steady hookup while I'm working this job. Is your dealer just a peddler or does he have access to quantity?"

"He just has what's on him, but he can get you more if you have the money."

Matt winked at her. "Of course I have the money. I have a job, don't I? It will be easier for me to get it here instead of having to drive back to Lexington. Levi won't be happy, but he'll get over it."

Crystal froze. "Levi is your dealer?"

"Yeah, is that a problem?"

"No, I'm sure Jared will love taking business away from Levi. They're rivals. They both grew up here and were partners in a pot operation, but then Levi said he wanted to go corner the drug market in the big city. Jared wanted to stay here. They've been competing every since. Come outside with me to meet my dealer, Eddie. He can take you to Jared. But first, let's do a hit. Then we can see Jared, and you can get more so we can really party tonight." Crystal tossed back another shot and tried not to stare as Matt pulled out a wallet flush with cash. He tossed some on the bar, and then Crystal was on him.

Her hands ran over his wide shoulders and down his rippled abs as she tried to get him to kiss her while they were walking out the back door of the bar. Her hands dipped to cup his package and then reached around to squeeze his ass. Either she wanted him here and now, or she was checking him for a wire. He used to wear those back in the day, but this year had changed him. He wasn't the squeaky-clean Kentucky state trooper anymore.

Matt picked her up, and her legs wrapped around his hips. He pushed her hard against the wall and shoved his hips against her as her dress rode up. "Or do you just want to do this now? You're getting me all worked up, babe."

"It's so much more intense when we're high. Come on, let's hurry up. I need a hit bad." She pushed against his chest, and Matt let her slide down his body. She stroked him through his pants, and with a giggle, left him standing there as she hurried out the back door.

Matt followed and was met with three men sitting on old drink crates, getting high and drinking straight from a vodka bottle. They all looked to be in their early twenties, but the one in the middle seemed to be the leader. The other two looked to him when Matt approached.

"You Eddie?" Matt asked.

"What's it to you?" the cocky little shit asked.

"Eddie, he needs a hit, and he's buying one for me, too." Crystal practically danced in place with the excitement of knowing she was going to get a hit soon. Her eyes never left the bag sitting at Eddie's feet.

"Did you manage to get your pea brain off a hit long enough to check him?" Eddie spat.

Crystal looked to the ground and nodded. "He's clear, and he usually gets his drugs from Levi." Her head popped up with excitement at telling Eddie the news.

Eddie's lips pursed and flattened to a look of disbelief.

"Yeah, right. Prove it."

Matt looked at him for a second and then started patting his back pockets. He pulled out the small zipped case and opened it. He pushed aside the needles and held up the bag with Levi's sticker on it.

Eddie grabbed it and stared. "Why do you want to switch dealers?"

"I'm working on the highway, and I'm tired of driving back and forth to Lexington to get it," Matt shrugged. "I like to buy in bulk. My buddies and I go through a lot on the weekends. But if you don't want the money, then I'll just go back up to Lexington."

"Nah, I can hook you up. What do you need?" Eddie asked as he opened his bag.

"I need a pound," Matt said and heard Crystal practically salivating.

Eddie's head shot up. "You got that money hidden on you?"

"No, but I can get it. The question is, can you?"

Eddie's lips slowly parted into a sinister smile. "I can get it."

"Jared has it," Crystal blurted.

Eddie stood up slowly and walked toward Crystal. She knew what was coming. She ducked her head but the slap still connected with her cheek. Matt ignored them and sighed out loud. "So, am I going to get high tonight or what?" he asked.

"I'll sell you a gram. It's $500." Eddie moved back to his bag and pulled out a baggie full of crystals.

"Bullshit. I'll give you $300 and that's that. If you think you can gouge me with a higher price, I'll stick with Levi."

Eddie nodded approvingly. "You know your drugs."

"I buy enough to know how much they cost." Matt pulled out his wallet and handed $300 to Eddie, who in turn handed him the baggie. "When can I see Jared?"

"Text me your number, and I'll let you know."

Matt pulled out his phone, entered the number Eddie gave him, and sent the text. "I'll need it by this weekend," he told Eddie before grabbing Crystal. "Come on, babe, it's time to party."

Matt watched as Crystal stuck the needle into her arm. She slowly pushed the plunger down as the drugs entered her bloodstream. With a sigh of pleasure and relief, Crystal pulled the needle from her arm and placed it back in her purse. Her body relaxed after its craving had been fed. She held the spoon out to him and he took it. "I'm going to run to the bathroom. Then I'll be ready to start our party."

Matt nodded and took out a crystal and placed it on the spoon. He held it over the flame and waited for it to melt. When Crystal came out of the bathroom, Matt was pulling the now empty needle from his arm.

Matt blinked. "Damn, this stuff is strong."

"Jared likes his ice to be as pure as possible." Crystal ran her hands down his arms as she straddled him in the chair.

"Tell me more about Eddie and Jared. Can they be trusted? How do I know they won't screw me over?"

"Jared likes to get to know his regulars. He's paranoid about being busted or of Levi sending someone in to steal from him. So, he'll want to meet with you first."

Matt laughed.

Crystal looked confused. "What's so funny?"

"The fact that I have to be interviewed by a dealer. Do I have to bring my résumé?"

Crystal giggled. "No, but Eddie will be passing along all your information, so a background check will be run before you're even allowed to meet with him. While we locals know his base of operations, most outsiders aren't permitted to know."

"What should I know before I meet with him?"

"He likes to be one of the people. He pretends to be just one of the guys, but you better show respect or you'll piss him off. Eddie will introduce you, but after that point he'll only be there to handle the payment and hand off if an agreement is made."

"Jared doesn't like to get his hands dirty?"

"Nah, he's a businessman only now. He's got a family to think about and his standing in the community. He takes this shit seriously. He's even in the PTA."

Matt laughed. "I know those types. I bet he doesn't even make the stuff on his property. Farms it all out so no one can bust him. That's smart."

Crystal nodded. "I met the farmer he uses once. It's all under his control, but Jared oversees it."

"I bet that farmer has a cool name like Smalls or Doc. They all do."

Crystal giggled as she worked at pulling off his shirt. "How did you know that? His is Tubbo."

"Is he super skinny?" Matt teased.

"No, this time the name fits. But enough talking."

"How much to move this to the next level, babe?"

"Five hundred."

Matt whistled. "I don't have that much cash on me now. I spent it all on this," he held up the baggie of drugs and shook it.

Crystal looked at the bag with greed in her eyes. "Maybe we could work out an exchange."

"What kind of deal are we talking about?" Matt asked.

Crystal leaned forward and whispered in his ear. Matt grinned as she gently bit his neck before pulling back.

"I think I can make that work." Matt handed her the baggie of drugs. While Crystal stood up and placed the baggie in her purse Matt poured two shots of gin into the motel's dirty glasses.

When he turned around, Crystal was unzipping her dress. "Let's have a drink to celebrate, babe."

Crystal tossed back the drink and dropped her dress on the floor. She sent him a wink and climbed onto the bed and promptly passed out.

Matt let out a sigh and strode to the adjoining door. He knocked, and it swung open. Two scruffy-looking men in ripped jeans and dirty sweatshirts stood there.

"What have you found out?" Matt asked as he pushed his way into their room.

"I'm running Tubbo's name through our drug database for a hit," DEA Agent Tate told him.

"And I'm pulling up all the members of the PTA for the elementary schools in the county along with trying to find an old yearbook. We know how old Levi was from when you arrested him, so we know around the time to look for anyone named Jared," DEA Agent Forgy told him as he went over to look at his computer.

The drug undercover Kentucky State Trooper Matt Walz put in Crystal's drink would have her out cold for the rest of the night. Tomorrow, she would wake up naked in a messed-up bed with no memories. Matt would lead her to think she'd fulfilled her deal with him. She would drive home and sometime in the next day or two, be pulled over by a K-9 officer for a minor traffic violation. The K-9 would indicate the scent of drugs, and the crystal meth would be recovered. She had enough to last her three more days at least. She would be ordered to rehabilitation, and his cover would stay intact. No one would associate him with her arrest in the slightest.

Matt stumbled past his partners and fell onto the disgusting couch with unidentified stains on it. "Wake me in six hours."

Tate and Forgy grunted their response and turned on the news. As Matt fell asleep, the reporter was talking about the following day's election. Images of an athletically built, natural redhead found a way into his dreams—one he'd walked away from almost a year ago in order to stay undercover.

Chapter Three

Riley had never been so exhausted. She was pretty sure she'd stopped at every retirement home, shopping center, antique mall, tractor pull, and farm in her district. She had spoken passionately about what Small Town, USA, stood for and how she wanted to represent their interests in Frankfort. She'd answered countless questions about being single, as if not being married somehow made her less qualified to lead. She'd talked about her college degree and how her time managing her father's farm had prepared her to better understand the concerns of her constituents. And finally, that morning, she had headed to Keeneston High School to vote.

"Have they started to come back with any numbers yet?" her mother, Gemma, asked as she hurried into the living room with a steaming pot of coffee.

"Not yet," her father, Cy, called out, and her mother went around filling Riley's campaign team's coffee mugs. Campaign team was a fancy term her sister had thought of. Riley's team was really made up of her enormous family and all of her friends. The Rose Sisters, the trio of elderly sisters closing in on 100 years old, had brought brownies. Others had brought drinks, chips, and a bottle . . . or five, of bourbon.

Riley took a seat on the couch next to her younger twin brothers, Porter and Parker. Her sister stood behind her and anxiously began pacing. "The polls are closed, why aren't they releasing the results yet?" Reagan asked for the tenth time.

"Rae, they closed two minutes ago," twenty-one-year-old Parker said for the tenth time.

"Shhh! Here they come!" Riley's best friend and cousin, Layne, called out as she turned the television volume up.

"Well, Dan," the same perky blonde television reporter who had interviewed Riley last week said from outside Keeneston High School. "The first numbers are coming in on the hotly contested House race out of Keeneston and Lipston. With one percent reporting in, it's almost a dead heat at 127 to 123 votes. Right now, Jamie Skites has a slight lead over Riley Davies, but with results like these, you can bet both camps will be up until every vote has been counted."

Riley groaned. It was going to be a very long night.

"Riley, wake up," Porter said as he jostled her awake. Riley bolted upright and wiped her hand over her face. Reagan was still pacing somewhere behind her. Her mother was still refilling coffee cups. However, there were only four bottles of bourbon left.

"What is it?" Riley asked as she blinked the sleep from her eyes.

"They're ready to announce a winner," Reagan said with barely controlled anxiety.

Riley leaned forward and watched Dan and his hairsprayed helmet of hair look over the card he was just given. She didn't think she took a breath as he looked seriously into the camera.

"With one hundred percent of the votes counted, we can announce Riley Davies as the winner."

Riley didn't hear how much she had won by. She stared at the graphics on the television showing her face with the official checkmark next to it in disbelief. She had done it! But with that realization, she also had another. It was now up to her to protect her town.

"Dude, wake your ass up."

Matt rolled over on the smelly couch and looked at Tate. "Is it six already?" he asked, a little pissed off. He was in the middle of a dream where Riley Davies was stripping out of her dress and standing naked before him. Too bad it was only a dream, since the reality was that she didn't think of him that way.

"Nah, it's only three, but you just got a text from Eddie. He says Jared wants to meet. Now."

Matt sat up slowly and rested his elbows on his knees and read the text before sending his response. The phone vibrated a second later.

"Eddie is outside the motel now." Matt cursed as he jumped up from the couch and headed through Tate's dark room toward his own room. "You know I can't have anything on me for command to listen to. You'll have to be my backup."

Matt didn't even need to say it since Tate and Forgy

were already strapping on bulletproof vests and sliding their badges onto their waistbands. In the darkness of the room, lit only by the glow of the television, the two agents were already checking weapons and slipping out the back door to their unmarked beat-up truck.

Matt kicked off his shoes, stripped out of his shirt, and unbuttoned his jeans before flipping the light to his room on. Matt nodded at Eddie and opened the door just enough for Eddie to see Crystal lying naked on the bed and to see Matt zipping his pants up.

Eddie smirked. "Wild night?"

"You know it."

"You have that money on you yet?"

"Why?"

"Jared isn't going to give you the goods without being paid. You said you wanted it. I thought you were serious about it," Eddie challenged.

"No problem. Give me one minute." Matt closed the door on an incredulous Eddie. He guessed most people were afraid of him, but not Matt. He was just an underling. Matt popped off the air vent and pulled out a bag of cash. He rustled through it to find the GPS tracker and tossed it under the door to Tate's room. Eddie was trying to hide it behind his back, but Matt had seen the small device used to check for bugs and trackers in his hand.

Matt opened the door as he buttoned up his shirt. With the duffle bag of cash over his shoulder, he declared, "Okay. Let's do this."

"Not so fast. I'll take the bag," Eddie demanded and held out his hand.

Matt shook his head. "I don't think so. And run off

with my money?"

"I need to check it."

"Then check it while I hold onto it. I'm not dumb enough to hand over ten grand just to have you steal it."

Eddie was turning red. It was likely he had never been questioned before. He was used to his own underlings following every order he gave. "Fine. Hold it out for me."

Matt held the bag out but kept a tight grip on it as Eddie unzipped it and looked around the inside before running his tracker around the bag. With a nod of his head, one of the underlings started to pat Matt down before taking the tracker and running it over Matt's body.

"Are we good yet, or do you want to play with my balls, too?" Matt said with a hint of boredom to his voice.

"We're good. Let's go."

Matt followed Eddie to his truck and got in. He didn't look around for Tate or Forgy as Eddie drove through the small town, around curving mountains, and into a small subdivision of houses that were larger than most around town. They had expansive yards and American flags on porches decorated with pots of mums. Minivans and a couple of luxury sedans were parked in driveways. Swing sets were in the backyards and bikes were tossed on the sidewalks.

"This is where Jared lives? The big bad drug dealer?" Matt laughed incredulously.

"This is the best neighborhood in the entire county. He has a wife and kids to think about. Besides, what better way to keep an eye out than a freaking neighborhood watch?" Eddie grinned as if this were the best idea in the world.

Matt shook his head as they pulled into a driveway in front of a pretty two-story tan house with a little red wagon in the front yard and kids' toys stacked on the porch. It had a black front door, black shutters, and flower baskets under the windows. Eddie parked the car behind a minivan with five stick figures on the back window and a massive tricked-out black Ford truck. Matt slowly got out of Eddie's car. He looked around at the family-friendly neighborhood and wondered if the residents knew what went on at this house.

A light shone through a door on the side of the house that led into the garage. A pretty yellow curtain covered the window in the upper half of the door with different-sized handprints on it. The small date under the handprints showed it to be a Christmas present from the kids. Eddie pushed a button and the door unlocked. With a quick glance, Matt saw the house had a high-tech security system, including a doorbell to the garage with a night vision camera built into it.

Eddie walked into the converted garage and Matt followed. He didn't hide the fact that he was curious about his surroundings. Most people would be if they walked into the second-biggest drug dealer's house in the state. The garage was impeccable. The floor had nice glossy epoxy on it that resembled white and gray marble. Two large rectangular worktables with stainless steel tops sat in the middle of the room. Behind them, along the entire length of the wall, were custom storage shelves from floor to ceiling. Pretty canvas storage baskets of all sizes and colors filled the shelves. They had initials and names embroidered on them as if they stored nothing more than little Timmy's old clothes.

Matt turned to his left. There was a sitting area with old leather furniture facing a television hanging on the wall. Coffee tables had magazines ranging from sports and parenting to gardening and gourmet cooking on them. Behind the sitting area, close to the entrance to the house, was another stainless steel table. This one was shorter and sitting behind it in a leather chair was Jared.

You expect drug dealers to look a certain way, but Matt had discovered that wasn't always true. Underlings, yeah, they looked a certain way. But the actual brain behind the operation of illegal drugs was not your average street criminal. He, or she, was smart and focused on business. They were often part of the community. They were members of a church, the president of the PTA, and local business owners who coached Little League. And Jared fit the bill just as Levi had. When Matt busted Levi, it was after he'd finished volunteering at the soup kitchen with his son's Boy Scout troop.

Jared had pictures of his family lining the wall behind him. Pottery made by his children sat on his desk. He was in his late thirties. Styled hair, khakis, and not a single piercing or tattoo in sight. He was your average suburban father.

"So you're Levi's client," Jared said with a smile and stood up to shake Matt's hand as if they were at a bank meeting instead of a drug deal.

"That's me. I'm Matt Wilson." Matt shook his hand and looked around. "Your kids are into soccer?"

"Yes. They love it. Every Saturday morning at eight we're at the fields. Do Levi's kids play soccer?"

Matt shook his head. "Basketball and ballet."

"Eddie said you were looking to leave Levi," Jared said as if Matt were simply looking to change brokers.

"I'm down here for the next year working on this highway. I'm getting tired of driving back and forth. In full disclosure, when I move back to Lexington, I'll probably switch back. You know, it's a matter of convenience."

Jared nodded. "I can understand that. What's your budget while you're here?"

"Ten grand a month."

Jared's eyes widened. "You have that kind of money?"

"Nah, man. I have friends I go in on it with," Matt laughed. "Damn, I'd be dead in under a month if it were just me."

"Is this what you've been buying from Levi?"

"Yup. Varies on our employment, of course. But lately, I've held some pretty steady jobs. A year working in Versailles, a year on a project in downtown Lexington, and now another potential year or two on this highway job."

"Why you?" Jared asked as he motioned for Matt to take a seat in the sitting area.

"Why me what?" Matt sat down and Jared sat in a chair near him.

"Why are you the handler?"

"Oh, because I ain't married. Wife and kids get nosy. We learned that after Carlos got married, and his wife found the stash when she was spring cleaning."

"Unless you have a very understanding wife like I'm blessed with. She decorated my office for me," Jared said with pride.

"Nice." Matt took the opportunity to look around

again. "I like the basket organizer thingies. I had a girlfriend once who had those in her closet for all her laundry."

"These hold things more valuable than laundry. Now, Eddie said you wanted a pound."

"That's right." Matt knew the deal was coming.

"Then you have a problem. I normally charge $15,000 for a pound."

"Then you're overcharging," Matt said immediately before pausing. "No disrespect."

Jared grinned. "And you're either smarter or dumber than most of my clients. They wouldn't dare question my price."

Matt held up his hands. "Like I said, no disrespect, but they're the stupid ones. I can get a pound from Levi for ten grand. If I bother to drive a little farther east, I can get it for eight. But since I heard your product was purer, I thought I'd go with you."

That caught Jared's attention. "Who would you go to?"

"One of my buddies has a contact in Beattyville."

Jared shook his head in amusement. "You don't want to be buying from Skunk. He cuts his drugs with antifreeze. Why do you think it's so cheap?"

Matt shrugged. "We all know bigger cities have bigger price tags. Like I said, I want to do business with you. However, I'm not going to be taken advantage of either. Ten grand is fair." Matt stood up and held out his hand. "Let me know if we have a deal. Eddie knows how to reach me."

Jared waved him away. "Sit. We have a deal. Just don't tell anyone the price or more of my clients will demand the lower price. And you have no idea how expensive it is to put three children through private school."

"Then let me make a contribution to their education." Matt tossed the bag to Jared who unzipped it and dumped the cash on the table before heading over to the shelves. He pulled out a pale pink container from the second shelf from the top. The initials MLB were embroidered on it in script. Meth, one pound. That was Matt's guess.

Matt watched as Jared took out a pink plastic bag of crystal meth, walked it over to a worktable, and pulled out a scale. Matt joined him and looked down at the scale reading 16.03 ounces. "Are we good?"

Matt smiled. "We sure are. I like the pink."

Jared set the scale back. "My wife again. She loves to color-coordinate."

"I look forward to trying it out this weekend and doing business with you in the future." Matt put the drugs in the bag he'd brought the cash in and zipped it up.

"Just let Eddie know when you need a hookup and we'll schedule an appointment. I'm the only one authorized to handle bulk orders. Eddie can handle the rest."

Jared held out his hand and Matt shook it. Eddie led him out of the garage and back into the car. Eddie talked basketball and girls until they made it back to the motel. Matt entered the room to find Crystal still passed out and Tate leaning against the open adjoining door.

"Since we didn't hear gunfire, I assume it went well."

Matt tossed him the bag and when Tate opened it, he let out a low whistle and showed it to Forgy. "His wife color-coordinates the drug packaging to the embroidered fancy baskets they're stored in," Matt told them.

Forgy looked up quickly. "The wife is part of the operation?"

"At least the decorator. It could be more."

"Okay. Let's hold off on the bust. We need to keep your cover anyway. We need to see what the higher-ups say about his wife. What's your feel on the situation?"

"I think they're partners. He referenced her more than any other dealer I've taken down," Matt told them.

"I'll get a background on her and see if anything pops out," Tate said as he moved to his computer. "In the meantime, stick tight."

Matt groaned. "Damn. This means I actually have to work on the highway now."

"Yup," Forgy grinned. "You know they will be checking you out. Good thing we have your cover all set up. You report to work at six in the morning."

Matt looked at his watch. "You mean in two and a half hours."

"Have fun at your first day of work, honey," Tate taunted as he pushed Matt out of their room and closed the adjoining door.

Chapter Four

Four months later . . .

Riley took a deep breath and walked into the large beaux-arts-style Capitol. Designed with French influence, the granite and marble building was stunning. Every time she came to work at the Capitol, she promised that would be the day she saved Keeneston. She had been sworn in two months ago after the New Year and had made it known immediately that she was going to fight this highway with everything she had. Kentucky's legislative session would be over in another month, and she felt the pressure weighing her down with each passing day.

  Today her vote was required in the House chambers on a dog-fighting bill, and then she was going to lock herself in her office and continue following the paper trail she had slowly been uncovering. If her instincts were right, this road issue went a lot deeper than she had first thought. It had started when the governor had proposed the new highway in her road budget plan. While she didn't say where she had gotten the idea, and considering the new governor was from Bowling Green, which was nowhere near Frankfort nor Lexington, it didn't take a genius to know someone lobbied her for the highway. Riley was just having trouble finding out who was really behind the push for the highway.

The governor wasn't talking, and Riley was sure this highway was either part of a political trade or possibly a bribe from a donor. Riley had combed the donor records. While many of the major donors were in road construction, none stood out from the pack. This left her thinking it was a political favor. Even so, it was risky. The House Appropriations Committee got the budget first and right now everyone and their third cousins were making amendments to it—Riley included. She was lobbying committee members to make an amendment to strike down the new highway.

Then the budget would go to the Senate Transportation Committee where, again, everyone and their sister's hairdresser's third grade teacher's brother would change it so the money went to their counties, to their roads, and to their constituents who needed highway jobs. Riley was also preparing for what came after. There would be three very different budgets. The governor's, the House's, and the Senate's. It would come down to the House and Senate being locked in a room, hashing out deals to come to one final copy of a budget that the governor would sign. And Riley was determined that final budget wouldn't provide funding for the new highway designed to destroy Keeneston.

Riley slipped in the side door and shook off the cold winter breeze. Spring was near but winter wasn't giving up the fight easily. "Morning, DeAndre," Riley smiled to the guard who alternated between the Capitol building and the annex where her office was. With her long hours in Frankfort, she had gotten to know most of the guards as well as the other Capitol staff.

"Morning, Riley. Watch out, it's going to be a doozy today."

Riley groaned. DeAndre Drews knew everything that went on around the Capitol. He was like John Wolfe back in Keeneston, except he was twenty-three instead of ninety-something, six-foot instead of a shrinking five-nine, handsome with rippled muscles and smooth black skin instead of John's potbellied and sagging translucent skin that came when you passed ninety years.

"What have you heard?" Riley asked in a whisper as she looked around to see if anyone was listening. The Capitol had ears that would make Keeneston's grapevine look nonexistent.

"I heard that Wilkerson submitted his estimate for the proposed highway to go through Keeneston. There's a secret meeting during the vote today to talk about the highway."

Riley cursed and DeAndre chuckled. Earl Wilkerson was the state-contracted engineer who estimated the price of a job and secretly submitted it to the committee. No one knew Earl's estimate—it was sealed. And the contractors would submit sealed bids as well. When the project passed and the budget committee set their price, the bids were all opened at once and compared to Earl's estimate. Lowest bid would win.

"Another House meeting?"

DeAndre nodded. "I've heard that only some members of the House committee even know about it, and this particular meeting includes not only your mentor, but also the Speaker of the House, the Senate Majority Leader, Gregory Peel, and a handful of reps and senators."

"Son of a . . . Senator Peel," Riley smiled as the man in question walked through the door. Senator Peel was from Eastern Kentucky. He was the head of the Senate Transportation Committee and would be very influential in whether the highway went through or not. "How are things in Lumpur?" In Kentucky, the town name was pronounced *lump-her*. Many Kentucky towns had unique pronunciations for their town names. The senator was what you expected for a politician—middle-aged white guy with an overinflated ego. Since he had a reputation for sleeping with every hot secretary, intern, and aide he could, he was called the senator from Humpher behind his back.

Senator Peel eyed her questioningly. The last time they were together, Riley almost jumped across the table and strangled him. Instead, she's just said, "Bless your heart" before politely stating the reasons he was wrong.

"Going well. How is your crusade to stop progress?"

Instead of resorting to violence, Riley pasted on a fake smile. "By progress you mean destroying a historic town? I saw the updated design. It calls for not only the last two buildings on Main Street being destroyed, but all the way to the bank so that a large retaining wall can be built blocking the highway from the town. That includes a law office, a world-famous fashion house, an antique store, and, well, *half of a town*."

Peel nodded his graying hair. "I saw that. It makes sense. Since your town is so against the project now, they won't have to see it. The retaining wall also enhances your town by cutting down on noise pollution from the highway."

"You think this is funny?" Riley asked with steel in her voice as Peel chuckled. "I guess it was a good thing I got the votes to ban cockfighting and am attaching it to the dog-fighting bill this morning. Reminds me . . . Lumpur is the 'capital' of animal fighting, isn't it?"

Peel's face reddened as he stepped into Riley's space in an act of intimidation. Too bad for him it didn't work. "You mess with my town, and I'll make sure there's nothing left of Keeneston, little lady."

"You haven't even begun to see how I intend to mess with you, old man. And you certainly won't enjoy it like you do with your secretary."

A snarl formed on Peel's lips as he hissed out in anger. "You don't stay in office for twenty-five years without knowing how to play the game. You're way out of your league. You've been warned. Step back and let the big dogs handle things. Vote how you're told or bad things will happen, little lady."

Riley let him push past her although she made sure her elbow jammed him in his soft midsection on the way by. "Oh, Senator!" Riley called out sweetly to his back. "Give your wife my best."

"Damn, girl." DeAndre swore. "Have you thought about having a security detail? After today, you have an even bigger target on your back."

"I came here to do what's right, not play games. If they don't like it, fine. I'm a big girl and I can definitely handle myself. Thanks for the heads-up on today's meeting. I'll talk to Angela and see what I can find out."

"Only for you," DeAndre called out.

It could be true, but Riley didn't know how many people DeAndre kept in the loop. They had hit it off on the day she was sworn in. A random meeting in the annex cafeteria turned into friendship, and now they saw each other almost every day. She didn't ask how he knew what he knew, and he didn't ask how she knew as much as she did about boxing. DeAndre was an amateur boxer in his private time.

Riley passed under the large rotunda painted in ivory, blues, and pinks and climbed the gray and white marble staircase to the third floor. She headed for the House chambers at one end of the building, opposite from the Senate. When the House and Senate let out at the same time, they look across the multiple marble staircases at each other.

The large doors were open, and Riley stepped onto the blue carpet. The room had a massive windowed ceiling that allowed light in. The walls were salmon-colored marble and the Speaker of the House sat front and center, facing all the reps' desks.

Riley found her mentor talking with a group of women and headed toward them. Angela Cobb was the head of the House Appropriations Committee and the head of the CWKY—Congressional Women of Kentucky Group. CWKY was a nonpartisan mentor group that matched up new congresswomen with women who were already in office.

When Riley won the election, Angela invited her to a group luncheon. There Riley met the tall, thin woman with fading black hair always pulled into a bun. She was in her early fifties and from Cairo, Kentucky. And since Kentuckians never pronounced cities the conventional way, it was pronounced Kay-ro, like the syrup. Riley was instantly drawn to Angela's steel and determination to do what was right, not necessarily what was popular. Over the course of a few meetings, Riley had found herself asking Angela for advice and they'd formed a mentor/mentee relationship.

Angela's brown eyes locked onto Riley's as she gave her a smile from across the room. Representatives were coming in as they prepared to vote. Interns were running errands, and groups of people were clumped together around the room, talking. "Just the woman I wanted to see. Excuse me, ladies. I look forward to seeing you at lunch today."

Riley stopped ten feet from the group, and Angela made her way toward her. Reagan had made sure Riley was dressed for success, but Angela was the real deal. Black fitted tea-length suit with a white blouse and colorful chunky jewelry that somehow made her look hip for her age while commanding respect.

Riley smiled at her mentor as she approached. "Thanks. I just heard through the grapevine you have an important meeting after the vote."

Angela let out an amused laugh that wasn't loud enough to draw too much attention. "I swear, how do you know everything? I've been here almost twenty years, and you already have a better network of spies than I do."

"A girl never reveals her secrets," Riley teased.

"Well, I'm glad I got a word with you alone. First I was

going to tell you about the meeting, but second, I wanted to warn you about Marge. She was cozied up to me to find out how I was going to vote on the budget. I thought she was on our side with the highway proposal, but I'm afraid even I make mistakes. She's entered an amendment that would support the highway with the addition of an exit ramp to the Milan Frontier Museum."

Riley whispered a curse, and Angela nodded in agreement. Milan, like all Kentucky cities named after foreign towns or countries, was pronounced differently than you would expect. Versailles, Kentucky, wasn't pronounced like the city in France, but like Ver-sales. Following suit, Milan was nothing like the beautiful town in Italy, but Ma-lawn.

Milan had an old fort from the time when pioneers hadn't made it any farther into what would become Kentucky. The fort had been turned into a museum where people wore period dress and pretended it was still 1779. Milan had a major bone to pick with Old Fort Hill—now known as Old Fort Harrod State Park in Harrodsburg, the first English settlement west of the Alleghenies and founded in 1774. One year later, Lexington was named by a group of Virginia militia camping at Middle Fork of Elkhorn Creek, now known as Town Branch, in honor of the Battle of Lexington in Massachusetts leading up to the Revolutionary War.

Fort Harrod had reconstructed the original fort and was named a state park. However, Milan had partial remaining buildings and a couple of original buildings, but hadn't been given designation by the state. They were also a little peeved at being the "second" oldest city in

Kentucky. They waged a tourism war against Harrodsburg, and this highway would give them an edge against Harrodsburg, especially if the highway connected to the interstate as some legislators were advocating.

"And," Angela continued, "she asked me a lot of questions about you specifically. I think she's joining Peel in standing against you on this highway. I'm sorry." Angela laid her hand on Riley's arm as Riley's mind took in the consequences of this allegiance.

"I made it known to Peel I wasn't going to back down. I guess I'll just have to do the same with Marge. I hate this. How can they stand by and let a town be destroyed? Sure, only part of the town will actually be knocked down, but with the highway and now a retaining wall so Keeneston can't even be seen, and with no exit ramp, the new industry we have brought into the town will move. Plus, over time, the farmers will sell their divided land or just let it go into bankruptcy and move to more rural areas to buy larger tracts of land. Fifteen years from now, Keeneston will be a very different place if I don't stop this."

"If anyone can do it, it's you," Angela said reassuringly as the Speaker called the House to order.

"Thanks. I'll think of something, even if I have to find *incentives* for each and every person voting for it."

"Careful, you're starting to sound like a politician."

Riley sent a weak smile to her mentor, and they took their seats. Her mind wasn't on the vote as she thought about how to move forward with saving her town.

Riley finally shut off her computer and turned off the light to her office. It was two in the morning, and she had finally found a bill she could support that might sway Marge from voting for the highway. It was a long shot, but in a couple of hours she would try to meet with Marge to feel her out. Right about now, Riley would sell her soul to gain the remaining votes needed to cut the highway from the budget being sent over to the Senate next week.

Keeneston was only thirty minutes from Frankfort, but that night it felt like forever as Riley buttoned her coat and locked her office door. The security guards were already gone for the night, and the Kentucky State Police patrol would be making random drive-by security checks, but she never knew at what times. That meant during this past week she was working the longest hours of anyone at the Capitol, and she had gotten used to walking the echoing halls alone.

Her father had been a former CIA spy and had taught her and her siblings how to defend themselves. It was a must in the Davies family, but she had never appreciated it so much as she did walking the empty annex at night. It gave her the creeps. Shadows played in the soft yellow glow of the hall lights left on at night as she made her way to the elevator. Somehow, taking the stairs in the barely lit stairwell seemed worse than the creaking noise of the elevator.

Every night she'd laughed at herself as she tightly gripped her bag and looked around before stepping out the door to the parking lot. But it didn't stop her from doing so again that night as she stepped into the cold. There was a new moon and the night was dark, darker than normal, with the heavy cloud coverage trying to decide if it would rain. As if answering her question, thunder rumbled and heavy rain began to fall. Riley had parked her truck under a light but the brightness was beaten down under the heavy rain.

Riley shrugged her shoulders up and made a dash toward her truck. If it hadn't been so cold and rainy, she would have noticed the movement sooner. As it was, the shape she had thought was just the tree trunk near her truck moved toward her. An arm reached out, and Riley screamed as it clamped down hard on her shoulder. She dropped her bag, all the lessons from her father kicking in as she fought with everything she had to free herself.

"This will teach you to toe the line. Vote for the highway, or else we'll come for you again. And next time in the dark of night, you won't get away with just a warning," a man's voice said through the pounding rain as he squeezed her painfully on her arm.

"You haven't done your research on me, or you would know I don't take kindly to threats," Riley yelled as she lashed out with a hard kick to the man's leg. She felt her heel tear through cloth and collide with bone.

He released his bruising hold on her arm and screamed, "Bitch!"

It was all she heard before a fist connected to her face.

Riley had been hit before while sparring with her cousins, but never at full contact or without pads on their hands. Riley's eyes watered with the sharp pain of the punch. She instinctively wanted to cover her face with her hands. However, she kept her one good eye open and landed a punch of her own. The man stumbled back with surprise, his foot hitting the curb and sending him sprawling to the cold, muddy grass. Riley followed him and landed a kick to his side. She didn't recognize the voice, and the face was masked in the darkness of a UK basketball cap. That only narrowed it down to most of the males in the state of Kentucky outside of Louisville.

"You." Kick. "Will." Kick. "Not." Kick. "Intimidate me!" Riley punctuated her tirade with another kick to his side. The man rolled into the fetal position and tried to protect himself.

Bright lights cut through the rain. When Riley turned to look, the man grabbed her legs and tugged. Riley felt herself falling and knew there was nothing she could do to stop it as she crashed to the ground. The cold dampness shocked her as she landed with a splash in the grass. The man scrambled up, gave her a swift kick to her side, and disappeared down the nearby residential street.

"Dammit!" Riley yelled as she lay in the water-logged grass holding her side. The sound of a car pulling to a stop and a door opening halted the string of curse words she'd intended to yell into the night sky.

"Police! Are you okay, miss?"

Riley pushed herself up with a groan and turned toward the headlights. A uniformed man was getting out of the car with a slicker on and flashed a Maglite at her. She shielded her eyes with her hand and called out, "I am now. Thank you, officer."

"What happened?" he asked as he hurried toward her. "Are you injured?"

Riley felt the sensitive skin by her eye and hissed in pain. "Doesn't feel broken, just a black eye."

"What's your name, miss?"

"Riley Davies. I'm the representative from Keeneston."

"Aw, shit. You're Matt Walz's friend. I'm Jacob Tandy. I was in Matt's training class, and we've been friends ever since. He told us guys to keep an eye out for you since you're . . . how did he phrase it?" Jacob pondered.

"Stubborn. Confrontational. Don't take any shit. Take your pick, Officer Tandy."

Tandy held out his hand and helped her to her feet. "Something like that, miss."

"Call me Riley."

"Okay, Riley. Why don't you tell me what happened, so I can make a report."

"Don't worry about it. I'm better off than he is. Besides, I'm cold, wet, and I have to drive home."

Tandy shook his head. Water sprayed from the wide brim of his tan hat. "Sorry, Riley, but I'm not pushing this under the rug. I saw a man run off. What can you tell me?"

"Someone wants me to shut up and vote for the highway that will destroy Keeneston. This was my warning. He was about five foot eleven inches and one hundred ninety pounds. Middle-aged, probably forty years old. His accent placed him from Eastern Kentucky," Riley rambled off.

Tandy blinked. "You got all that?"

"Yeah. My mother always told me to be aware," Riley said with more snipe than she meant to.

"And he punched you?"

"He grabbed me and squeezed my arm while threatening me. I kicked him in the left shin, injuring him with my heel as I tried to get away from him. He punched me, and I fought back. I'm tired, my face is throbbing, and I'm exhausted. Can I please go home? I have to be back up here at eight."

Tandy nodded. "Come on. I'll take you home."

"It's okay. My truck—"

"If you don't get in my cruiser, I'll insist on taking you to the hospital to be checked out."

Riley grumbled but got into the front seat. She was asleep before they were off Capitol grounds.

"What the hell happened?"

Riley blinked her eye open as her father stared down at her from the passenger door of the cruiser. "Dad, it's three in the morning. What are you doing up?"

"I always stay up to make sure you get home all right. I've told you I don't like you driving so late at night. And then I see a cruiser coming through the gate, and your eye's all bruised. What happened?" Cy Davies demanded in such a tone that Riley would have rolled her eyes if one hadn't been swollen. However, the tone had Officer Tandy snapping to attention and spilling all the details.

"I'll have someone pick her up in the morning, sir." Tandy practically saluted. Didn't he know her father was CIA, not military?

"Thank you, Trooper, but I'll take her to Frankfort tomorrow *if* she even goes."

"Dad," Riley sat up and prepared to argue that she was a grown woman.

"Don't even argue. If you insist on going, then I'm taking you and staying the entire day to make sure you get home safely."

"Oh my gosh, Dad. I'm a grown woman," Riley began to argue as her father escorted her inside.

Chapter Five

Matt stood next to Jared in the moonless night. It was almost three in the morning, and he could smell the rain moving in. This deal needed to go down fast, or he was afraid it would be ruined. The distributor was thirty minutes late. It was cold. It was about to rain, and Jared looked like he was going to shoot someone.

For the last few months, Matt had worked construction on the highway during the day and became friends with Jared. He even invited him to bring a pound of meth to one of his parties. Of course, Jared didn't know the party was full of undercover agents and informants. But it had gained the trust Matt had needed to get into Jared's inner circle. When Jared found out Matt was handy with his fists, well, then he started using Matt to stand by as some of the major deals went down. Matt had a log of Jared's bigger customers and had just recently been included in the expansion effort. Jared was branching out to Miami.

It had taken three weeks, but by keeping his head down and being a loyal friend, Matt had finally learned the entire plan from Jared. Tonight was it. The head of the Miami ring was coming up to meet face to face with Jared and swap $8 million dollars in cash for 500 pounds of meth hidden in personalized bourbon barrels. Normally, the barrels held 53 gallons of aging bourbon, but these only held 43 since a false bottom was built into each barrel to hide the meth. With the new Miami distributor selling a pound for $25,000 to $35,000, depending on the Miami market, he was set to make a killing on this deal. Eight million to the Miami mob was a drop in the bucket. But to Jared, it would be a significantly higher income stream. However, when you dealt with the mob, you had to make sure your product was good. Tonight was the sampling, and if all went well, the trade would follow.

Jared had taken Matt to his processing plant the week before to make sure there was enough product for the deal to go through. The DEA had the place under constant surveillance, thanks to Crystal's information. Like many dealers, Jared didn't use his own product. He tested the meth chemically to verify the purity. If the mob was happy with the drugs and this batch sold well in Miami, then they would begin a long-term arrangement. Too bad for them they were all getting busted tonight by the DEA and Kentucky State Police. During the bust, Matt Wilson would make a daring escape into the woods as agents shot at him. He would disappear off the face of the planet.

"Where the hell is he?" Jared yelled into the wilderness. Birds shot from the trees at the noise and disappeared into the darkness. They were parked on top of a small mountain, watching the only road to the clearing where they stood.

"They're city boys," Matt reminded him. "They're probably driving 20 miles per hour on these country roads. Wait, I see headlights."

Jared pulled out a hunting rifle and looked through the scope. "It's a box van. It has to be them."

"Do you see anything else?" Matt asked as he looked suspiciously around the area. DEA agents were in the woods. Night cameras with audio enhancement were on trees, but technology today made them invisible. A helicopter circled out of earshot waiting to move in. Agents would be laying tire strips on the dirt road after the box van drove up, effectively stopping anyone from getting off the mountain.

Jared scanned the area. "I don't see anything. Are you worried?"

Matt shook his head. "Nah. I just heard Eddie got a speeding ticket a couple of weeks ago. I want to make sure we're all covered, if you know what I mean."

Jared looked behind him to where Eddie stood, talking with his crew of minions. "You think he was compromised?"

Matt shrugged. "I don't think so. I know he's always carrying, but he didn't say he was searched. And he hasn't been acting differently, has he? You're around him more."

Jared thought for a few minutes and then hesitantly shook his head. "I don't think so. When Crystal was pulled over and busted, she was arrested. I have sources who told me she has kept her mouth shut in rehab. If Eddie talked, then I would have found out about it."

Matt nodded. He had suspected some of the local police might be paid to keep Jared informed, but now he knew for sure. But his mission was now complete. He'd planted the idea that Eddie had turned on him. By the way Jared was suddenly nervously looking around again, it seemed he had bought it. The DEA would make sure to affirm it when they patted Eddie on the back after cuffing him. They'd also put him alone in a separate police car on the other side of the clearing and offer him coffee. Jared would draw his own conclusions.

Jared raised his rifle again and scanned the area. "We're good. I don't see anything outside of the ordinary."

Matt hid his smile as Jared relaxed. The car lights approached and finally pulled to a stop in the level clearing overlooking the small town of Lumpur. The front doors opened, and two men in tan linen slacks and loose-fitting, vibrant pink and blue guayabera shirts got out. They looked ready for a Miami nightclub, not the mountains of Eastern Kentucky.

"Fuck me," the driver in the bright pink shirt billowing in the wind cursed. His black hair was slicked back and his tan was so dark his ethnicity was undetermined. "I thought Kentucky was in the fucking South."

"Barely. I'm Jared Caudill. I'm glad you found the place."

"Me too. It's in the middle of nowhere. My GPS told me to park and walk the rest of the way to my destination. Tony Carolla," he said as he shook Jared's hand. "And this is my partner Nicholi, but everyone calls him Little Nicki."

Matt looked at the man who easily stood six and a half feet and weighed close to three hundred fifty pounds. Guess country boys weren't the only ones who liked ironic nicknames.

"And this is Matt," Jared nodded toward where Matt stood, slightly behind him. His hand wasn't far from his firearm, and he knew Little Nicki's wasn't either. On a silent nod from both Jared and Tony, Little Nicki and Matt moved to check all parties for wires. When it was all clear, Jared smiled and rubbed his hands together.

"Eddie, show the man his product."

Eddie and his crew jumped to their feet and hauled the bourbon barrels out of the back of the truck and placed them upside down. They popped off the false bottom to reveal the bottom of the barrel was full with crystal meth in neat little baggies, put together by weight in their color-coordinated pouches by Jessica, Jared's wife.

"Nice," Tony whistled as he flicked his wrist at Little Nicki, who pulled out a giant rectangular suitcase and unzipped it. Cash in neat bundles filled it. When Jared motioned to Matt, he headed over to the cash and wanded it to make sure it was clear of any tracking or listening devices.

"It's clean," Matt called out.

"Would you like to test the product?" Jared offered with a gesture toward the product.

"Yes, thank you." Tony pulled a switchblade from his pocket and randomly cut into a bag. He pulled out a crystal and placed it a test tube before heating it. As soon as it, melted he waited to see how fast it recrystallized. The faster it did so, the better the quality. Tony then opened a second bag and pulled out another piece before dropping it in a small amount of water in a second test tube. They used an extremely tight strainer over the top of the tube and poured out the water as soon as the meth had dissolved. If a lot of solids were used for cutting the product, they would be left behind in the tube, meaning the quality of the meth was lower.

Jared rocked back on his heels with a smile on his face. These were extremely un-scientific ways to test meth. And what Matt had learned was Jared didn't do anything subpar. He wasn't running meth labs out of broken-down trailers or the back of cars. He had a full, scientific, state-of-the-art lab set up in the mountains with ventilation and a very specific formula for making the drug.

"This looks great. It's going to sell like gangbusters in Miami. You wouldn't believe the crap we have down there. We have a deal. And the price is locked in, right?" Tony asked.

"Yes, for the first year, just like we agreed upon. I need three weeks' notice for large orders if you want the highest quality. I still have my area to serve, after all," Jared said as he motioned for Eddie and the boys to seal things back up.

"We can work with that," Tony held out his hand and shook Jared's. "I look forward to a very profitable relationship with you."

Matt got ready. It would all be going down as soon as the exchange took place. Eddie and the boys pulled the barrels from the pickup truck bed and carried them to the box van. As soon as it was being slid inside, Tony handed Jared the cash and all hell broke loose.

The helicopter light turned on in the distance, sirens flashed at the base of the mountain as vehicles raced up the dirt road, and agents poured in from the woods behind them. Jared cursed. Little Nicki started firing. Tony leapt into the box van with the back still open. He spun the tires and pulled a 180. The barrels slid toward the open back door. DEA returned fire, and Little Nicki leapt inside. Tony slammed on the gas, and the van jolted down the dirt road.

The barrels bounced against the back of the van, some bouncing out the back and splitting open, others rolling out the open door. They careened down the hills, scattering the drugs as bourbon splashed out before the barrels finally came to a stop. The van was blocked in by the DEA vehicles heading up the mountain.

"Run!" Jared yelled. Matt didn't need to be told twice. While the agents were rounding up Eddie and his boys, Matt and Jared took off toward the side of the mountain. Shots were fired as they slid down the loose dirt. Jared grunted and started rolling out of control down the steep side of the mountain.

"Jared!" Matt yelled as he turned his body sideways to better control his descent down the side of the mountain. A bullet hit at Matt's feet, and he lost his balance. He rolled to a stop ten feet from Jared's writhing form.

"Son of a bitch. They shot me in the leg. I can't stand up. Run, Matt! Get to my wife before they do."

"I can't leave you," Matt called as he scrambled nearer the downed drug dealer. He tried to lift Jared, but Jared's leg wouldn't hold him.

"You're a good friend. Save yourself," Jared told him, looking over his shoulder as the wall of agents advanced down the mountainside.

Matt gave Jared a grim nod and then took off. He ran as if his life depended on it — because it did. His cover had to stay intact if he didn't want to keep looking over his shoulder for the rest of his life. His shoes slid on the loose rock as he plunged through the cover of the woods. Matt heard Forgy yelling at him to stop and breathed a sigh of relief. Not all of the agents were in the loop. But if Forgy was there, then the plan was working. Forgy shot, but the bullets kicked up dirt three feet to his left.

Matt didn't look back until he was sprinting on solid ground into the line of trees. Jared was being cuffed as two agents hefted him up by the armpits. Jared gave him a brief sad smile before Matt disappeared into the woods.

Matt slowed his running. Forgy and Tate would give pursuit but would come back and make sure everyone heard that Matt had been wounded but had gotten away. They would order an APB on him, but it would come to nothing since Matt Wilson was now gone. Matt Walz would be picked up at a prearranged safe house and taken back home. Home—he was finally going back home. Exhaustion hit him as it sank in that his undercover work was finally done.

It had taken an hour to reach the abandoned mobile home at the base of a nearby mountain four miles away. The mobile home was cold, but it blocked the wind. Spring in Kentucky wasn't all sun and roses. Cold fronts blowing in at night could be brutal. He had been sitting in the musty trailer listening to the scurrying feet of rodents in the cabinets and waiting for his ride to show up. Matt wanted to close his eyes and sleep, but he didn't want to miss his ride. He was too eager to get home. His small ranch house in Keeneston seemed like paradise right now.

He heard the engine of a car and stood up, moved to the side of a window, and looked out. He breathed a sigh of relief as he saw the familiar DEA vehicle. He waited, though, to verify the identity of the driver before making his presence known. When Matt saw Tate's lanky form get out of the car, he finally emerged from the trailer.

"How did it go?" Matt asked as he shook Tate's hand before getting into the passenger seat.

Tate chuckled as he drove out the valley and back onto the small country highway. "Forgy slapped Eddie on the back with a huge smile on his face. He even took off the cuffs after he got Eddie in the car. Jared saw and lost it.

"Forgy called and said the likelihood of you testifying is slim to none. Eddie spilled his guts to Forgy during the car ride to the jail. It was all caught on tape. Including Forgy reading him his Miranda rights. Eddie told us everything you did and more. He begged us to keep him far away from Jared and to protect him from Matt Wilson, Jared's new right hand. Jared had apparently screamed some very specific ways on how he was going to kill Eddie for turning on him. Your plan of us being friendly to Eddie after the arrest worked better than we ever dreamed."

"I planted a bug in Jared's mind right before you arrived, too," Matt told him as he looked out at the mountains and hills of Lumpur passing by. In twenty minutes, they'd be on the parkway, heading to Keeneston.

"Well, it worked. His wife will be going away for a long time, too. When they busted into the house, she used her kids as a shield and fired at the agents. One agent managed to sneak behind her and stun-gunned her."

"What about the kids?" Matt asked sadly. Their whole world was taken away from them that night, and he knew how that felt.

"The wife's sister is in Texas and owns a large cattle farm. She's going to take them. We called her after the bust and woke her up, but she said she'd be on a plane at six in the morning to be here for them. She's never met her niece and nephews. Their parents were users, and she hated it. The sister moved out at eighteen and hasn't talked to them since. She cut off communication when Jessica married Jared. She had no idea the kids even existed. She was actually more surprised that her sister and Jared were still alive. Her sister likes heroin; Jared made it special for her. That's how they met," Tate explained.

"What a romantic story," Matt said dryly. "But this sister will take the kids? Is she a saint?"

"She and her husband can't have kids. Her husband's a rodeo star but a particularly bad fall damaged his boys. He has two prosthetic ones now. As soon as she was told what happened, she offered to take the kids. She cried when she heard about them. We'd already vetted her. She's thirty-one. He's thirty-six. They've been married for eight years. Have a 1500-acre farm where they run cattle. They pay their taxes, are active in their community, and have no evidence of drug or alcohol abuse. It's probably the best thing to happen to these kids."

"Good. I hate when children are involved. And the processing plant?" Matt asked.

"We rounded up the night shift and left their cars there. There are ten people who work during the day. We have agents waiting to arrest each worker as they come inside the plant. In a few hours, the whole operation will be shut down."

"And the Miami guys?"

Tate turned onto the parkway and left Lumpur behind forever. "They aren't talking. But it's only been a short time. We'll see what we can find out when we dig further.

For now, you can go home and rest."

Matt closed his eyes. Rest sounded good. Seeing his friends again. Having a meal at the café. Not worrying about being shot if you say the wrong thing. It would be heaven.

Chapter Six

The sound of the radio going off in the car had Matt's eyes popping open. He'd only been asleep for fifty minutes but already they were out of the Eastern Kentucky mountains and into the rolling hills of Central Kentucky. They would be in Lexington soon.

"Tate, do you have Walz with you?"

Tate picked up the radio and spoke into it. "Yes. We're ten miles from Lexington. What's up?"

"There's a state trooper by the name of Jacob Tandy trying to relay a message to him. Matt's boss contacted us and told us to pass it along once the operation was over," dispatch said.

Tate handed the radio to Matt. "This is Walz. What's the message?"

"He wanted you to know your friend Riley Davies was assaulted in the annex parking lot at two this morning. She has a black eye and some bruises on her side but was otherwise unharmed. Suspect is unknown and on the loose."

Matt shot up in his seat. The exhaustion was replaced by a myriad of emotions—rage and worry the predominant ones. "Where is she now?"

"Officer Tandy drove her home and left her in the care of her father. He wanted me to relay that she intends to be back at work tomorrow. He has notified the guards on duty, and there will be extra trooper presence in the area. He said to call if you want more information." Dispatch rattled off a number that Matt had in his phone at home.

Matt snatched Tate's cell and dialed his friend. When he had left for this undercover job, he had hoped Riley would win. It didn't matter that they had left on uneasy terms. He wanted someone he knew to be there if she ever needed it. Matt just didn't think she'd ever need it. Riley was stubborn and independent almost to a fault, but she was smart, too.

The afternoon before Matt left for this undercover job, he found Riley working on the ranch. He couldn't tell her where he was going or what he would be doing. They had been dancing around each other, and he had wanted to know if he had a chance with the fiery redhead. He'd admired her for many reasons, not including his physical attraction to her. She was smart, kind, confident, and when she allowed it, she was fun.

Matt had first noticed her when he'd driven by the town's water tower late at night and had seen all the cars parked in the field. He'd thought he was busting up a teenage drinking party but instead had found the Davies cousins and their friends celebrating Sydney and Deacon's upcoming wedding. Matt had been off duty and had been instantly invited to join the fun.

Riley had a drink in her hand and was standing on the truck bed dancing with Sydney. The former supermodel should have drawn his attention, but it was the long, shapely legs of Riley in her short cutoff jean skirt that had him agreeing to join the party. Riley had worn a jungle green cami that made her slightly curled red hair shine in the headlights of the cars circled around. Her rounded breasts swayed as she danced to the music and Matt thought he'd never seen anything so seductive in his life. He must have been staring because Sydney whispered something to Riley, and Riley turned and looked at him. She sent him a laughing smile and lifted her beer bottle in a silent salute. Matt saluted back with the beer one of her cousins had given him and thought it was going to be the start of something.

But it wasn't. They flirted, but nothing ever came from it. Riley ran hot and cold, and Matt didn't know what to do. When he was sure she was interested in him, he would approach her to ask her on a date, and she would suddenly turn uninterested. She would stop talking or limit her responses to "yeah" or "nah," and Matt would lose his nerve to ask her out. He would be thirty-one this year, and he didn't know what this woman wanted.

He had gone to see her before he had left for this undercover assignment with the DEA. He was hopeful she would give him a hint as to her feelings. He had found her washing horses at one of the barns. Her headphones were on, and she was dancing and singing, badly, to a country song when he'd pulled up. When she finally heard him, she had turned five shades of red and practically hid behind the horse.

Matt assured her he liked it, and slowly Riley had come out from behind the mare. He'd told her he wanted to talk to her, and she suddenly became very interested in the mare's neck. He didn't know what to think, so he just pushed forward and asked her out to dinner that night. She had stammered out a "thanks but no thanks" response. Something about a horse and her sister—Matt didn't follow it but he got the gist. She wasn't interested. It had made leaving a lot easier. But it didn't mean that he had stopped caring. Was he in love with her? No. Was he still interested in her? No. But could he walk away from something that had tantalized him for over a year as if he'd never had feelings for her to begin with? No. And that's why, after tipping his dark tan cowboy hat at her, he had gotten back in the car and called Tandy and the new guy who would be covering Keeneston to ask them to keep an eye on things for him.

Matt snapped out of his recollection and looked over at the speedometer and finally had to admit to himself he might have lied. He could try to be disinterested, but the truth was Riley meant something to him. Tate was being a good agent and going the speed limit. What agent or police officer ever went the speed limit? Matt leaned forward and flipped on the flashing lights. "It's time you gunned it."

Tate pressed on the gas and the powerful engine under the unremarkable sedan body responded. They were going a hundred miles per hour in no time. "Am I taking you straight to this woman's house?"

Matt thought about it and shook his head. "No. Take me to mine so I can get some clean clothes and my own truck. Just hurry."

"She must be some woman."

"She's something," Matt said. He just didn't know what she was to him, because the feeling he got at hearing she had been assaulted signaled that he wasn't as indifferent about her as he'd thought.

"Dad, stop," Riley complained as her father put some foul-smelling paste on her eye. She'd lost track of which home remedy this one was. She's already had the range of cayenne red pepper to pineapple pulp applied to her eye. When it didn't magically go away in the hour, her dad turned to herbs instead.

"This works wonders for the swelling. I used this when I was in China," Cy said as he dabbed the thick paste around her eye.

"Dad," Riley practically whined.

"Sorry, kiddo, but I will not have your mother waking up to find your face a mess."

Another opportunity to roll her eyes at him missed due to the swelling. "Thanks to Mila, we know all about how you and Mom met. She was kidnapped by a crazy black market dealer with strong ties to terrorism, and you think she'll pass out from a little bruise?"

"It's completely different when it's on your child. And yes, I know how old you are, but you're still our little girl. Now hold this there for thirty minutes." Her father pressed the paste to her eye and put some cling wrap over it. Riley sighed but moved to hold it while her dad went to clean up the kitchen. She didn't know how her mom had slept through the science experiments as her dad made these various concoctions, but she still hadn't come downstairs.

Instead of hearing the pots in the sink, she heard the clicking of a magazine clip being loaded into a gun. "Dad?"

Her father didn't look at her as he flipped the safety off on his pistol and headed to the door. "Stay here," he ordered in a voice that sent chills down her back. "And don't take off that compress for fifteen more minutes."

Riley shook her head. How had her dad known she was taking it off in order to grab a gun to back him up? Instead, she made a sound of annoyance and watched as Cy listened at the door. Suddenly he flung open the door with his gun aimed.

"Good evening, Mr. Davies."

Riley shot up from the couch. She hadn't heard that voice in months. What was Matt doing here?

"Matt. How was your undercover work with the DEA? What have you done to your hair?" her father asked as he lowered the gun and flipped the safety back into place.

"How did you know I was undercover with the DEA?" Matt's voice grew closer as he approached the porch stairs. "Wait, don't tell me—John Wolfe?"

Her father chuckled. "Who else? He has spy skills I could have only dreamt of. I guess you heard about Riley? You didn't leave your assignment, did you?"

With her one unpasted eye, Riley darted a look around the room for a place to hide. She didn't know why. She'd known Matt for years now, but one night at the water tower had changed everything. Riley had had boyfriends in college. It wasn't easy since her father would mysteriously appear via video chat on her boyfriend's computer in the middle of the night just making sure she wasn't in bed with him. College boys just didn't have the balls to handle that. And honestly, after what happened, she wasn't complaining too much.

But that night at the water tower, when she had been dancing with Sydney and looked at Matt, she knew he was interested in her. She could see it in his eyes, and she freaked out. Her father ran away any man she liked. Yes, she was a strong woman who stood up to her father on a regular basis, but that didn't mean she didn't suddenly get dumped, too. "What did my dad do now?" was her standard question as the men went running for the hills.

Sometimes it was nothing more than showing her boyfriend his weapons room. Sometimes it was knowing incredibly private things, like what the last picture he took on his cell phone was or — her dad's favorite — the STD results of the guy's latest blood tests. It was one thing if the guys were in Lipston or Lexington. Riley wouldn't run into them all the time. And they had been fun, but she hadn't experienced that *feeling* her mother had told her she would feel when she met the one. Until she had seen the way Matt had looked at her. And when he had taken her in his arms for a dance, she knew that feeling her mother had described. Then she'd thought about her past and all the ways her father would screw up any relationship she had with Matt. She was sick with the feeling of loss before she even had someone to lose.

So instead of going for it with Matt, she had hidden from him. Sometimes Riley had forgotten to hide her feelings and they flirted, danced, and talked. The *feeling* was so strong it scared her. If those feelings grew, would she be able to handle the inevitable loss? She didn't think she could handle the rejection, so Riley had decided it was not better to have loved and lost and had opted with not knowing love at all. But here Matt was, on her father's doorstep within hours of hearing about her attack. He had been somewhere working undercover for the DEA, and he'd left that to see her.

The good eye teared up. Riley swiped at it and decided hiding as much of her face as possible with the paste was the way to go. She sat ramrod straight and steeled her heart as her father opened the door wider.

"No, sir," Matt said casually as if it were normal to be talking to her father at five-thirty in the morning. "I completed the bust a couple hours ago. I'm home now. Tandy got a message to me through DEA dispatch. Since I was just getting home, I thought to check in on Riley. Is she okay?"

Riley pushed back the emotions clogging her thoughts. It was better to never know love than to lose it, she kept reminding herself as Matt walked into the room. He was about an inch taller than her father, standing close to six feet two inches of broad muscle and . . . lean? Matt wasn't lean. He was athletic. But as Riley squinted, she took in long, black hair instead of his normal short, dark blond scruff that was an hour away from being a beard and malnourishment. Matt had dropped at least twenty pounds and seemed lanky now. The only thing that looked the same were his deep blue eyes that were so deep she'd call them navy. And they were tired. And haunted.

"See for yourself," her father said as he gestured to where she sat in the softly lit room.

Riley saw his eyes harden before softening and filling with concern. She also saw him sniff the air. "Is that pineapple?"

"Yes," her father nodded. "It's good for . . ."

"Black eyes. Helps with the swelling. The vitamins and enzymes in the fruit aid the healing process," Matt mumbled as he moved toward her.

Her father sent her an I-told-you-so look, but all Riley saw was Matt kneeling on the rug at her feet. "How bad is it?" he asked softly.

Riley removed the paste and heard Matt suck in air. "Are you in a lot of pain?"

Riley shook her head. She wanted to throw her arms around him and cry into his shoulder but then her father would learn the truth and ruin it. "Are you okay? You don't look too well," she said instead.

Matt's face fell as he let out a long breath. He looked like he was about to fall over with exhaustion. "I'm better now that I'm home."

"What were you doing?"

"I'm sorry, Riley. I can't tell you that."

Riley nodded and choked down the emotion making her throat feel as if it were being squeezed shut.

"He was posing as a meth user to bust the largest crystal meth ring in the state for the past six months. It all went down tonight. He's just arrived back home. Life of a druggie isn't easy," Cy told her as he took a seat in the nearby chair. "And put that paste back on."

Riley slapped the paste back on her eyes, and Matt shook his head.

"What?" her father asked. "You said you couldn't tell her. That didn't mean I couldn't tell her. Besides, John would have said something tomorrow, and it feels good to finally beat him."

Matt moved from where he was kneeling before her to

sit beside her on the couch. "Do you have any idea what this was about?"

Riley nodded as she moved her leg to make sure their knees didn't touch. If they did and she felt his warmth, there would be nothing stopping her from throwing herself into his lap and her father shooting him. "They said it was about the budget vote. I needed to fall in line and vote in favor of the highway coming through Keeneston. And it's gotten worse. They're going to destroy even more of Main Street — all the way to the bank for a giant retaining wall. Not only will our farm, Uncle Pierce's, Will's, and Mo's farms be cut in half, but quite a bit of downtown will be destroyed."

"Then what happened?" Matt asked.

Riley told him what she'd told Officer Tandy and her father. She was already getting sick of telling the story. "But I won't be intimidated. I have a meeting this morning, and you can bet I won't sit quietly by not saying anything about this incident."

"You will do no such thing," Matt and her father said at the same time.

Riley's feeling of wanting to curl up and cry on Matt's shoulder died instantly. "Excuse me?"

"You were just attacked. You will not be going anywhere alone. You just pissed whoever is behind this off even more. And . . ." Matt grabbed her hands with his. They completely encased hers and were so warm and strong that the desire to crawl into his arms came rushing back. "I'm so proud of you for handling yourself. They weren't prepared for you, and they underestimated you. You're your father's daughter, but now they are smart and will not come softly again. I don't think you should be alone in Frankfort. There are too many chances for something to happen to you."

Her father looked impressed at Matt's assessment. "I agree. I told her if she insisted on going, then I would take her."

"Yes. You'll be safe with your father," Matt said, thinning his lips. Reluctantly, he took his hands from hers and stood up. "I'm glad you're not more seriously injured. Let me know if you need anything. Anything at all."

Riley felt empty when her hands dropped in her lap. Instead of hugging him, she looked down at her hands in her lap. "Thanks," she said, keeping an eye downward. Had they somehow changed just by being held? "But you need to take care of you. Every woman in Keeneston will be bringing you casseroles, pies, and cakes as soon as they see how skinny you've gotten." Riley finally looked up at him and gave him a wobbly smile. "Goodbye, Matt. Thanks for checking in on me. It means a lot to have a friend like you."

Riley saw the muscle jump along his scruffy jawline, but he didn't say anything else to her. Instead he looked to Cy and repeated his offer to help if he was needed. "I have a month's worth of time off before going back on duty. I'll just be sitting here fattening up."

Riley watched her father stand and shake Matt's hand. They walked to the door with their heads down as they talked to each other, and then he was gone. It took everything she had not to chase after him. But her father started planning the rest of the week, and Matt wasn't mentioned again.

Chapter Seven

Matt stopped at the door to his truck and glanced back at the two-story house. It had been a punch to his gut to see the swollen and bruised eye on Riley's beautiful face. Her hazel eye was barely peeking out from her puffy eyelid. He had wanted to gently kiss her and tell her he would protect her. He wanted to keep her safe, but then she had called him *friend* and her father had said he had everything under control. Riley simply didn't need him.

"Psssst!"

Matt took his eyes from the porch and swung toward the sound. There, in a pair of flannel pajamas with big red lips on them, was Riley's mom. She tiptoed to the side of the house and waved him to her. Gemma Davies was a former gossip reporter who bought *The Keeneston Journal* after marrying Cy and moving to Keeneston from L.A. But then she'd written a book. Then another and another. Her books had been bestsellers and had been picked up for movies with the hottest stars in the leading roles.

Matt looked around again as he moved to the side of the house. "Good morning, Mrs. Davies. Are you okay?"

Gemma peeked around the corner and then hid against the side of the house once again. "Oh yes, dear. I'm fine. I just wanted to talk to you about Riley and my husband. See, I heard Riley come in and tell her father what happened. They were trying to be so sneaky, hiding it from me. As if you could hide that from a mother! Anyway, I heard you all talking. Now, don't get me wrong. I love my husband and have every faith in his ability to protect our daughter. But," Gemma looked nervously around again. "He's not as young as he used to be. I can see him falling asleep while Riley works late or running out of steam by the end of the week."

Matt nodded as if he understood what Mrs. Davies was talking about.

"I heard you offer help."

Matt perked up. "Yes, ma'am. Anything."

Gemma smiled and patted his arm. "You're such a good man, but bless your heart. I agree with my daughter. You need fattening up. And rest. It must have been very hard doing and seeing the things you did while undercover. I'll send Nora Owens from the Fluff and Buff to your house tomorrow, too," Gemma said, eyeing his hair.

Matt felt useless again. Did he really look that bad?

"But I need your help."

The exhaustion fled. "Just tell me what you want me to do."

"Give my husband today. As you know, it takes a lot of energy being so observant. If you promise me you will do nothing but eat and sleep, then I will ask for your help in protecting my baby."

"Yes, ma'am. I'll do just that. I'll pick her up for work tomorrow. Will any of her cousins be helping?" Matt asked. Ryan Parker, the eldest of the Davies cousins, was the head of the Lexington FBI office. His brother was FBI hostage rescue and their cousin Dylan was something mysterious. He never said, but he was something that involved danger and the military.

Gemma shook her head. "It would be too obvious if Ryan, Jackson, or Dylan showed up. Besides, Jackson and Dylan are both working somewhere. I heard you're off duty, so I was hoping you would go as a reporter for *The Keeneston Journal*. Maybe do an in-depth profile—a week-in-the-life type of story. I can get you cleared with security and a press pass that will allow you to go almost anywhere with Riley except behind closed-door meetings."

Matt felt his lips split into a smile. "You're sneaky."

"You're just now figuring that out?" Gemma winked. "Now, here's what I want you to do."

⁂

True to his word, Matt did nothing but sleep and eat for twenty-four hours. He'd taped a sign to his front door begging for sleep and when he first awoke at noon he opened the door to find a stack of casseroles held by Nora who had come to cut his hair and dye it back to its original color.

The cakes and pies started arriving at three. Matt would bring them inside, heat one up, and eat. He'd stumble back into bed and would wake up three or four hours later to find more desserts waiting for him. This process repeated itself throughout the day.

In twenty-four hours, he had eaten two whole casseroles, one pecan pie, and one marble cake with chocolate icing. At nine o'clock that night, Gemma had texted him to let him know Riley was back home, and Cy was asleep on the couch. Riley had followed through with her threat and had taken the opportunity to stand up in the cafeteria and tell everyone there if they were behind this, they'd have to kill her to stop her from voting down the highway proposal.

The plus side was, she gained support for an amendment to kill the highway proposal and created a great opportunity to have a reporter hanging around. The bad news, it wasn't just the highway funding that was looking to be killed.

Didn't tell R that you were picking her up, but she's expecting her dad at seven. I talked Cy into letting you handle things tomorrow. He wanted you to know he still likes shooting things, but I think he was just irritable from being bored. Politics was never his thing. Look outside and thanks for your help – Gemma

Matt read Gemma's text again and shook his head while softly chuckling. Cy had either defended his manhood or threatened to kill Matt if he didn't do a good job. Either way, it amused Matt. He liked Riley's parents. They were unlike anyone he'd ever known before. Well, except for the rest of his friends' parents. They were all a mix of sweet and scary.

He looked at the clock. It was midnight. A perfect time for a snack and a little more sleep. He opened the door and found an envelope with press credentials, a Capitol badge, a notebook, pens, and a summary of journalism terms. Matt brought it inside and flipped through everything while heating up a baked spaghetti left by Nikki Canter, the president of the Keeneston Belles. The Keeneston Belles was supposed to be a charitable organization for women out of college, but it was really a husband-hunting organization. And they were perfect shots. They nailed down the best bachelors Keeneston had to offer—most of the time. Nikki was in limbo after thinking she was a shoo-in for Zain Ali Rahman's wife, who would become a princess of Rahmi. Instead of fulfilling Nikki's desire to be a princess, Zain had married a German interpreter named Mila. The couple had just gotten back from happily traveling the world on diplomatic and charitable projects, which had left Nikki needing to find a new victim, er, husband.

Being a lowly state trooper, Matt hadn't thought he would be in her sights, but when he found a G-string in the notecard welcoming him back to town, he knew he'd been wrong. However, the fear of being hunted by Nikki didn't outweigh his desire for baked spaghetti.

Matt ate while standing over the small island in his kitchen. He pulled up pictures and layouts of the Capitol and the nearby annex to study them. He wanted to know where every possible exit or ambush location was. He took notes on the pad Gemma had left for him before polishing off the spaghetti. Matt yawned, and with a full stomach and an initial game plan on how to protect Riley, he headed back to bed for a few more hours of sleep.

Riley smashed her alarm with her hand. Yesterday had been a disaster, even though her father had kept her safe.

How could he not have when he wasn't more than two feet away from her at all times? But then he'd rolled his eyes during a meeting, and she was pretty sure he'd hidden the word *bullshit* under a cough during floor debates. Sure, she agreed with his assessment, but the representative presenting the bill had heard him and Riley had wanted to hide under her desk.

And today was another day to spend with her father — a father who had growled when a handsome staff member had approached her and offered to escort her to her car. Riley rolled out of bed and was thankful Reagan was busy flying these next couple of weeks. Reagan was transporting horses to England so they could start preparing for the spring races. Afterward, she'd be flying horses from all over the world to Aqueduct, Santa Anita, and Tampa for horses to prepare and qualify for the Derby in May. If Reagan were here, she would be just as smothering as their father. Reagan was the business-minded sister. While they were both wild, to an extent, Riley was the more carefree of the two. Her sister would want to take charge with her very practical nature.

Riley tossed her oversized *Got Bourbon* T-shirt to the corner of the bathroom floor before kicking off her underwear and turning on the shower. While the water heated up, she looked into the mirror and tried not to cringe at the ugliness of her eye. Riley was not overly concerned with her looks, but this was hard to stomach. The swelling was going down and the colors around her eye now resembled abstract Goth art.

The steam from the shower covered the mirror, preventing her from wallowing further in self-consciousness. Riley stepped into the shower and let the hot water relax her. She was rinsing the conditioner from her hair when she heard the doorbell. Her dad was early. "Door's open!" she yelled as she stuck her head out the shower door.

When the door closed, she yelled again, "I just need one minute!"

Riley hurried through washing her body and turned off the shower. She wrapped the towel around her and secured the corner between her breasts. She'd pick up her clothes that night. Now she raced out of the bathroom and into the hall heading toward her bedroom.

"Take your time. I'm early."

Riley stumbled upon hearing Matt's voice come from the living room. She reached out quickly to grab the wall and fell clumsily to the floor, landing hard on her butt. The towel came unwrapped and fell on the ground around her, right as Matt raced from the living room.

"Are you all right?" he asked as he fought his lips from spreading into a grin.

Riley sat frozen for a second as he ungentlemanly took his time looking at her sitting on the floor naked. His eyes took in her breasts, and when they dipped lower she finally snapped out of her shock and grabbed at the towel. "What are you doing here?"

"I'm filling in for your dad. He thinks politics is boring," Matt said, no longer fighting the grin.

"Oh no," Riley shook her wet hair, "it was bad enough with my dad there. How can I explain why there is a trooper by my side the entire day?"

Matt dug into his pocket and tossed something at her.

She instinctively dropped her death grip on the towel, causing it to fall again as she caught the object. "You're an ass," Riley mumbled as she covered herself again.

Matt just chuckled as she looked at what he had tossed her. "A press pass for *The Keeneston Journal*?"

"Yup. I have a month off work, and your mom hired me to do an in-depth story on your fight to save Keeneston. It's a real personal piece that will require me to spend all day, every day with you until the matter has been resolved one way or another."

"She did not! You did not! But, but . . ." Riley sputtered.

"You're making it seem as if you don't want to be around me, Red."

Riley paused as Matt stared at her. He seemed to be searching for an answer to some internal question. "Fine, but don't call me Red," Riley huffed as she stood up with the towel clenched to her body.

"There's my firecracker. Now, get your cute butt moving or we'll be late."

Riley stood with her mouth opening and closing, not knowing what to say to the order or the nickname as Matt spun around and whistled his way back to the living room.

"Ugh!" Riley groaned in frustration before slamming her door to the sounds of his laughter.

Chapter Eight

Matt was learning quickly that Cy had been right. This was boring—painfully so. He had met DeAndre, who was outraged over what happened to Riley and offered to help in any way he could. After talking to Riley about DeAndre and his John Wolfe-esque ability to know things before they were public, Matt decided he could read the guard into the situation. It always helped to have an extra set of eyes and ears.

But before he could do that, they were walking into the first meeting of the day—a banking and insurance committee meeting. The meeting ended just as Matt was about to stab his eyes out. He tried to talk to Riley then, but politicians all wanted to see the one brave enough to take a punch for her beliefs. A pack of them followed her to her next meeting—administrative regulation review. Matt had never experienced this kind of torture before. He gave up fifteen minutes into the ninety-minute meeting and quietly passed a note to one of the staff running around the room. The fresh-from-college young woman blushed when Matt thanked her and hurried to give the note to Riley. Riley read it and their eyes met across the committee room. She gave him a slight nod and went back to listening to the sixty-year-old man across the table from her.

Matt had told her he was going to make a round and be back in thirty minutes. She wasn't to leave the room. He knew there was a fifty percent chance that she would leave without him, but he'd risk it to escape from the meeting.

Matt headed to the main door of the annex building and found DeAndre at his desk by the metal detector. DeAndre looked up and gave him a chin nod. "What's up, man?"

Security guards at government buildings were under the Kentucky State Police, but they weren't troopers like he was. They were considered special law enforcement officers. While they didn't have the training Matt had received, they did have firearm training and had to keep current with it.

"I would like to interview you for this article I'm writing," Matt said as some congressmen walked by.

"Sure thing. What do you want to ask?" DeAndre asked as he stood up.

"Is there someplace private we can talk?"

DeAndre nodded again and called into his radio. "Doug will be here in a couple of minutes to cover for me."

While they waited, Matt found out DeAndre was born and raised in Frankfort. He didn't have the money for college and his grades weren't good enough for a scholarship. So he'd started working in a gun shop. He liked the perks of being able to shoot at the range after he closed and had met a lot of state police there. Two years before, one of them asked to see a gun and DeAndre showed him how it was used and fired it a couple times, hitting the bullseye each time. The trooper had asked why he wasn't in law enforcement. DeAndre went home and looked it up. He told Matt he just knew it was what he was meant to do. He wanted to join the state police but didn't have the required college credits. This job had come up, so he'd taken it while he took night classes to become qualified. Doug appeared and Matt followed DeAndre down the hall.

"I need a place that's completely private. I can't have anyone overhear us," Matt said in a low voice.

"What kind of questions are you asking me?" DeAndre asked with humor lacing his voice.

"The confidential kind."

"Then there's only one place to go here." DeAndre led them down into the basement and unlocked a door. A loud furnace was pumping heat into the building. "This is the only place I know that people can't hear you. I'm sure there are others, but here you don't have to constantly look around. So, what questions are so secret we had to come here?"

Matt reached into his back pocket and pulled out his wallet. He tossed it to DeAndre who looked at him skeptically before opening it. "Man, you're with the state police?"

"Yes. And my territory is Keeneston. I am on a month-long leave after wrapping up another job. I'm friends with lots of people in that town, including Riley and her family. Her mother asked me to watch over her until this guy is caught," Matt explained.

"Why aren't you doing what her dad did yesterday and scaring everyone who dares to look at Riley?" DeAndre asked.

"Because then the assailant wouldn't make another move. I want to blend in. I'm familiar with undercover work and have great results with it. Plus Riley would throw a fit if I played bodyguard."

DeAndre snickered. "That's the truth. What do you need?"

"I need you to keep my cover as a reporter, but mostly I need someone I trust to be an extra pair of eyes and ears and backup, in case we need it."

"Oh, man. Of course. Riley's real cool. Most of these people don't even pay attention to me. She's not a regular politician. She really does care about others. I'll help anyway I can. I do change buildings quite often, though."

"Not a problem. I'll get Riley's schedule and send it to your boss. You'll be at whichever building she is the most that day. Here's my number. Call me if anything unusual goes on." Matt sent DeAndre a text with all his info and felt better, having someone else know the game plan.

"Thanks for bringing me in on this. It'll be a great learning experience. I'll have my college credits required to apply to the Kentucky State Police in May," DeAndre told him.

"Well, you help me out, and I'll help you out. I'll help you study or go through the physical tests as much as you want."

"Really?" DeAndre's eyes got big, and he smiled with such enthusiasm Matt remembered even at twenty-three, he was still a kid trying to better his life.

"Absolutely." Matt held out his hand and DeAndre eagerly shook it.

Five minutes later, Matt was back in the most boring meeting in the world. A woman he recognized as Riley's secretary walked in and handed her a note. She stood back as if waiting for a reply. Riley read the note and her eyes shot to his. Matt straightened up. Something was wrong. Riley's lips thinned and she wrote a reply and handed the note back to her secretary who looked at it and shook her head before bending down and whispering in Riley's ear.

"I don't care," Riley said on a harsh whisper that interrupted the meeting. She ignored her secretary and turned back to the table. "I'm sorry, please continue."

Matt saw that Riley kept glancing up at him and sat very rigid as her secretary left the room. A second later his phone vibrated. He glanced down. It was a text from Riley. How? He had been watching her, and she hadn't looked down at her lap to type. Hell, he hadn't even seen a phone.

Peel and Stanley are in my office demanding I see them. I told Karen I didn't want to see them, but she let them in anyway. I have thirty more minutes here. If I swear to come straight to my office, can you go eavesdrop?

Matt gave her a barely perceived nod and stood back up. He had wanted to talk to these two anyway. Riley had told him about Senator Gregory Peel and Representative Marge Stanley and their desire for the highway proposal to succeed. Matt casually headed for Riley's office. There were four rooms and two doors to the office. The main door opened to the waiting room where there was a couch, a coffee table, and two chairs. Behind them was the secretary's desk. To the right was a small conference room for no more than eight people and a kitchen area, both of which were shared with the neighboring representative.

A left from the waiting room led to Riley's office. It was large enough to have its own sitting area, two large bookcases, filing cabinets, and a cherry desk. It also was home to the second, unmarked door leading to the hallway. It was that door Matt went in with the key Riley had given him that morning. The office door to the waiting area was half-open and Matt could hear Karen talking with Peel and Stanley.

Matt turned his phone to silent and set his bag down by the unmarked door back to the hallway. He slowed his breathing and crept closer to the partially open door. When he got close enough to hear, he relaxed his body and closed his eyes. He focused all his attention on the conversation coming from the next room.

"She wouldn't leave the meeting. I'm sorry," he heard Karen repeat.

"She has no respect for seniority," Peel spat. Matt silently agreed. Riley had respect for people who earned it, not someone who thought it was owed them. When he was working construction in Lumpur, he'd heard quite a bit about their senator. They thought he was a god. He brought jobs to the county and was one of the highest-ranking members in the state legislature. When he was home in Lumpur, he worked at his law firm, though Matt never heard of him actually having clients. It appeared his associates did all the work, and Peel would come out, shake hands with the clients, and collect his money.

"I didn't think some farmer from the middle of nowhere would be such a problem," a woman's voice said. That must be Marge. Matt hadn't had time to really look into her except to know she was from Milan, Kentucky, was a community volunteer, and the president of something that sounded a lot like the Keeneston Belles for married women. In Keeneston, married Belles became part of the Keeneston Ladies.

"That's what Karen is supposed to be handling. If you can't even get Riley to meet us, what are we paying you for?" Peel snapped.

Matt's eyes opened, and he fought the urge to step closer.

"You're only paying me to keep you informed of everything she's doing. As I told you, she's looking into talking to the historical preservation society about turning all of Main Street into a historical landmark."

"Dammit!" Marge cursed. "Where did she get that idea?"

"She got it after looking into you. You were the chair of the committee that did the same thing for downtown Milan," Karen said softly, as if expecting an outburst. The outburst came in the form of a hand slamming down onto a desk.

"Calm down, Marge," Peel said. "It took you years to get that done. Remember how many hoops you had to jump through? Keeneston is a couple years younger than Milan with no fort or historically significant landmarks. Since she's keeping us waiting, what else can you tell us she has going on? Has she said anything about the attack?"

He could hear Karen taking a deep breath and moving to get something from a desk drawer. It sounded like she was turning pages in a notebook. "Well, you all surely know about her speech in the cafeteria yesterday. Angela

Cobb was in here yesterday afternoon and told her that five more people have agreed to vote down the highway funding."

"Hmm," Peel murmured. "That leaves us only three votes ahead. We need to get some of those voters back. It shouldn't be that close."

"Let's go back to the war room after we talk to Riley and see who we can get to flip since it's looking less likely we can use reason with the girl," Marge said with disgust.

"Is there anything else?" Peel asked Karen.

"Yes. Her father was with her yesterday. He told me to keep an eye out for her. I was expecting him back today, but Riley said he got bored. However, there is a new guy with her."

"Who is he?" Peel asked.

"A reporter named Matt Walsh from *The Keeneston Journal*, her hometown paper. They saw the news on the attack and wanted to do an in-depth story on her and her fight to save their town," Karen said. Matt could practically hear her rolling her eyes.

"Do we need to worry about him?" Marge asked.

"I don't think so. He just seems to follow her around and write in his notepad. He hasn't really gotten in the way, although he's only been here a couple of hours. He's with her now in that committee meeting. He was sitting in the corner of the room looking as if he were about to fall asleep."

"What does he look like?" Marge asked again as she stood up and started pacing.

"Tall, skinny, dark blond hair. He's usually eating. He raided the kitchen before the first meeting."

"Let us know what questions he's asking. We don't want him to dig where we don't want him to," Peel ordered before cursing again. "I don't have time to wait here another fifteen minutes. Come on, Marge. We can use the time before my lunch meeting to see who we can flip to our side."

Matt didn't move until they had left the room and walked past the closed office door. Karen sighed loudly, and he heard her collapsing into her chair. Matt waited until she was typing again to sneak out into the hallway so he could walk in through the main door. As soon as he did, Karen's head popped up from her computer, and she smiled at him. She was in her mid-thirties, divorced, and had two kids, according to Riley. It was probably why she needed the money. Unfortunately, she also would need a new job soon.

"Hi, Karen. I don't know how she does it. That meeting almost put me to sleep. I had to get up and stretch my legs."

Karen gave him a flirty smile. "Oh, I know!"

"So, why don't you tell me a little about how you run the office? You know, the type of calls you take, who visits, and so on so I can get the feel for what it's like working here."

Matt took out his notebook and listened as Karen told him most of the truth. "I bet it can get heated when you have two equally stubborn forces on opposing sides. Anything ever get heated in here in terms of yelling?"

Karen shook her head. "Not that I can think of. I know it happens in committee meetings and sometimes on the House floor, but no one has ever charged in here and started yelling before."

"I'm surprised," Matt told her as he looked up from his notebook. "You would think the person who attacked Miss Davies would have talked to her before to find out she wasn't going to change her vote and only resort to threats then."

"Has she said she isn't going to change her vote?" Karen asked nervously. "I mean, after experiencing what she did, I would be afraid to vote either way. I would probably abstain."

"Miss Davies did make it very clear yesterday she wasn't going to change her vote . . ."

"And I'll make it very clear right now that I have no intention of changing my vote. I will do whatever it takes to make sure there is never funding for that highway," Riley said from behind him. "Now, where are the terrible two?"

Karen cringed slightly before pasting on a serious-looking face. "They left fifteen minutes ago. Here are your calls, and Ms. Cobb stopped by to see how you were doing today."

Riley walked past Matt and took the messages Karen held out. "Thank you. But I told you I didn't want those two in my office at all. My door is unlocked and they probably went into my office to snoop while you came and got me. I just hope they didn't see the application to become a historical landmark. They can't know about that. You're my gatekeeper, and I have to trust you to keep the people out I don't want to see."

"Yes, Miss Davies. It won't happen again. I promise," Karen said without giving away her deception.

"Do that," Riley ordered, striding into her office. Matt stood up and followed. They had some talking to do, and he wasn't going to let Riley run away this time.

Chapter Nine

"Can I ask you some questions about your meetings this morning?" Matt asked loud enough for Karen to hear as he closed the door. He held his finger up to his lips and walked to where Riley was moving to sit at her desk. Matt bent over and placed his lips by her ear. He smelled her soap that had a slight hint of lemon and vanilla when he breathed in. Matt found himself leaning forward as if to kiss her neck and stopped himself. He wanted her. He always had. He'd never stopped. It was time to admit that to himself. But now was the time to keep things professional. He didn't want to give Riley any reason to kick him out—not that he would have left—but she could make things hard on him, and all he wanted to do was keep her safe. The safest place for her was in his arms and in his bed. No one would be able to get to her then.

He looked down at her shoulder, and his gaze slid to the top of her breasts. She was holding her breath and her nipples were hard underneath her blouse. Pride, satisfaction, and lust shot through him. So, she wasn't quite unaffected after all.

"What?" Riley bit out in a whisper.

"Karen's a spy. She's being paid by Peel and Stanley to

tell them everything you're doing, including the historical landmark application, and about the votes you turned against the highway funding."

Everything Matt had heard of redheads' tempers were true. The words that came out under her breath were things the men on the highway job didn't even say.

"What I am supposed to do?" she finally whispered.

Matt leaned back down toward her as his hands cupped her shoulders and began to absently rub her tight muscles. "What do you want to do?"

"What I want to do would get me arrested," Riley answered sarcastically.

"That's my girl," Matt chuckled and Riley briefly stilled under his hands before relaxing back into him. She was back to hot and cold. It was time to see which was the true feeling and which was the cover. Matt continued to gently massage her shoulders as he moved toward her neck.

"I think you have two options," Matt said, bringing his lips to her ear and letting them graze her sensitive skin. She shivered but didn't pull away. Instead, Riley leaned deeper into his touch. "You could try to use her to relay false information to Peel and Stanley, or you can just fire her and find a bulldog to place out front who would stop anyone from getting past him or her."

Matt let his hands slide lower over her shoulders so his fingers brushed the top of her breasts. A soft moan escaped her lips, and she suddenly jumped from his touch. "I think I'll go with option two. I can't stand having to whisper for fear she'll overhear or worry that she'll report every person coming and going. It would be very hard to get the support I need with her sharing that information."

"Then let's find you a gatekeeper," Matt said as he straightened up and spun her chair around so that she faced him. "And it's about time you tell me what's really going on between us." This was a conversation a long time coming and Matt stopped caring about the perfect timing. He needed to know he wasn't the only one whose heart was already involved.

Riley froze. "What do you mean?" she cautiously asked. Her heart hammered so loudly she almost missed his response.

"I'm talking about you and me. You're a smart woman, Riley. You must know I have feelings for you. But every time I start to make a move, you freeze me out. I thought it was because you didn't have those feelings, but your response to my touch is like fire. Let's get to the bottom of this right now." Matt stepped up to the chair, forcing her to spread her legs as he stood between them. He bent over and placed his hands on the armrests cutting off any chance of putting distance between them so she could think.

"I . . . I . . . don't know what you mean," Riley finally got out with a degree of attitude behind it. She managed to lift her chin and look him in the eyes as if daring him to disagree. Instead of backing off like she thought, his lips quirked, and his navy eyes darkened as if she were looking into the deepest depths of the ocean.

"Then I'd better show you."

It was all the warning Riley got before Matt pulled the chair closer and bent his lips to hers. It wasn't a romantic kiss that started off slow and sweet. It was a set-you-on-fire kiss with power, heat, and an energy that made her whole body come alive in a split second. It robbed Riley's breath while at the same time was the only thing that kept her alive. Matt pulled back and Riley gasped for air.

"There's my firecracker," Matt said with a triumphant smirk. "We could have been doing that for the last year. Why have you been running from it?"

Riley blinked. The carefully constructed walls protecting her heart started to crumble. The risk was too great. The feelings were too strong. If she lost them . . .

"I never took you for a coward, Davies," Matt said as he shook his head and straightened up.

"I'm not," Riley hissed back. "I was protecting us."

Matt raised his eyebrows. "Protecting us? How? By denying our feelings for each other? By preventing us from having a chance?"

Riley was so embarrassed. She felt her eyes moisten, and she looked away quickly to regain her composure.

"Riley?" Matt asked forcefully.

"It's my father," Riley said softly as she kept her eyes on the books in the shelf to Matt's right.

"What does your father have to do with this? You're a grown woman. I'm a grown man. Nowhere does your father factor into my feelings for you."

Matt put his hands on his hips. His pants were still slightly baggy from the weight loss but he was already looking better. Soon he'd be back into filling those pants, and she wouldn't be able to keep from looking at him every time she saw him. "You don't understand. You know my dad's ex-CIA, right?" When Matt nodded, she let out a long-suffering breath and continued. "Well, he scares away every serious boyfriend I have. As soon as my emotions are involved, he swoops in and ruins it. They run from me the second he gets involved. And these are grown, intelligent men. The thought of letting you into my heart and then watching you run away from me as fast as you can is too much to bear."

Riley's eyes snapped from the bookcase and over to Matt when he started laughing. It was soft at first, but then he tossed his head back and laughed so hard the sound of it echoed in the room.

"You find this funny? I finally tell you that I have more than just casual feelings for you and you laugh?" Riley felt as if she'd been punched in the stomach.

Matt shook his head as he tried to stop laughing. "No, it's not that. I'm just relieved. I thought it was something we couldn't overcome. This is nothing. I think your dad already threatened me. I thought it was funny."

"Funny?" Riley said and then realized her mouth was still hanging open.

"Yeah, I think it's great. If a guy can't handle a little hazing by the man who could be his potential father-in-law, then he's not man enough for you. You'd be miserable with someone like that. You'd walk all over him. I'm just surprised you put up with it."

The smile and confidence on Matt's face had her feeling hope for the first time. "Are you saying you think my dad is doing me a favor by running everyone away, and you're up for the challenge?"

"Yes, and hell yes. Full disclosure—I'll probably do something similar if I ever have a daughter," Matt told her seriously. Riley sucked in air as if breathing for the first time.

"You know he'll hack your phone, find out what your last medical exam results were, and probably take you out hunting only to find yourself the one that's hunted, right?"

Matt shrugged. "Sounds fun."

Riley shook her head in amazement. A tornado of thoughts flew through her head. Her dad hadn't been torturing her, he'd been weeding out the ones he knew couldn't handle being with someone as strong-willed as she was. Matt didn't care that her father would look into him. He wanted to be with her anyway.

"You . . ." Riley stammered as her thoughts fell into place.

"And me. Together. What do you say?"

Riley saw that Matt was trying to be casual but questions filled his eyes. Her heart swelled, her throat was tight with emotion. He was willing to fight for her. Riley jumped up from her chair and straight into his arms. He wrapped them around her as their lips hungrily met. They moved frantically as if desperate to make up for lost time, while the promise of a future together drove them on. His hands were splayed across her back, and he drove his tongue in deeper. She matched him stroke for stroke as they stumbled across the room and fell together onto the couch.

Matt had one foot on the ground, a knee on the couch between Riley's thighs, a hand up her now untucked shirt, and was rolling her nipple between his fingers when Karen knocked on the door.

Matt groaned in frustration as he rested his forehead

against hers. "Can we pretend we're not here?" he whispered.

"No, then she'd just come in," Riley said softly as she pushed him off and stood up. "Just a minute!" Riley called to Karen.

"Are you going to fire her now?" Matt asked quietly as he straightened his clothes and gave thanks for Nora cutting his hair. Riley's messy hair was bad enough, but both of them with messy hair would have been a dead giveaway.

As Riley tucked in her shirt, he ran his hand over her silken hair and plucked at the curls to disperse the tangles caused from being crushed into the couch. "You're good," he whispered quickly as he sat on the couch and pulled out his notebook.

"Thanks," she whispered back and took a seat across from him. "I think I'll wait until the end of the day. Come in!"

Matt nodded absently as he started writing in the notebook as if they were in the middle of an interview. Karen came in and tried not to be obvious about looking around, but Matt caught her easily enough.

"Yes?" Riley asked.

"Here's the copy of the Milan historical landmark application you asked for," Karen said, handing it to Riley. "And you have to be on the floor at two."

"Thanks," Riley said to Karen and then turned to him. "Are we about done?"

Matt smiled professionally. "Not yet. But why don't we finish this up over lunch. I'm starving."

Both Karen and Riley found amusement in that. Hey,

he needed to gain some weight back. And after six months of working construction and eating cheap food he could make in his crappy motel, he was ready for some real nourishment.

"Sure. Why don't we just eat in the cafeteria?" Riley stood and brushed imaginary lint from her skirt as she waited for Karen to leave. "Is there anything else?"

Karen shook her head. "Just make sure he fills up, our kitchen mysteriously ran out of almost everything," she laughed.

Riley smiled and Matt looked offended. "I'm a growing man. I need to eat."

"You eat more than my teenage boy," Karen giggled before sending them both a smile and heading back to her desk.

Matt grabbed his bag and stuffed the notebook inside before he and Riley headed for the cafeteria. They got their food—three cheeseburgers for him and a club sandwich for her—and took a seat at one of the few remaining tables.

"Hey, guys. Do you mind if we join you?"

Matt looked up and saw DeAndre and a woman who might be five feet three inches tall if she stood really straight. She was DeAndre's age with double piercings in her ears. One held a small diamond and the other a large gold hoop. Her dark black hair was short and tapered with her bangs swooping over her warm skin. A one-inch hot pink stripe highlighted the outermost swoop of her bangs. Matt had thought Riley was curvy, but this woman had a lot going on in a small package. Large bouncing breasts were pushed high on her chest and provided the perfect display for her cross necklace. The tight black spandex shirt would have looked bad on anyone else, but this woman had so much confidence, it worked. Her jeans hugged rollercoaster curves and had rhinestones along the pockets. Spiked, hot pink heels peeked out under her jeans, leading Matt to believe she really wasn't over five feet tall.

"Of course," Riley smiled at them, and the woman took the chair next to Riley and DeAndre sat next to Matt.

"Thanks," DeAndre said. "This is my girlfriend, Aniyah."

Matt and Riley shook her hand and introduced themselves.

"So what do you do, Aniyah?" Riley asked pleasantly.

"I used to work customer service at Kentucky Cable, but they got bought out by some national company, and they laid me off last week. I've been looking for a job ever since I found out. Nothing yet though. Since I don't have to work, I thought I'd have lunch with my sugarbear," Aniyah explained before biting into her sandwich.

"I heard about that deal. I'm sorry you lost your job," Riley told her.

"It's okay, sugar. It's nice to not be yelled at every day while never being allowed to yell back. I had to be nice to all those people calling and complaining while cussing me from here to next Sunday as if I were the one personally messing with their cable."

Matt looked up from his burger and stared at Aniyah, then looked at Riley. When he did, he saw the same look on Riley's face. Had they just found the answer to the Karen problem?

"Have you ever thought of getting a job here?" Riley asked.

"I did for a brief second, but there are no openings. Besides, I can't stand bullshit, and that's all I smell here." Aniyah popped a fry in her mouth, looking completely unruffled at insulting the entire room.

"Baby, this is where I work. Miss Riley is a friend. Be nice," DeAndre cajoled.

"Oh no, sugar, I'm not talking about them. I was talking about all those stuck-up bullshitters I saw leaving for lunch. I heard them talking about blackmailing people and threatening them to get their way, all the while they're smiling as if they're feeding you a gourmet meal. Well, I know the difference between caviar and shit on a cracker and I don't need anyone trying to feed me their shit."

Matt choked on his burger. Riley pressed her lips together so tightly they were white, trying not to laugh.

"Baby," DeAndre sighed.

"What, sugarbear? It's the truth. From my lips to God's ears," Aniyah said as she pressed her hand to her cross and then offered it up to God above.

Riley set her sandwich down and turned in her chair to face Aniyah. "I just so happen to need a person who can tell the difference between caviar and shit. Someone who can stand her ground against preening peacocks who think they are entitled to anything they want at any time. Can you do that?"

"Sugar, if I can stay polite while a customer is telling me they'll track me down and shoot me for their cable going out during a University of Kentucky basketball game, then I can handle some old pushy politician."

"Then you've got yourself a job, and I have a spying secretary to fire." Riley grinned and shook Aniyah's hand.

Chapter Ten

DeAndre and the head of human resources watched as Karen packed up her belongings. Karen had kept her mouth closed and denied all that Matt had overheard. Instead of confessing, she had fought it. She'd even pulled up her bank records and had shown the head of HR there were no deposits from any suspicious sources; however, Riley wasn't buying it. She'd already sent a message to her cousin Ryan and asked that the FBI look into it. He texted back that he'd have Karen interviewed by one of his agents but warned it would be a hard case to prosecute unless there was physical evidence of money changing hands.

Karen paled as DeAndre gave her a nudge through the door now surrounded by as many staff members as could fit. It probably didn't seem real to her until Karen saw all the people whispering about her and knowing she was going to be scrutinized by every person on the Hill.

Riley saw Marge Stanley's assistant among them, texting everything that was going on. "Jean," Riley called out as the woman stopped midtext. "Tell Marge I want to see her immediately."

Jean looked like a deer caught in the headlights as all the staffers turned to look at her. "Um, she's in a meeting right now."

Riley smiled grimly. "If she can read your texts, then she isn't really paying attention anyway. Tell her to get her ass in my office, or I'll send the FBI in to get her."

The only sound was Jean swallowing hard and the sound of thirty staffers frantically texting their bosses.

"Excuse me. Please step to the side. I know this is all very exciting, but back to work, people!" Angela Cobb entered the office, clapping her hands and sending the staffers scurrying back to report all the juicy details to their bosses. She shut the office door and let out a sigh. "Oh my gosh, Riley. Is it true?"

Riley nodded. "I can't believe it. I know I'm a newbie, but spying? Peel and Stanley have gone too far. I'm filing ethics charges against them, and the FBI is now involved."

Angela shot a look to Matt and lowered her voice. "Who's he?"

"Matt, he's . . ." Riley started but Matt stepped closer and interrupted.

"A journalist with *The Keeneston Journal* here to shadow Ms. Davies until resolution has been made on the highway," Matt cut in and held out his hand.

Angela gave her fake smile and shook Matt's hand. "A reporter, great," she said in a way that made it clear she didn't mean it.

"It's okay," Riley soothed. "Matt has assured me I would have first look and veto rights to the final piece. We can speak freely in front of him."

"Honey, nothing is ever off the record when a reporter is involved. Excuse us, Mr. . . . ?

"Walsh," Matt provided even as Riley shot a confused

glance at him for using a different last name.

"I need a private, off-the-record, free-from-reporters talk with Ms. Davies." Angela smiled prettily before whisking Riley into her office and shutting the door. "Now what in the hell is going on? The FBI, really? It's going to turn this session into even more of a circus than it already is!"

Riley blinked in surprise. "You don't think I should take full recourse for spying and potential bribery, or the possible blackmailing of my secretary?"

Angela waved her question aside. "Of course I do, but it could have waited until after the session. Damn, we're so close to the end, and now we'll never get anything done. Haven't you learned that in politics it's all about timing?"

Riley stood straighter and crossed her arms over her chest. "If this puts their votes in contention, then I'd say the timing in pretty damn perfect. And no, I didn't run to be a politician. I ran to fix a flawed system that believes in waiting for a *better time* to punish those who break the law. Sorry, Angela, but I will not back down. First I'm attacked, then my secretary is spying for the opposition; I won't stand for it and I shouldn't be scolded for it either."

Angela's face fell. "Oh, no! That's not what I meant. I just thought you could have handled this better. If you had come to me first, I could have helped you get everything organized so it would happen at the end of the day after most of the people left the building. As your mentor, I just have to warn you that it will have the opposite effect from what you wanted."

"I don't understand," Riley said in confusion.

"Instead of being asked about how devastating the

highway will be, the media will only care about your secretary being used as a spy. The highway is as good as forgotten now. I'm sorry."

Riley collapsed onto the chair. "You're right. I didn't think about that. What do I do?"

Angela took her hand and squeezed it reassuringly. "We have until the end of the week to pass the budget so the Senate can look at it. I'm sorry, but without the media's focus on this, I don't know if we'll have the votes to send it to the Senate without the highway proposal in it. We need those three votes and right now this topic has just become a hot potato no one is going to want to get caught with. Nothing like the words *corruption, bribery,* and *spying* to turn chatty politicians silent."

"Well, that's not going to stop me," Riley said, sitting up straight. "I'll lobby for the rest of the week nonstop. I'll make every interview focus on the highway, and in two days when we vote on the budget, that highway won't be funded."

Angela stood up. "I hope so. Good luck, Riley."

Riley hugged her mentor and walked over to her desk. Friday was the vote on the House budget, and she wasn't going to rest until that provision was stricken from the bill.

Matt watched as Angela Cobb, the head of the House Appropriations Committee, walked gracefully from the room without bothering to acknowledge him. Matt wrote her name down and turned the lock on the door. Aniyah was with Human Resources having her application fast-tracked, but she wouldn't be cleared to work until Friday, and he wanted a moment to talk to Riley before anyone burst in.

When Matt walked into Riley's private office, he found her already on the phone with a House member. Matt took a seat to wait. They had many things, business and personal, to talk about. When there was a knock at the door, he knew it wasn't going to happen then.

Matt got back up and opened the door to find an irate Marge Stanley, the head of the Senate Budget Committee. "Where is *her highness*?" she snapped.

"Wait here, please," Matt told her. He tried to hide his smile as he went to Riley's office. He shouldn't find humor in this. Any of these people could be the ones behind her attack, but he was surprised to find Aniyah had the right idea. C-SPAN should start a reality show based on this stuff. "Real Congressmen of Kentucky" . . . it would be ratings gold with the backstabbing and doublespeak. He could see the confessionals now. *Marge said she'd vote for my bill and then she voted for Greg's instead.*

Marge didn't bother to wait. She shoved passed Matt as he opened the door. "Thanks to you and your little stunt that is playing all over the media, I just got a call from the governor. She wants her budget passed now."

"I'll have to call you back," Riley said into the phone without taking her eyes off Marge. Matt slipped in behind Marge and watched quietly. "Am I supposed to be sorry that you were caught spying on me?"

"Spying? I wasn't spying. All I did was ask *your* secretary where you stood on the budget. Is that spying? You freshmen always come in guns blazing and thinking everyone is out to get you. As if you haven't tried to ascertain who is in favor of the Keeneston Highway. Grow up, Riley, and learn how to play the game before you're taken out of it altogether."

Matt straightened up. "Is that a threat?"

Marge wheeled on him. "Who are you?"

"Matt Walsh, reporter for *The Keeneston Journal*." Matt saw Riley look confused again. She didn't understand why he was giving a different name.

"Ah, and all reporters have drug track marks on their arm. I don't think so. Get out."

Matt saw Riley's eyes dart to his forearm where his sleeve was rolled up, but Matt didn't back down. He dug into his pocket and tossed the press pass at her. "I'm not going anywhere. And for your information, I'm diabetic. I bruise easily and have to move my sites around. Now, I asked you a question. Was that a threat?"

Marge's face transformed. "Of course it wasn't a threat," she said condescendingly. "I was simply educating the freshman representative how things work. How else is she to learn? Now, if you excuse me." Marge spun on her heel, slamming the door hard as she left.

"Walsh? Drug marks? What's going on Matt?" Riley asked softly.

"I can't have people looking me up and finding out I'm a state trooper, or they will know you're being protected. Your uncle Cade put together a fake identity for me," Matt explained, hoping Riley wouldn't ask about the needle marks.

"And the drug tracks? You're not diabetic, Matt," Riley said softly.

"And I'm not a saint either," Matt said more harshly than intended. "I tried to get close to you, and you pushed me away, and now you expect me to tell you everything all at once? I know we're giving us a shot, but give me a break, Riley. I'm not the same person I was when I had a crush on you last year."

He saw her suck in a breath as her eyes narrowed.

"Look," Matt said more softly this time. "All I'm saying is you have no idea what I went through while I was undercover. I had to do a lot of bad things in order to gain the trust of some even worse people, and I don't need you judging me for it when the whole reason we couldn't talk about this before was because of your daddy issues."

"Get out," Riley whispered, but Matt could hear the command.

Dammit. He hadn't wanted to start this, but he couldn't stop himself. "No. I won't. You've been so focused on your little world and protecting your feelings that you haven't thought of me."

"Then tell me!" Riley yelled as she slammed her hand on her desk.

"You tell me the real reason you won't stand up to your father. Tell me why you were so scared to admit you have feelings for me even when you knew I did," Matt countered.

"I told you," Riley said as her throat worked hard to keep her voice level. Matt saw it but pressed on.

"I don't believe you. Why are you hiding? Why is the girl who climbed to the top of the water tower naked on a dare, or who rides horses with no fear, scared to let me get close to her?"

Riley swallowed repeatedly and Matt backed down his harshness. "What is it, Riley? What happened?"

"I had to know who I was first," she said softly. "I'm always the wild twin, the one who is only good for getting into trouble or doing something outrageous. As you know, Reagan and I went to the University of Kentucky and roomed together. I love my sister. I do. But I needed to be my own person. Reagan was dating a guy, and it was getting serious our freshman year. He wanted me to meet his cousin for a double date. He had heard I liked to party and had said his cousin had quite a wild streak. Reagan pulled me aside and told me she didn't trust my blind date. I didn't listen. I was too concerned about being different from my twin to care. I got into a fight with Reagan and she left.

"My date said he understood and listened as I ranted about my sister. Then we were on the dance floor, and he started pushing me too much. He tried to feel me up right there in front of everyone and then he tried to do more. I pushed him away and told him no. He apologized and everything was fine for the next hour as I downed a couple more shots. I know I was underage, but I didn't care. We were dancing, and I was hot, so he offered to get me a drink. The next thing I know the world is spinning. I pushed past him saying I was going to get sick. I made it to the bathroom and managed to send a text to my dad."

"What did it say?" Matt asked softly as he slowly stepped closer to her. He didn't think Riley saw. She was lost in the past.

"SOS. I knew he had a GPS tracker on my phone. I knew he'd come. I just wasn't able to hold out until he did." Riley swallowed hard once again. "I remember being picked up off the bathroom tile by my date, and I remember a car. It's kind of hazy, but I remember trying to push him off me and the car slamming to a stop before my door was thrown open. Uncle Miles reached in and pulled me out. I remember seeing my dad and the rest of his brothers, but that's it. I woke up later at my parents' house with my mom beside my bed."

"What happened to the guy?"

"I don't want to know. My dad tried to tell me, but I didn't want to hear it. I never wanted to think of him again," Riley sobbed. "My father told me to move home after that, and I was happy to do so. I lived in fear for months until Aunt Annie forced me to come over for self-defense lessons with Bridget. I told her I knew all of it. I mean, as if my father didn't teach me! But she dragged me to Bridget and Ahmed's gym every day. It took three weeks, but I finally found my confidence again. The trouble was, I had lost myself in the meantime. I wasn't the risk taker I had been. I faked it. I faked the happiness. I went on dates and was happy to let my father scare them off. It prevented me from having to examine why I didn't care that they left. It didn't bother me until you. Okay, that's not exactly true. It started getting on my nerves as soon as I moved back to Keeneston after college, but you changed all that."

"Me?" Matt moved to pull her against him, and she rested her head in the crook of his shoulder as one hand encircled his waist and the other rested on his chest.

"Yes, you. I finally cared about someone again. I wanted to take a chance. The trouble was I didn't know how. I blamed my father, but it was really me. I was just using my father as an excuse because I didn't know how to open up anymore. Plus, after seeing man after man run from my father's inquisitions, I found myself thinking if I opened up, it wouldn't matter since they were all leaving anyway. It's why I threw myself into this highway project. I wanted to find myself again. To stick up for those who couldn't stand up for themselves — to regain my power. Then I thought I would have the courage to tell you that I liked you. However, what I told you earlier was also the truth. I was scared you wouldn't fight for me."

"Then fight for us, Riley. I'll always fight for you. Will you do the same for me? You're not the only one looking for yourself. I told you, I've changed and not for the better. I feel lost," Matt said softly as he ran his hand over her hair.

"You? But you're always so sure of yourself."

Riley looked up at him with her damp eyes, and he did the hardest thing he had ever done. He started talking. "My mother was a drug addict. It started with pain pills after the car accident my father died in when I was ten. But then the grief was too much, and the high from the pills wasn't enough, so she turned to illegal drugs. I was in my senior year of high school, two weeks from graduation, when a state trooper pulled me from class to tell me my mother had died of an overdose."

"Matt, I had no idea," Riley gasped, her trembling hand cupped his cheek.

"No one does. The trooper, Simon Walz, worked with children's services so I could stay with him until I was eighteen. It was only two months, but in those two months, he taught me what it was to be a man, to be a police officer, and he encouraged me to apply for college. I hadn't planned on going. I was headed for a job in construction like my father. But with Simon's help, I enrolled in community college and then transferred to the University of Louisville for my junior and senior year. Before graduating, I changed my name to Walz to honor him."

"What about your father?"

"He was a louse who slept around on my mother and hit us whenever he felt like it. Yet my mother still mourned him." Matt shook his head. "When I changed my last name, I had hoped to leave the nightmare behind me for good. But you understand it's never gone. Simon and his wife became my family. At the age of seventeen, I was able to start my life over again. Banish the darkness and fight for good. Protect people like I couldn't do for myself when I received beating after beating. But then this last job—" Matt took a deep breath.

"The drug ring my dad talked about?" Riley asked softly.

"Yes. It all came back. I had to take meth to prove I was who I said I was. I felt the high. I felt the low. And after doing it enough, I felt the tug that a little more wouldn't hurt. My mother used to say the drugs called to her. I didn't have to use all the time I was undercover. Only a handful of times, really. The other times I shot up with saline solution if I was able to use my own product. But I felt it, Riley. I felt the drug calling me as I stood in a room and threatened a man in front of his wife and young daughter to hand over the money he owed to the drug boss. I felt it when I helped sort out the merchandise. I felt exactly what my mother said she felt."

Riley gasped and shook her head in disbelief. "Why?

Why would you threaten?"

"Because it was my job. I had to get in with the dealers and the boss. To do that, I had to take the drugs that were offered, and I had to prove myself. I proved myself through collections and loyalty. It's over now, but I still feel stuck in the shadows," Matt confessed.

"And then I drag you into another undercover operation. Why do you do them? You can turn them down, can't you?" Riley asked.

Of course he could. "I want to protect people. By sacrificing six months of my life, I took down the state's second-biggest dealer, which, I hope, brought some mothers and fathers back to their children. Did I fix the drug problem? No. That will never happen. Although, in one year I've cleared out the top two bosses in the region and that feels like justice to me. I mean, you should see the money trail alone that I cut off. People's hard-earned savings . . ."

"The money!" Riley said so quickly that Matt's eyebrows rose. Riley rose up and kissed Matt's cheek. "Thank you for forcing me to talk and for trusting me enough to tell me what you've gone though."

Riley pulled away from Matt with a peace to her soul she hadn't felt since that night at the bar she was drugged. She'd confided her secrets and her fears, and Matt hadn't thought she was overreacting. He hadn't left. He had his own secrets, and sharing them was a soothing balm to years of worry. But then he had given her an idea.

"I have an idea. Hear me out. Friday, the House votes on the budget. The governor wants this budget fast-tracked, which almost never happens. Why? Because everyone and their mother throw in clauses and amendments to repay those who donated to their campaigns or who can help them in the future. So, what does it come down to?"

Matt smiled as he picked up her train of thought. "Money."

"Exactly. Now I can worry about Friday, or I can turn over the lobbying to Angela and follow the money. Regardless of how the House will vote, the Senate will muck it all up again, and the real budget won't get settled until we all get together and hash it out. And what will we use to hash it out and make deals?"

"Money," Matt smiled again.

"Right. I'll promise a senator that I'll support the bill sending jobs to his region or whatever it is he wants in order for him to support getting rid of the highway, which will earn me money and votes from my constituents in return. It all comes down to money and votes. If I can make it unprofitable to vote a certain way, then no one will touch it. And what is so toxic that it trumps money?"

"You got me there," Matt shrugged.

"Scandal. You think there aren't laws being broken in all this wheeling and dealing? I just have to follow the money and uncover the skeletons."

"Then what are we waiting for?" Matt winked at her, and Riley wanted to hug him. Well, hugging was the least of what she wanted to do with him, but it would have to do for now.

"First, you need to go to a Narcotics Anonymous meeting while I figure out where to start following the money," Riley ordered before turning to her desk and pulling out the exact language of the bill and her notes on who the supporters of the bill are.

"But I don't have a problem."

"You worry about turning into your mother. That's enough. Drugs affected you enough to feel the pull. Please, at least think about it. I'm going to be locked in my office until tonight. I promise I won't leave this room without you."

Riley tried not to hold her breath as Matt thought about it. "You're right." Matt took a deep breath and she saw the light lines around his mouth relax. "I should stop it before it becomes a problem. I'll ask DeAndre to keep an eye on you. I'll only be gone a couple of hours. Keep your phone on you at all times. And thank you."

Riley went into his arms then. Sometimes words weren't needed to convey feelings. They had both felt it—the relief of someone knowing their secrets and loving them anyway. She watched Matt head out of the room and then picked up her phone. "Angela, can you come back to my office? I have an idea."

Chapter Eleven

Two hours later, Riley had talked to every supporter of the highway to find out why he or she supported it. Some were straightforward with her while others caused her to channel her father's CIA interrogation skills. It was worth it, because now she had a list of suspects, and she had even more knowledge on how the road building process worked.

The lock tumbled on her door and Matt strode in. "Everyone's leaving for the day," he commented as the stream of assistants and policy advisors walked down the hall toward the exits to the parking lots.

"How did it go?" Riley tried to ask casually.

"Well, it was hard to go through, but I do feel better now. They understood what I was talking about. They understood the drug calling to you and shared what worked for them. I feel as if I have a plan now. How is it going for you?"

Matt took a seat on the couch, and Riley grabbed her notepad and sat down next to him. He put his arm around her and pulled her closer. She kicked off her shoes and curled her legs under her as she leaned against his chest. The touch and feel of Matt's body was so new and exciting.

She savored the heat, the feel of the muscles bunched under his shirt, and the way he absently rubbed his thumb on her shoulder.

"Peel and Stanley are the loudest proponents of the highway. However, I found out from another freshman senator that he was approached to support the bill from Luttrell Food Industries, and another supporter of the highway said that LeeRoy Hager pushed for the highway after making a really large donation to her campaign."

"LeeRoy Hager, as in the owner of Hager Road Construction?"

"The one and only. She said LeeRoy sounded very confident in his ability to get the new highway contract." Riley paused as a memory tried to surface but she couldn't grasp it.

"I worked for Hager when I was in Lumpur. They're based out of Lexington but hire a lot of employees from whichever county they are working in. From what I heard, they usually get any contract they bid on," Matt told her as he looked down at her notes.

"Why's that?"

"Because they have their own asphalt processing plant. It allows them to bid lower since they don't have to pay the trucking fees to import the asphalt. They have so many resources in the area that they pretty much get any job in an eighty-mile radius of Lexington. Each major city has its own go-to construction company. Either that or they could pay off the state-contracted engineer to know what his bid will be. Then they're guaranteed the contract that way, too. But what does Luttrell Food care about the highway?" Matt asked.

"They moved their corporate offices to Keeneston, close to the Lipston border. With the new highway, they could get a service road connected to it and save a ton of driving time," Riley explained.

"So, what's our first move?"

"Let's go back to Keeneston tonight and have dinner at the café. I'm starving for some good food. We can ask my aunt and uncle to meet us there. Morgan and Miles worked hard on trying to prevent Luttrell's move to Keeneston and can provide some insight for us. Tomorrow, we can pay a little visit to Harvey Luttrell. After that, I think we need to have a chat with LeeRoy Hager."

Matt kept his eyes on the road as he drove Riley toward Keeneston. Miles and Morgan Davies would be meeting them at the café. Miles ran his own company that supported the growth of small family farms through consolidating their voice under his company. If a major restaurant or grocery chain needed a product, they'd place an order with him and he'd organize which farm or farms could fill the order. Morgan, who during her high school years had been the black sheep of Keeneston, now ran a public relations and crisis management firm on retainer with her husband's company. According to Riley, Miles and Morgan fought against the tax breaks the mayor had given Luttrell Foods since they would threaten the local farmers' livelihoods.

Riley finished telling Matt what she had found out about Luttrell, and they lapsed into a comfortable silence. Matt glanced over at her and felt his heart warm. She was here with him. *Him.* She had trusted him enough to tell him of her past, and she was the first person besides Simon Walz who knew his own past. It was freeing to not hide the secret anymore. It was also scary. Riley knew his vulnerabilities. It should worry him more, but it didn't. It felt good.

They had not talked about their relationship since that morning, and that was scarier to Matt than anything. He was turning into a talker. He wanted to express his feelings. He wanted to tell her he was proud of her for what she was doing. Instead, he reached out and covered her hand with his. Riley smiled at him and went back to looking out the window. Her hand was so much smaller than his. He found it fascinating, thrilling, and comfortable all at the same time.

"If I haven't told you yet, thank you for being here for me," Riley said softly as she moved to lace her pinky finger with his.

"Anything for you. Always," Matt said with the realization that he meant it. He had thought he was over Riley when he left for Lumpur, but even then he had made sure she would have people watching out for her. He never could let her go. Even if he pretended he could forget about her.

Matt pulled into a parking space near the Blossom Café on Main Street in Keeneston. The lights spilling out of the large plate-glass windows warmed the cloudy night. Matt loved the café. Daisy Mae Rose and Violet Fae Rose originally ran it. Their sister, Lily Rae Rose, ran the bed-and-breakfast up the street. However, they called in reinforcements when they turned ninety. Two very distant cousins from Alabama, Poppy and Zinnia Meadows, now ran both businesses for the Rose sisters. However, that didn't stop the sisters and their husbands from having a reserved table in the middle of the action.

"I see the Rose sisters and their husbands," Matt said with fondness as he opened the truck door for Riley.

"Good. Maybe John will have some information for me. I still don't know how he finds things out, but I'll be grateful for any little tidbit."

Matt let his hand rest of the small of her back as he guided Riley to the door. "I think he has bugs in everyone's houses."

"I know aliens is the leading theory, but I think he might be psychic. Or maybe he just knows by asking a Ouija board."

Matt opened the door and Riley walked in. Heads turned as people shouted their greetings, but then grew silent as Matt stepped up behind her. He placed his hand on her shoulder, leaned down, and whispered in her ear that he'd spotted Miles and Morgan. When he looked up, he noticed the stares. Eyes were taking in the placement of his hand on her shoulder, the closeness of his head to hers, the way Riley leaned back into his body. Then chaos erupted.

The Blossom Café wasn't just the best, and only, place to eat in Keeneston; it was also the headquarters for all gossip and the town's betting pool. Keeneston gave Vegas a run for its money on all wagers relating to gossip: dating, marriage, and babies. "So, this is what if feels like," Riley whispered as they both gave the patrons nervous smiles while working their way toward their table.

"Don't make eye contact. Keep your head down and a smile on your face and whatever you do, don't stop to talk to anyone. We're almost there," Matt whispered.

"Yoo-hoo!" a voice called, though with her over-injected lips she sounded more like a drunk slurring her words.

"Shit," both Matt and Riley cursed at the same time as Nikki Canter, the fluffed and puffed president of the Keeneston Belles, called out to them.

"Don't look!" Matt whispered. "She's like Medusa with those lips. You look once and you can't look away."

"And you haven't seen the newest addition . . . have you?" Riley suddenly accused.

"Of course not. I've only slept, alone, and been with you since getting back. Doesn't really give me time to see anything. What's the new addition?"

"Butt implants," Riley giggled as she kept her eyes glued to the ground, moving closer to the table.

"Really?"

"Don't look! Last month she showed them off by balancing a glass of sweet tea on her ass," Riley said with a roll of her eyes. "She's turned desperate after losing out to Mila for the role of Zain's princess. Even Kandy, the head bitch in town back when my parents were young, questioned her butt implants."

Matt felt a pull at his arm and gripped Riley's waist for dear life. He saw one spiked boot and then another. They encased calves, knees, and thighs before skinny jeans appeared and a soft cream shirt covering humongous boobs. Oh god, he couldn't stop. His eyes rose to the lips, and he was trapped. The lips quivered, and he thought

Nikki was trying to smile.

"There you are. I wanted to let you know I'll be over tonight to help out with the G-string I gave you."

Matt felt Riley tense under his hands and wanted to plead for Nikki to go away except he couldn't tear his gaze from her lips. If they stretched any further, they would explode.

"I'm sorry. Riley and I have plans tonight," Matt said as he forced himself to blink. The lips scowled. Well, kind of. This was it. They were pulled so tight he was sure they would split in the middle.

"Don't worry, sexy, I'll wait for you at home while you tuck her safely in at her own house. Then we adults can have the whole night to play. After all, when you have curves like I do it, takes all night to worship them."

Nikki ran her hands over her large breasts, down her small waist, and then over, over, over her enlarged bottom. Matt's eyes followed the marathon path her hands were taking. Holy crap. It looked like two beach balls ate some watermelons whole and attached themselves to Nikki's ass. She would probably be four inches taller when she sat down than when she stood up.

"G-string?" Riley hissed, but it was loud enough for Nikki to hear and pounce.

"Yes, I left it at his house yesterday. Why don't you run along and let the adults speak now," Nikki said condescendingly.

"And how about you back off my boyfriend before I flatten one of your tires. It would be pretty hard to sit with one implant deflated."

"I'm sorry, honey," Miss Lily asked from across the

room, "did you say *boyfriend*?"

Riley nodded. "And I'm not going to let a sore loser mess it up. Let me guess—you set your sights on Gabe, but he's been traveling so much that you are ready to move onto your next victim."

Nikki huffed. "Implants! I've just been working out. And he's not yours until he puts a ring on your finger. And even then, he's not *only* yours."

"You can cross me off your list, Nikki. Riley is the only woman I'm interested in. Now, please excuse us. We have dinner plans."

Matt slid past her as Nikki hissed. "I'll be in your bed in no time. Everyone knows Riley talks a big game but doesn't put out. Call me when your blue balls need releasing." Nikki spun, her ass hitting Matt, sending him careening into Neely Grace and her daughter Addison's table.

Neely Grace shook her head and *tsked*. "Addison, I believe you may need to overthrow Nikki to save the Belles when you move back to town. They've lost their way again," she sighed. Back in her day, Neely Grace had cleaned up the Belles and their boyfriend-stealing ways.

Finally, they made it to where Miles and Morgan sat. Their dark hair was starting to gray together, but Morgan's violet eyes held amusement as she silently held up a twenty and waited for Zinnia to come take her bet. It would do no good to shout. It was as loud as the opening bell at Wall Street right then as people placed their bets on the potential of a wedding between Matt and Riley.

Maybe he should place a bet just to mess with them. All he knew right now was that he'd liked Riley for over a year. They'd become friends and after their talks earlier, he felt as if they finally understood each other. While that was progress, it wasn't time to go ring shopping. He had a rather intimidating family to win over, as well as Riley's heart.

"So, you think Harvey Luttrell is involved," Miles said with his deep voice and straight-to-the-point attitude. He didn't like to waste time.

Riley nodded as she sat down. "What can you tell me about him and his politics?"

"He goes wherever he gets the best deal, and he usually gets that by paying people off. I don't know what the mayor got in return for the tax breaks she gave him, but I notice she has a nice new car," Miles told her as he slipped a twenty to Zinnia. "Two weeks," he whispered.

Matt felt his eyebrows rise but he didn't say anything. Miles gave him a shrug. "Davies family members tend to know what they want and don't bother waiting for the sake of waiting. Though, I guess you're not a Davies. Honey, what did you bet?"

"Three months," Morgan answered.

Miles let out a breath. "Good, we're covered."

Riley felt herself turn red and was too embarrassed to look at her uncle so she talked to her plate of food. "Luttrell donated heavily to a couple of key congressmen. Why would he be so interested in seeing the highway go through?"

"I think he wants close access for shipping. But with him you never know. He gets grand plans, and if he can't buy his way into them, he just ups and leaves. He's moved their corporate headquarters four times in the past ten years. He's always looking for the better deal. The area that will let him do whatever he wants. That's why we are so worried about his headquarters being moved here," Morgan explained.

"I'm going to have a chat with him tomorrow," Riley told them as the food was delivered. She just didn't know exactly what she was going to ask him yet.

"You should play to his ego," Miles suggested. "I know it's hard to do, but it could get him to tell you more than he should."

"I just wonder what his connection is to LeeRoy Hager of Hager Road Construction. He's the other donor pushing congress to pass the highway. I mean, I guess it's almost a done deal that he'll get the bid, but it just seems strange that they're both pushing for it," Riley told her aunt and uncle.

"It could be nothing. I haven't heard of them having any connection," Morgan said with a shrug. "That doesn't mean they don't; it just means that there's no gossip or pictures of them together or anything."

Riley let the conversation drift to family news as they talked about their daughter, Layne. She was now the primary physical therapist for the NFL's Lexington Thoroughbreds football team. Years ago, she had helped one of the players out, and he'd told his friend who had called her with a knee injury. Over time, she'd treated every player who needed help. They liked the fact that Layne was not easily impressed and didn't give a crap who they were. To her, they were just bones and muscles.

"You know how she's very involved with military

charities," Morgan smiled proudly as she squeezed her husband's hand. Miles had been a high-ranking Special Forces soldier after college with his brothers, Marshall and Cade. "Well, now that's she's making so much working for the Thoroughbreds, she's taking on local veterans who have been injured in the line of duty. She's even opened her own charity and has a friend of hers also donating time. Has she told you about him?"

Riley shook her head. She was close to her cousin Layne, but Riley had been so busy recently, she felt out of touch with her girls. "No. Who is he?"

"He went through PT school with her," Miles grunted unhappily. Just like Riley's own father, Miles didn't approve of any man Layne dated, though she was pretty sure Miles hadn't gone so far as to tap her phone . . . maybe.

"Aaron Ornack," Morgan answered as she smacked her husband. "I hope there's something more going on between them. I don't know why, but every relationship seems to end before it begins."

Riley shot a look at Matt, who just shook his head. They all knew why those relationships ended before they began—because of the hulking man sitting across the table from them, a man who was currently trying to look innocent but not really pulling it off.

"Ornack? Isn't his family part of the Lexington bluebloods?" Riley asked as she tried to remember the family.

"Yes, but he doesn't seem to be as caught up in society as the rest of his family." Miles growled again while his wife ignored him and easily turned the tables on Matt and

Riley. "I bet your parents are thrilled you two are together. How long have you all been dating?"

Riley looked to Matt and gulped. She wasn't really ready to answer questions about them. Their relationship was old yet new at the same time. If she made too big a deal about it, her father would ruin it. But she didn't want Matt to think she didn't care. She should have put her foot down with her father long ago. The truth was, she let him do it because she was scared.

"Well, we've been wanting to date for a while now," Matt told her aunt and uncle as he took Riley's hand into his. "But sometimes you just have to find your own path and hope it leads back to each other. In this case, it did."

Riley sent him a thankful look as Morgan smiled and sighed. "I'm just so happy for you two. I hope Layne can find that someday."

"Someday when I'm dead," Miles mumbled.

"Oh hush, you'll turn into a pile of mush when you hold your grandbaby in your arms," Morgan said with a look in her eyes that was becoming very noticeable in all of Riley's aunts' eyes, not to mention her own mother's.

"I don't know if they'll let me hold a baby in jail, and that's where I'll be if Layne ever . . ." Miles took a shuddering breath and turned his intense hazel stare onto her. "Does your father approve of this?"

Riley swallowed hard. "Umm . . ."

Miles' lips quirked. "He doesn't know yet." He turned his amused stare to Matt. "You're a dead man."

Matt grinned with amusement. "I'm not worried about it. I really like Mr. Davies."

Miles just shook his head as he looked at Matt like he

was the dumbest son of a bitch he'd ever seen. "That was before you started dating his daughter."

"You men need to knock this off, or we'll never have sons-in-law or grandbabies. And y'all do not want all your wives teaming up on you," Morgan warned.

Miles scoffed. "I've led warriors into battle. I think we can handle wives suffering from baby fever."

Riley sucked in her breath and held it as Morgan's violet eyes blazed before a genteel smile formed on her lips. "Yes, dear," Morgan said instead of the blistering response Riley was expecting. But Riley wasn't fooled. Miles was in very hot water and didn't even know it.

Matt cleared his throat. "Well, thanks for talking with us tonight. It helped a lot."

Riley took the hint and started to stand up. Matt held out her chair and placed his hand on the small of her back again. "Yes, thank you both."

"Good luck," Morgan said and hugged Riley.

Chapter Twelve

Matt drove to Riley's house at the back of her parents' farm. It was a very beautiful spot, and luckily a good distance from the main house. They had collectively held their breath as they drove through the gate and past the farmhouse with the lights on. Somewhere inside, her parents were doing whatever they did now that they were empty nesters.

Matt pulled the truck into the garage and told Riley to stay put. He wasn't all together surprised when she just rolled her eyes and got out. "I wanted to clear the house before you come in," he told her as he pulled his service weapon from his waistband.

Riley quirked her eyebrows, walked over to a large gun safe, and entered the combination. She pulled out a Walther PPK handgun and turned to him. "Ready."

He could fight her on this, but he knew she was capable. Her father's overprotective streak did give her quite a few skills that most civilians wouldn't know.

Matt pushed open the door leading into the mudroom and felt Riley at his back. It both terrified him and reassured him at the same time. The thought of something happening to her had him checking every nook and cranny of the house before declaring it safe.

He put his gun on the coffee table in the living room, and Riley set hers next to his. It was then Matt realized they were well and truly alone together. He had the woman of his dreams all to himself, and they'd finally passed the barrier that had prevented them from moving forward. They were an *us* now. All those fantasies he'd had about them could turn into a reality. He just had to make a move, and he'd know what it was like to strip Riley naked and sink into her. But was it too soon? While they acknowledged what they felt for each other today, their feelings had been building for a year. It wasn't like he picked her up at a bar and took her home an hour later. Not that he hadn't done that with a few women in the past, but he wanted everything to be perfect with Riley. He wanted to give her everything she deserved, from rose petals on the bed, to romance, to making love all night long. Riley looked at him and absently licked her lips as her eyes traveled over him.

"Screw it," Matt said, his voice graveled with need.

They clashed in the middle of the room. The second Matt took a step toward her, Riley took a step toward him. When he looked into her burning-with-desire eyes, he knew her expression mirrored his. They were frantic to succumb to the desires they had been denying each other since that night at the water tower. Riley frantically ripped his shirt over his head at the same time he divested her of her blouse and shoved her pants to the ground. She kicked them off and stood before him in nothing but a nude bra, panties, and black heels.

"You're even more beautiful than I imaged in my

dreams," Matt said, his voice husky with desire. He wanted to explore and worship every inch of her body. When Riley reached behind her and removed her bra, his heart pounded, and he knew he wouldn't be able take it slowly. His erection was hard and straining for release. When Riley shimmied out of her panties and stood in front of him in nothing but her heels, he gave up on the idea of going slow.

His brain shut off and his primal need to consume her took over. He had her legs hooked over his hips and was pressing her against the front door before he knew it. His erection strained against his jeans as he rubbed against her. Her body was hot and pliant against his touch. Their tongues battled, and his hips pushed eagerly against her core as her breasts filled his hands. Matt lost track of who was moaning as he squeezed her nipple between his fingers and she nibbled his lower lip before sucking it into her mouth.

Knock.

Matt's hips pushed her into the door again as he moved his hand between them to unbutton his pants.

Knock.

"Matt," Riley whispered frantically as she clawed at him.

"I had a feeling you might like it this way," he whispered in her ear as his erection sprang free and Riley scored his back with her nails. "And I'm more than happy to give you everything you want."

"Open the damn door, Riley!"

Matt froze and looked into Riley's panicked eyes. He didn't waste any time. He stuffed himself back into his pants and had his shirt on in no time. Riley stood frozen as the door reverberated under the heavy pounding.

"One second, Mr. Davies," Matt called out as he scooped up Riley's clothes and shoved them into her arms before flinging open the door. Riley stood plastered behind the door with fear in her eyes and her clothes bundled in her arms.

"What the hell is going on here?" Cy demanded.

"What do you mean?" Matt asked innocently.

"I heard banging on the door." Cy stepped inside and looked around the living room.

"Banging . . . oh, that was me. I was killing a spider. That's why I didn't want you to open the door. I was right behind it." Matt told him as he put his hands in his pockets and stepped back, allowing Cy to walk into the room. Matt kept his back against the door so Cy couldn't close it and find Riley hiding behind it.

"Where's Riley?" Cy asked suspiciously.

"She went into the garage to look for bug spray," Matt said casually. "Did you need her for something?"

Cy's eyes narrowed. "No. It was you I wanted to talk to. Miles called."

Matt's grin slipped from his face. "I figured he would."

"I want to know what's going on, and I want to know now because if you so much as touch my daughter—"

"You'll kill me?" Matt asked. "It's worth the risk."

Cy made his move so fast Matt didn't even have time to react. It was a little embarrassing that a man twice his age could grab him by the collar so fast.

"Cyland Davies!"

Matt and Cy turned to the censuring voice and found

Gemma marching toward them. Shit. He could practically hear Riley cursing behind the door. "Mrs. Davies. It's nice to see you again," Matt smiled as Cy kept his grip on his shirt.

"You too, Matt," Gemma smiled kindly. "Cy Davies, you better put that man down and get out of Riley's house this instant. I will not let you interfere with this one."

"This one?" Matt muttered more to himself than anything.

"Boyfriend," Cy spat as if the word had a bad taste. "And why not? Riley is my baby girl. No boy is good enough for her," he whined to his wife as he kept his grip on Matt's shirt.

Gemma put her hands on her hips and stared her husband down. "We will talk about this at home, but right now you leave them alone."

Cy made a disgruntled noise and dropped his grip on Matt's shirt. "You didn't even fight back," he grumbled.

"I would never hit the man who could potentially be my father-in-law," Matt answered seriously.

"See, I told you," Gemma said cryptically to her husband. "Now, let's go home." Gemma grabbed Cy's arm and tugged him out the door.

"Tomorrow, dinner at our house at seven. Tell Riley I expect you both there." Cy issued the invitation as if it were a threat.

Matt grinned again and waved goodbye. "I look forward to it!" he called as Gemma shoved Cy into the car.

Matt closed the door and found Riley with a death grip on her clothes. "I . . . I'm going to kill them!"

Riley tossed the clothes onto the ground and put her hands on her hips. "Did you hear my mother?" Riley asked, but it was rhetorical and Matt smartly kept his mouth shut. "She knew about all the others. She *let* my father chase them all away."

Matt nodded, and Riley noticed his eyes weren't looking at hers but lower. She felt herself flush knowing she was standing completely nude in front of him while he was fully dressed.

"And I also heard her telling your father to back off. I think I have her approval. But, Riley," Matt finally looked up from her body to her face and Riley's breath caught. His navy eyes were so intensely focused on her it stole her breath. "I don't give a shit what your parents think. I would hope they approve, but I care more about what you want."

Riley's nipples tightened under his gaze. Matt was stepping slowly toward her, and his voice had dropped to a low timbre.

"What do you want, Riley?" The deep rumble of his voice sent tremors through her body.

"You," Riley answered. It was the easiest question she had ever been asked.

Matt strode forward, and she was in his arms before she could catch her breath. He didn't give her a chance to suggest they go to the bedroom or to even think twice about anything as his hands and lips laid siege to her body. All thoughts of her parents, Frankfort, the highway, and anything else in her life disappeared from her mind.

He kneaded her breasts, slowly circling her nipples tauntingly, causing Riley to arch her back, pushing them into his hands, begging him to satisfy her. His head dipped and, as his mouth covered her breast, she speared her fingers through his hair. She held him tight against her and unconsciously ground against him, looking for completion. Riley moaned as he pressed his knee between her legs and pushed upward, allowing her to ride his jean-clad thigh.

Sex had been something she'd done before, but this was different. It was feverish. It was desperate. It was two bodies recognizing they should be together, and she let all inhibitions go as she pulled the shirt back over Matt's head and ran her hand over his shoulders, down his chest, and over the rippled muscles of his abdomen. Her body demanded it of her, and she knew why. She loved him. And if you loved someone, you could let your guard down. You didn't care if you looked pretty as he was going down on you. Didn't care if you made cute little noises as he made you come, or if you were a sweaty mess by the end. Because when you were with the person you loved, it was all about the connection you two shared. The love of every shared touch, whether it was hard and fast or slow and gentle.

Riley felt Matt kicking off his shoes and pushing his pants to the floor. She felt powerful and free under his touch. She boldly took what she wanted and basked in his desire. And when he balanced her against the wall and thrust inside her, Riley knew she would never be the same.

In the dark of the night, the car doors opened. The figures masked in the shadows of the parking garage appeared and formed a circle. The mood was not as pleasant as their last meeting. Their plan wasn't progressing as they had anticipated.

"I'm afraid we should have backed Stokes."

There were some nods of agreement and a lot of grim looks.

"Can Riley be controlled?"

"She's starting to ask questions."

"I'll handle it."

A figure shook his head. "You've let it get too far."

"I'll get her under control."

"And if you don't?"

"Then Riley Davies won't make it to the vote. She'll be dead long before then. I'm not willing to risk all we have worked on." The harshness of the statement left everyone silent as they contemplated Riley's future, or lack thereof.

"Do it anyway. Now. I don't want to risk it. You kill her now and enough time will have passed that her supporters won't rally around denying the highway funding and ruining our plan."

"Now?"

The shadows nodded and then floated away. Cars, but no lights, were turned on as they drove away in different directions.

Chapter Thirteen

Riley snuggled closer in Matt's warm embrace. She was almost afraid to wake up from her dream. Last night had been better than anything she had imagined, but when she opened her eyes it would allow the world back into their lives. Riley would have to get to work, making sense of the tangled web of donations and votes and figure out how they were all connected.

Matt's hand dropped from where it cupped her breast and slid under the sheet to between her legs. Well, the real world would just have to wait a little longer.

The alarm had Matt and Riley groaning. They lay panting in each other's arms as the alarm progressively grew louder and louder.

"Just shoot it," Riley grumbled.

Matt shut off the alarm and smacked her ass. "Come on, sweetheart. It's time to catch some bad guys."

Riley wanted to snarl, but Matt tossed off the covers and stood. She enjoyed the view of his muscled back leading to a narrow waist and hard ass. Matt had been eating almost constantly since getting back to Keeneston, but the evidence of his time undercover was still visible when he breathed in and his ribs showed a little too much.

"Why don't you take a shower first, and I'll make breakfast," Riley offered. There were two ways to make breakfast: the healthy way and the Southern way. The Southern way would help him fill out his jeans better.

"Sounds great." Matt leaned over and placed a quick kiss on her lips. Riley hurried from bed and slipped on Matt's long-sleeved T-shirt. It hit her mid-thigh and was the softest thing she'd ever felt.

As she pulled out fresh butter, eggs, and sausage, she hummed to herself. While they didn't declare their feelings last night, Riley wasn't sure they needed to after what they'd shared. This was not just a one-night stand. They both completely let go and dove into their every desire. They shared a mutual trust. She would never have done that thing where he held her off the ground and she bent over, and well, suffice it to say it was something you couldn't do with just anyone.

"Smells good," Matt said, walking into the kitchen with jeans slung low on his hips and his blond hair almost brown with dampness.

"Good. It's just a breakfast scramble, but I have a lot of it so eat as much as you want. Let me get ready, and we can visit Luttrell first."

Matt pulled up to the guard at the entrance of Luttrell Food Industries. He had to give Riley credit, she talked herself — well, lied — her way into the compound. It was relatively small, only a shipping warehouse and a large square corporate building, but small fields of crops were all around them. It was really quite beautiful out there, and

Matt could see why they had brought the property.

"How do you want to play this?" Matt asked.

"What do you mean? I thought I had a good set of questions to ask," Riley said worriedly as she looked at the notes she had taken.

"I mean about me. How do you want to explain me?"

"Oh, I hadn't thought about that."

Matt turned off the car and wondered what to do. "I could be your chief of staff. But if these people are connected to Frankfort, then they'll have heard of me in relation to being a reporter."

"Be Matt Walsh. I'll talk you into the building, but I don't know if I can talk you into the office. Just keep an ear open and an eye out for anything that might seem strange."

Riley opened the door herself, and Matt hurried to catch up to her. He kept a half step behind her. As much as he hated it, he had to let her do her thing. He couldn't be there protecting her the entire time.

They entered a large lobby with a curved reception desk around four feet tall, with an assistant's head barely visible from the lower inside portion of the desk. She perked her head up, asked, "May I help you?"

Riley smiled sweetly and Matt almost laughed. It wasn't sweet exactly — it was kind of predatory. It was the look many Southern Belles had perfected by the age of thirteen. It said, "I'm going to get my way one way or the other, so you might as well make it easy."

"Good morning. Representative Riley Davies to see Harvey."

Matt stood quietly behind Riley as he took the time to

look around. There was only one exit through the lobby. Two sets of double doors were behind on either side of the welcome desk. Above them was a mezzanine that overlooked the lobby.

"Of course, let me just check . . ." The woman let her voice trail off as she looked at the computer. "I'm so sorry, Representative Davies, but I don't see you on the calendar."

"It's okay, hon. Regardless of what your calendar says, why don't you just pick up that phone and give him a ring. And when you do, also mention I have a journalist with me."

Riley smiled again and Matt had to turn around so the secretary wouldn't see him smiling. Riley was damn impressive.

"One moment please."

Riley turned away from the woman and took a couple of steps toward Matt. "You think they will let me in?"

"Yep. But I don't know if they'll let me in. If they don't, I'll stand right here until you come out. There's only one exit from the lobby. Since there are two hallways behind the desk, I'm guessing there are two exits out the back. If you have to run, I'll see you running through the parking lot." Matt nodded to the large windows covering the front of the lobby. "Plus, if you scream really loud, I'll probably hear that, too."

"Representative Davies?" the young woman called out. "Mr. Luttrell will see you now."

Matt moved with Riley toward the middle-aged man in a dark brown suit, who had just opened one of the double doors. "I'm sorry, sir, but this is a private meeting."

Matt gave a nod and smiled encouragingly at Riley. Then, before he could go after her, the glass doors closed, and he was stuck staring after the woman he loved as she walked into the lion's den.

Riley casually glanced around. She doubted she was in danger. After all, another person had come with her to this meeting. She couldn't simply disappear without raising some flags. Riley followed the man, who led her to a corner office. Inside, she saw Harvey Luttrell behind his desk, laughing into the phone.

"Anything for the kids," he smiled as he waved Riley to sit down. "Look, Cheryl, I have a guest who just came in. I'll send the check to you today. You just better save me a seat at their first game now."

Riley watched as the man who led her to the office quietly left the room, closing the door behind him. Riley crossed her legs and smoothed her olive green suit skirt over her thighs. In Kentucky, the weather was everyone's favorite thing to complain about. It could be as cold as a frosted frog one day and then hotter than a billy goat's ass in a pepper patch a week later. However, the days that fell in between winter and summer were spectacular. Today was one of those days. It had been chilly that morning, but by the time Riley and Matt had finished breakfast she had the windows open as the warm spring air blew in, bringing an extra pep to everyone's step, even Harvey's.

The middle-aged cross between a farmer and a big city banker smiled into the phone as he promised to throw out the first pitch at Little League. His brown hair was average in color but expensive in cut. It was parted on one side of his head and swept the other way in a look Riley was calling SPH—standard politician hairstyle. Apparently it also extended to CEOs. His bland suit color said he was nothing special, but the cut of the suit told Riley he was anything but ordinary. He was fit, but not overly fit—just an average look. On the surface, everything about Harvey Luttrell cried normal. But when you looked deeper, that's when things got interesting.

"I'll talk to you soon, Cheryl. Give my best to Jeb and the boys. Uh-huh, bye now." Harvey hung up the phone and turned the full force of his good-ole-boy smile onto Riley. "Now, this is a wonderful surprise. I've heard your name quite a bit around these parts. It's an honor to meet you finally, Representative Davies."

Riley could *out-deb* anyone if she put her mind to it. While none of the Davies group wanted to become debutantes, that didn't stop their mothers from beating in good manners and etiquette. Riley smiled as if the pleasure were all hers—as if there were nothing she wanted more than to see this man shaking her hand.

"Mr. Luttrell, the honor is all mine."

"Thank you, thank you. Now, what can a farmer like me do for a big shot like yourself?"

Oh, he was smooth. Him a simple farmer . . . ha! And as if Riley hadn't grown up and now managed a farm. "You flatter me," Riley blushed and then threw in a giggle. "But I came to ask you about your involvement with the proposed highway we are currently discussing in Frankfort." Riley kept the smile on her face as if they were talking about her mama's recipe for apple pie.

Luttrell was good, but not as good as she was. His lips

quickly twitched in annoyance, smoothing back into his fake smile she thought resembled her own. If only he had the experience of maintaining a straight face while being grilled by the Rose sisters for relationship information, then he might be her equal. If there was something any true Keenestonite under the age of sixty-five could do, it was weather an intense interrogation. The words *just wanted to know how your love life was doing* let you know you were next on the long list of romances to be bet on at the Blossom Café.

"The highway?" Luttrell laughed. "Why would a farmer like me care about a highway?"

Riley just smiled larger. This man would be mincemeat under the Rose sisters. "Oh, Harvey, you can tell me. I already know anyway. I just wanted to hear it from those little lips of yours," she cooed as her eyes narrowed in warning.

Harvey picked up on it and let his smile drop from his face. "How about I tell you what *you* are going to do about that highway, young lady? You're going to march that little ass of yours back to Frankfort and vote in favor of a project that will give jobs to your constituents and benefit the local economy."

Riley saw his hands turn to fists before he sat back and assumed the power position behind his desk. It was the pose where he leaned back and placed a Gucci-clad foot on his knee and pretended that everyone would hurry to do his bidding.

"No," Riley said simply as she too sat back and stared at the man across the desk from her.

"I must not have heard you correctly. Do you have any

idea who I am and what I'm capable of?" Luttrell leaned forward as he kept his eyes locked on hers.

"No, why don't you tell me? I'm just a freshman representative, so I'm not familiar with how things work," Riley said sweetly even though it killed her. On the inside, she wanted to leap across the table and put his tie in the shredder while it was still around his neck.

"It's very easy to understand. You do what I tell you. Besides, you're already bought and paid for. Now, let the real men get to work. You have a vote to make in favor of my highway." Luttrell leaned back and tried to dismiss her.

"I'm sorry. I don't understand. Why is it your highway? I would think it was LeeRoy Hager's since he's the one who will probably be building it."

"He builds, and I benefit. Don't ask questions. Just do what you're told."

Riley sighed. "I feel as if there's an *or else* that you left off."

"There is. And you'll find out what it is if you don't do what we picked you for!" Luttrell finally let the rest of the façade drop as he slammed his hands on the desk and shot up.

Riley felt her heart pumping as a shiver of fear shot through her. How much trouble was really associated with the highway and why? However, there was one thing she knew about herself, no matter what, she wasn't going to back down. Stubbornness was her area of expertise.

Riley stood and held out her hand. "Thank you so much for fitting in the time to see me, but you can kiss my little ass as I vote down the highway and make your life a living hell. Never, ever piss off a redhead." Riley squeezed his hand tightly before pulling her hand free and walking out.

Matt leaned against the car, chatting with some men on break as he kept an eye on the building. He wondered if her meeting had gone as well as his. So far the workers were more than happy to tell him they were forced to donate to certain campaigns—campaigns of congressmen who just all happened to support the highway proposal.

"Do you know why this is such a big deal?" Matt asked one of the men who was taking a drag on his cigarette. He seemed to be the most knowledgeable of the group.

"Has something to do with all the land around here. I don't know what that really means, but I heard that it's really expensive, and Luttrell can't afford to buy it."

Another man nodded. "Yeah, it's the soil. Best in Kentucky. Most expensive in Kentucky, too. Some is owned by horse farms and some by crop farms."

"What makes the soil so much better here?" Matt asked. He was from Louisville, and sometimes it felt as if they were in a bubble. They even had their own basketball team and were known as the "big city" to the rest of the state.

"The limestone. Kentucky basically sits on nothing but limestone and underground water, but it's especially present here. It makes the soil nice and rich. Crops love it because it keeps the soil at a perfect pH for them. It's also high in calcium and that helps the horses develop strong bones for racing. The water's filtered naturally through the limestone, making our bourbon so good, huh, boys?" The man with the cigarette smiled.

The door to the headquarters flung open and the group turned and watched Riley striding toward them with nothing more than a pissed-off, determined look on her face.

The man with the cigarette let out a low whistle. "She looks madder than a wet hen. Good luck, man." He dropped his cigarette and used his foot to put it out before he and the guys made a hasty return to work.

"You look like Joan of Arc preparing to ride into battle. Was is that bad?" Matt asked as he opened the door for her.

"That arrogant son of a bitch. He demanded I vote for the highway or else," Riley huffed as steam practically blew from her ears.

"What are you doing?" Matt asked, watching her as he drove out of the plant and headed for stop number two, LeeRoy Hager.

"I'm sending out a town text. I want all the information, gossip or otherwise, people have on Harvey and LeeRoy. I have a feeling they are in this together with Peel and Stanley."

Matt listened as Riley told him exactly what Harvey had said to her and tried to connect the dots with what the workers had said about the surrounding property. "Hey, could this have to do with land?"

"Well, yeah. The land the government will take to build the highway," Riley answered as she started reading the texts the townspeople were sending back. So far there was nothing earth-shattering.

"No, I'm talking about the land around Luttrell Food Industries."

Riley shook her head. "Not that I know of. That wasn't brought up at all." Riley stopped talking when her phone rang. "It's Neely Grace," she said before answering it.

Matt watched from the corner of his eye as Riley nodded to herself and listened to Neely Grace. Suddenly she sat upright and yelled, "I did what?"

Five minutes later, Riley hung up, looking stricken. "What is it?" Matt asked impatiently. Riley wore a look of defeat, and she never gave up.

"A photo was just released to the media, showing me accepting a check from LeeRoy Hager at a private event Will and Kenna hosted. The check, the press learned, was for $50,000 and was the reason I was able to make that big push the week of the election. Furthermore, there are pictures of me with all of his higher-ups at the road construction company. The piece is all about how Hager's campaign money got me elected and is filled with quotes from so-called constituents who are so glad I saw the error of my ways and will be voting in favor of the highway to bring jobs to the district. It's being picked up all over the state."

"Do you still want me to take you to see Hager?" Matt asked quietly.

Riley shook her head. "No. I want to go home, change clothes, and get on the phone to see what I can find out."

"Don't give up. You're my firecracker, after all."

Riley shot him a daggered look. "Give up? I'm not going to give up. I'm going to destroy those bastards!"

Chapter Fourteen

Riley paced back and forth through her house as she made call after call. She talked to the media, gave interviews, and swore that she was not part of a vote-buying operation. It didn't seem to matter. Public opinion had turned against her. She was being branded as untrustworthy and bought by big money.

Riley slammed down the phone and took a deep breath. "I need to shoot something."

Matt just nodded and pulled out his gun.

"Let me go change, and we can either go for a horseback ride or an ATV ride to the shooting range on the other side of the farm."

"Sounds good to me. Do I need to run home and get my rifle?" Matt asked.

"You're free to borrow one of mine, but you will have to recalibrate my scope," Riley told him as she reached under her skirt and yanked off the horrid invention called panty hose. She hopped on one foot as she tried to pull it over her heel.

"If you can give me fifteen minutes, I'll run home and get mine. I haven't shot it in six months and would like to. And stop undressing or I won't leave." Matt sent her a suggestive wink and Riley deliberately started to slowly unbutton her shirt.

"I may still be naked by the time you get back."

"Just promise not to get into any trouble while I'm away. Well, any more than you already are in," Matt groaned, tugging her shirt from her skirt and slipping his hand underneath to cup her breast as he took her mouth in his. Matt had her grinding her hips against his in seconds. Her body was flush, her breasts felt heavy, aching for his touch, when he pulled away and shot her a grin. "I can be evil, too."

Riley tossed a throw pillow at Matt as he laughed his way out the door. She headed to her bedroom to finish undressing and found herself humming. It was going to be a hard week until the end of session, but she had someone she could talk to about it. Shooting and riding had always been her go-to for relaxation and brainstorming. When Riley would let out her breath and slowly squeeze the trigger, she found it wasn't only the target she hit. The moment she lowered her gun or jumped a fence on her horse she would hit upon some of her best ideas.

Riley shrugged out of her blouse and tossed it on the end of her bed. She unzipped her skirt and shimmied out of it, and tossed that on the bed, too. In the back of her closet were her boots and a small gun safe. This safe held her favorite guns. Riley opened the closet and pulled out a light flannel shirt. It was warm out that day, but the sun would be going down, taking the temperatures with it. She slid the red and navy shirt up her arms, but didn't bother to button it as she shoved her clothes away from the back of the closet to reach her boots and gun.

"What?" Riley squinted her eyes into the dark corner at the far end of her closet. She couldn't be sure, but she thought she saw the shadows moving. Riley blinked and stared. She saw the outline of her boots sitting slightly past her safe and decided she was seeing things.

"I've gotten so worked up that I'm imagining my boots moving," Riley said to herself as she shook her head and put her thumb to the lock on the safe. Her fingerprint unlocked it and she reached farther into the darkened closet and grabbed her gun and ammo.

Placing the gun and box of ammo on the bed, Riley threw a pair of jeans onto the bed along with some socks. All she needed were her boots. The question was did she really want to get dressed or not? She had teased Matt, but was it really a tease if she followed through?

Grinning, Riley picked up her jeans and socks and placed them on the nearby chair. She grabbed her suit and hung it on the hangers at the front of her closet before reaching into the shadows for her boots. Riley had one hand on a lower clothes rail as she patted the floor for her boots. She turned her head to look into the back when she saw that one of her boots had tipped over.

"There you are."

Riley reached for the boots, but when she grabbed them it wasn't the feel of her boots that greeted her. It was undulating scales. She heard the shake of a rattle, and as if the fog were lifting from her eyes, Riley adjusted to the darkness and what she saw caused a scream to lodge in her throat as she tried to leap back. It was too late. All she saw were fangs sinking into her hand. The bite made her feel as though her heart was stopping. She fell backward as the varying shades of brown and rust-colored snake fell from her hand. She had woken a den of sleeping pit vipers.

Riley tried to keep calm as she scrambled backward, but seeing the poisonous copperheads, timber rattlers, and the nonpoisonous black rat snakes slithering out of her closet sent adrenaline surging through her body as she reached back for her gun. It felt as if someone was stabbing her hand over and over again with a knife as she fumbled with the box and ammunition and loaded the clip. Riley didn't hesitate to start shooting. Her back was to her bed as she took out the copperhead that had bit her. Thank goodness it hadn't been the rattlesnake. But, she killed that one next as it slithered toward her. She didn't care that the bullets lodged in her floor or that near-dead snakes were twitching at her feet. She fired until she was out of bullets, slammed the bedroom door, and ran outside.

Her hand throbbed, her head pounded, and it felt as if her blood pressure was dropping fast. Riley collapsed onto the porch swing and dangled her bitten hand over the side of the swing as she lay down and went completely still.

"Shit," Riley whispered to the universe as she realized her cell phone was inside her bedroom. There was no way in hell she was going back into her room to get it. Her stomach rolled with slight nausea as she tried to move as little as possible while taking off her shirt. She wrapped it around her arm, right above her wrist, and used her teeth to pull it tight. It was the best tourniquet she had at the moment.

Two red marks with blood trickling from them were clearly evident on her hand that was already swelling and starting to bruise, which indicated this was no dry bite.

Everyone in Kentucky was familiar with copperheads. Riley tried to calm herself as she waited for Matt to arrive. Keeping still would help prevent the fast spread of the venom. Her hand hurt so badly, but she knew that most copperhead bites weren't fatal. Now, if she'd been bitten multiple times or by the timber rattlesnake, then she'd have a lot to worry about. Now, her main concern was how much venom was injected and whether or not she was allergic to it. If she was, she'd die of cardiac arrest or anaphylactic shock. Luckily, so far she wasn't feeling any of those symptoms.

How did a den of snakes end up in her closet? And how long had they been there? Had she been reaching in to get clothes and shoes for the past week or month with them curled up, their bodies intertwined this whole time? Riley was so freaked out by the slithering, undulating, hissing, and rattling she had heard, seen, and felt that even as she knew she killed them, or at least most of them, she was fighting panic. Every whisper of the wind. Every rustle of the leaves. Every shadow of a cloud past the sun—she worried it was a snake. She feared if she opened her eyes they would be above her, below her, or coiled around the chain of the swing as they reached out with their forked tongues at her.

A tear leaked out of her eyes as she squeezed them close. She had to remain calm. Her father had taken her and her sister to the woods when they were little and explained about copperheads. If you get bitten, get away, lie down, and keep the part of you bitten below your heart. Use a tourniquet to slow the spread of poison and stay calm. Help will be here soon, she told herself over and over again as she felt the pressure of her hand swelling to the point that it felt as if someone were repeatedly slamming her hand in a car door.

Matt beat his hand against his steering wheel in rhythm with the music as he drove up to Riley's house. He had his gun, and he had an idea to put a tail on both Luttrell and Hager. If Hager was playing the media card, there was nothing stopping Riley from doing the same. He knew he was only playing a reporter, but there was enough circumstantial evidence to anonymously pass along to a certain bulldog reporter in Lexington to change the tide of the media coverage, all while making Riley look as if she were above such things. Which, he knew, she wasn't. She would happily get her hands dirty if it meant doing what was right.

When Matt pulled to a stop, he blinked and then smiled. Riley was waiting for him on the porch swing in nothing but her underwear. Matt responded instantly by ripping off his shirt and trying to get out of the car quietly. He kicked off his boots and shucked his pants. After the previous night, he knew Riley was up for anything. But sex in the middle of the day outside where anyone could see them? Seems he was up for it in more ways than one.

Matt tiptoed up the few stairs and paused. His mischievous grin fell along with his erection. "What the hell happened to your hand?" She had a shirt tied tightly around her forearm, but that didn't hide the swelling and discolored hand.

Riley jerked as she opened her eyes as if she were afraid of something. "Viper den in my closet. A copperhead bit me. Why are you naked?"

Matt was by her side in an instant as he examined her hand. It looked as if it were starting to swell but not as badly as he had heard it could be if someone was sensitive to the venom. "How's the pain?"

"It might feel better if you shoot my hand off," Riley tried to joke, though he could see she was serious.

"When is the ambulance getting here?" Matt felt as if his whole world was coming to a shuddering stop. The sight of the woman he loved battling off the pain of a poisonous snakebite was even worse than when she was attacked. At least then she could fight back. Now they were helpless.

"I haven't called one yet. My cell phone is in my room and there's not a chance in hell I'm going back in that house," Riley told him as she put her other arm over her eyes and took a deep breath.

Matt cursed and leapt down the stairs right as he heard the sound of another vehicle coming to a stop. It was an old town car, and it had three white heads with their faces plastered to the windshield in it. The car rolled to a stop as Matt picked up his pants and pulled his phone from the back pocket.

He heard the sound of a photo being taken but he was already dialing 9-1-1 and didn't care that the Rose sisters were getting a kick out of seeing his "winkie" (their word, not his).

"This is Trooper Matt Walz. I have a copperhead bite victim." He noticed the Roses instantly grew quiet as he rattled off the address along with the pertinent medical information the emergency responders and the hospital would need to know for proper treatment.

The Rose sisters pushed past him as he finished with the call. By the time he pulled up his pants, he heard more cars coming and figured he'd better get dressed or it wouldn't only be Riley's life in danger. He had just shoved his feet into his boots when Miss Lily shuffled by him and pulled a quilt from the car at the same time Cy and Gemma's slid to a stop, kicking up dust.

"Where's my baby?" Gemma asked with fear etched in her face.

"On the porch," Matt responded as Gemma raced by. "Emergency services are on their way. The bite was ten minutes ago. Her reaction is mild to moderate, thank goodness. There appears to be no allergic reaction," Matt rattled off as he jogged up the stairs next to Cy.

"Let Daddy see," Cy cooed as the Rose sisters let him through. Riley was fighting tears, and Gemma was as pale as a ghost as she stroked Riley's cheek and whispered soothing words to her. Miss Lily's brightly colored quilt covered Riley from the neck down, but it didn't take Cy long to notice that was all she was wearing. Matt could hear Cy's teeth grinding from where he stood slightly behind him.

"It's not bad, baby. I know it doesn't feel like it, but as soon as they give you the pain medication, you'll feel a lot better." Cy leaned forward and kissed Riley on the cheek as her mother tried to hide the tears threatening to escape down her cheeks.

Matt fought the urge to push Cy out of the way so he could be at Riley's side, but it wasn't his place. Not yet. One thing that had been made shockingly clear was he was in love with Riley. Not the kind where you think you *might* be, but the full-blown die-for-her type of love. And right now seeing her in pain was ripping his heart out.

Cy stood up and quietly walked toward Matt. Before Matt knew what was happening, he had a fist to the face. "You want to tell me why my daughter is naked, and you were putting on your boots when we arrived?"

Matt rubbed his jaw. At least he hadn't seen him naked. He shot a glance at the Rose sisters who stared with open mouths and wide eyes and figured it was a 50/50 shot that the picture of him naked was already being circulated.

"Dad," Riley cried. "Stop! It wasn't Matt's fault. He wasn't even here."

Matt's gut twisted. She needed to stay calm. "It's okay, sweetheart. Just let me have a talk with your father. You just rest." Matt pulled Cy off the porch and to his car. "We were going to go shooting. I went back to get my rifle. While I was gone, Riley was going to change out of her suit and also get ready. She said she went for the boots in her closet and reached right into a den of vipers. She said there were copperheads and timber rattlesnakes, along with some nonvenomous snakes. She was bitten by a copperhead and then shot as many as she could and ran out here to get away from them."

"I won't bother to ask why you arrived without boots because I think I know. And if I'm right, I'll castrate you."

"I think Mrs. Davies might have a problem with that. She wants grandkids, and I'm the only man not afraid of you. I actually like you. Anyway, what I'm more curious about is the timber snakes. They're not generally found in

Central Kentucky. And while they do nest with copperheads and the other snakes Riley described, that's typically in a forest, not a closet."

Cy's eyes narrowed and Matt could see his mind churning. "You think they were planted?"

"I don't know. I've heard of plenty of copperheads in houses, but hardly ever a timber rattler. And while they are generally more docile than copperheads, their bite is more deadly. If Riley hadn't reacted as quickly as she did, she would have been bitten multiple times by multiple venomous snakes less than an hour after Harvey Luttrell threatened her. Coincidence? Maybe. But I don't like coincidences."

Cy nodded. "I have a friend who is a snake expert. He'll tell us if they were naturally in the house or if someone put them there. He's a professor at the University of Kentucky. I'll have him meet us at the hospital. In the meantime, get your gun and get my daughter some clothes."

Chapter Fifteen

Riley felt good, really good after the hospital had given her morphine for the pain. Two shots in twenty minutes had left her unable to stop smiling.

"Why is she giggling?" Miss Violet asked quietly.

"You're awesome, Miss Violet. I miss your bread pudding, though. Zinnia does a pretty good job, but her bread pudding doesn't make me orgasm like yours does. Just a little *zing* to your hoo-ha when you take a bite. I miss that," Riley sighed.

Matt stood by the door, shaking his head and trying not to laugh. The Rose sisters, Gemma, and Riley's cousin Layne were all crammed into the small, curtained room. At that moment, he was content with not being seen.

Layne's father, Miles, was with Cy at Riley's house with the snake expert. He had left only after doctors had assured him Riley was perfectly fine. Her hand had swollen, but with medicine, it was slowly coming back down. She hadn't needed anti-venom but would be kept overnight for pain management. While she had received a bite, the envenomation was local to her bite. The doctor told her it would hurt for 24 to 48 hours as the pressure from the swelling receded, and then her hand may be a little stiff for a month, but it shouldn't hinder her. She had been lucky and had shown no sensitivity to the venom.

Miss Lily clucked. "It's a sad day when a pretty woman like you is reduced to orgasm by dessert."

Gemma rolled her eyes at Miss Lily and Riley giggled again. "What do you expect after *the incident?* And when I'm over that, Dad goes all crazy on anyone I date. And all it did was let Reagan get away with . . . oops," Riley's eyes got comically big as she slapped her unswollen hand over her mouth. "That's a secret," Riley whispered to the entire room before giggling again.

"At least one of your daughters has apparently been getting some." Miss Daisy chuckled as Gemma lightly swatted at her.

"That is not something I need to be worrying about or knowing about," Gemma whispered.

"It is if you want grandbabies," Miss Lily said seriously, though her eyes danced with amusement.

"Babies!" Riley said happily before sighing. "I want babies. Not now, though. Good thing, too, since Matt used a condom, and I don't know if he even loves me, but I hope so. Talk about your hoo-ha *zinging,* though," Riley said, fanning herself as a loud growling noise filled the room. Matt didn't need to turn around to know that Cy and Miles were back.

"It's a good thing I love him. I'll let him make my hoo-ha *zing* every day. Every breakfast, lunch, snack time, and dinner. Basically anytime I eat, I could have sex. They say sex is better than chocolate and Matt sex is *waaaaaay* better."

The room gasped as the growl grew louder, and Matt

was glad he was already in a hospital. He prided himself on being a strong man, a man who never backed down, but there was no way in hell he was going to turn around right now or he'd need emergency care. He could feel the anger rolling off Cy, standing behind him.

Riley sighed again as Layne frantically tried to get Riley to talk about something else. Riley pushed her cousin's hand away from her mouth and narrowed her drugged eyes at Layne. "You of all people should understand. I mean, remember that super-hot guy you were boinking before Uncle Miles found out and scared him away? Where are the real men? Men who aren't afraid of some old dads," Riley asked as if she were giving a speech in the House of Representatives. Gemma stifled a laugh. She apparently didn't fear for Matt's life and any future grandchildren as much as Matt had hoped. A second growl, deeper than Cy's, sounded behind him as Layne frantically tried to quiet Riley, but she was on a roll.

"Men with balls. And big penises! Who know how to use them," Riley added as a second thought. "Men who can stand up to our fathers and say, 'I'm going to love your daughter. I'm going to *zing* her all night long because a good man gives good orgasms,' right, Layne?"

"Amen!" Miss Lily called out.

Layne groaned and covered her face with her hands.

"You and I need to have a little talk." The barely formed words coming from right behind Matt sent shivers down his back. And if that weren't enough, Cy's hand clamped around the base of Matt's neck to pull him away from the room.

"Oh! There he is. Hi, Matt. You have a nice penis and

know how to make my hoo-ha *zing*!" Riley called out before she caught sight of her father. It would have been comical if the hand squeezing Matt's neck didn't suddenly tighten.

Riley's eyes were so round they might've popped out of her head. Then she shook her head, lifted up the hospital sheet, and looked under it. "I'm sorry, hoo-ha, no more *zinging* for you." She put the sheet down as Cy dragged Matt away. They heard her call out, "Before you die, know I love you, Matt!"

He was probably going to die. There was nothing "old" about Cy. He still ran every day and sparred with professional bad-asses. However, all that fear was cast aside when he heard Riley tell him she loved him. Okay, it was a drug-induced declaration, but he'd take it since it wasn't a whispered "I love you" like you say when you aren't really sure and don't want any of your friends to know. Nope, she had screamed that she loved him, and he was going to find a way to tell her he loved her, too.

Cy shoved the door leading to the stairwell open, sending two nurses scurrying back into the hall. He didn't say anything as he took a deep breath, and Matt decided he was tired of waiting for his demise. He might as well face it head on. "Would it help if I told you I loved your daughter?"

Cy shook his head. "That's my baby girl."

"I know. And I know about what happened to Riley in college," Matt said with more seriousness than he'd ever had before. This was his whole future, and he wasn't going to lose it.

Cy stopped clenching and relaxed his fist. "She told

you about that?"

Matt nodded. "Don't forget we've known each other for years. Just like you and I have. And have I ever not been there for you or your family? Have I ever hurt Riley or given any indication I ever would?" Cy didn't say anything, but he hadn't killed Matt yet either, so Matt went on. "I would have asked Riley out over a year ago, but I think we needed to go our own way for a while to see if our paths came back to each other. And they have. My feelings haven't changed. I love her. I did last year. I will next year. I hope you'll approve of our dating, but it won't change anything if you don't. I want to be with her, and I'll leave that up to Riley if she feels the same."

Matt held his breath. Cy relaxed more and started to pace the small landing of the stairwell. "I guess I can be a little overprotective," he admitted as if under extreme torture.

"I've already warned Riley that I will be, too," Matt said as he dared to allow his lips to quirk upward.

"After the text she sent in college . . ." Cy shook his head as the memory came back. "Luckily, my brothers and Ahmed where playing poker with me that night. Cade had her location pinged instantly, and we all took off after her. My heart stopped beating from the second I read that text. I don't know if it has ever fully recovered. Someone tried to take my little girl from me."

Matt nodded solemnly. It caused his heart to constrict even thinking about it.

"Riley doesn't remember most of it, but I do. We found him in a deserted parking garage near the bar she had been at. He was over halfway up and parked in a dark corner."

Matt felt his brows knit in confusion. "Riley said she remembers the car slamming to a stop."

"No. She must have mistaken my ramming his car with that. I lost my mind when I saw his silhouette grabbing at my daughter. I slammed my car into the back of his so his car was pinned on the front by the cement barrier and behind by my car. He wasn't going to drive off before I dealt with him. Riley's shirt was torn. He had his pants down and was trying to . . . Riley was fighting with everything she had, even if she doesn't remember it. But she was so weak. She wouldn't have been able to hold him off much longer. I reached in and pulled him out at the same time Miles got Riley. He and Marshall had her rushed to the hospital where a drug test was taken, and they pumped her full of liquids to flush her system. Emma discharged her and took her home with Marshall and Miles after the hospital did everything they could. It's handy to have an ER doctor as a family friend."

"What happened to him, and why doesn't Riley know?" Matt asked.

"I may have crossed the line and injured him. However, all parties witnessed him slipping down the stairs as he tried to run away. My brothers took him to the police station, and Ahmed drove me to the hospital. Riley doesn't remember it. She didn't even remember being in the hospital. I asked her if she wanted to know what happened, and she said no. She knew she hadn't been raped and just said she wanted to put it behind her. I should have forced her to talk about it. I should have made her see a counselor, but she refused. She does have a stubborn streak," Cy said, knowing full well that streak came from him.

"And the guy?" Matt asked.

"Was put in jail. Riley's blood test showed she was drugged. Furthermore, she had clawed his face. The doctors collected the scrapings from under her nails. When the police got involved, they ran his DNA against open rape cases and found two matches. He's serving twenty years for rape."

Matt drew a deep breath. "And Riley has no idea because she just wants to shut the whole incident out. She needs to know. She doesn't think she does, but it scarred her more than she wants to admit. However, she did say Bridget and Annie helped her get her confidence back."

Cy nodded. "I called them. I knew I was too involved. I was too close to it and she wouldn't listen to me. Anyway, I didn't mean to say so much. It's just that, because of this, I *might* have been a little hard on the men she was dating."

"I'm not going to complain," Matt said with a grin that had Cy relaxing his shoulders. "I just want you to know you don't have to protect her anymore. I want the honor of that position. I want to be there for her for every up and every down."

"I can't do that. I'll always protect her, but I'd be happy for the help." Cy held out his hand and Matt quickly took it. That was the closest thing Matt would ever get as a blessing, but he'd take it.

Chapter Sixteen

Riley blinked her eyes open. It was Friday. The vote was that day. She put her hand to her head and groaned at the headache pounding behind her eyes.

"How are you feeling?"

Riley let her hand fall and looked around the curtained room. She found Matt pushing off a flimsy blanket from where he sat in a hard plastic chair next to her. She gave him a weak smile and then looked at her hand. It was a nasty color of black and blue, but the swelling had started to go down. She could even bend her fingers again.

"Hand is feeling better, but my head is killing me."

"They took away your happy juice," Matt chuckled.

"The what?" Riley tried to remember all the medicine they had given her. Quite frankly, she didn't care what it was. All she cared about was the pain had gone away.

"Morphine. You're not sensitive to copperhead venom, but you are to morphine. It made you a happy, giggly, talking mess."

Riley blinked as she tried to remember what she had said. She remembered the Rose sisters, her mother, and Layne being there. "I remember just talking with the girls. Then I dreamed about wolves growling and stealing

Layne."

Matt's shoulders shook, and he gave up the fight and let loose with his laughter. "Honey, those weren't wolves. Those were your father and your uncle Miles. Your girl talk was all about sex. Miles swooped in when you started talking to Layne about, your words not mine, 'that hot guy you were boinking.'"

Riley was mortified. She would never deliberately tell Layne's secrets. Oh, no. What other secrets did she tell? "What else did I say?"

"You said enough to get people wondering what Reagan's up to, but you didn't spill the beans. You also let Miss Violet know her bread pudding gave you an orgasm, and you told your mother we practice safe sex and I gave you a better orgasm than the bread pudding. And that's when your dad hauled me out."

Riley was about to find out if you could die from embarrassment. "And you're alive?"

Matt grinned at her, and she decided she'd rather not die of embarrassment and partake in one of those orgasms again instead. "We're good."

"Say what?" Riley must not have heard him right. Matt was probably in the chair because both legs were broken, and he was higher on drugs than she apparently had been.

Matt stood up so he could take a seat next to her on the bed. No broken legs. No broken anything. He looked perfect. He lay against the back of the bed and brought her into his arms. She rested her head against his chest and listened to his heartbeat. "There is something I want to tell you," Riley said slowly.

She felt Matt's chest rumble as he said "Hmm."

Riley took a deep breath. It was only speaking the truth, and you should never be afraid to speak the truth. "I've fallen in love with you. I think I've loved you since that night at the water tower."

"I know," Matt said softly as he kissed the top of her head.

"Wait, what? You know?" Riley shot up and was about to punch him when she saw the grin on his face.

"You might have mentioned that yesterday, too." Matt stopped laughing and cupped her face with his hands before kissing her gently on the lips. "And I love you, too."

"There is something I need to do, though, before I feel I can put the past behind me and move on. I need to find out what happened that night in college," Riley said softly as she buried her face into his shirt. Just thinking about the man still alive was enough to keep her heart from truly being free.

"I think it's time, too."

Riley sat up as her dad walked in and took a seat next to her bed. "You're not here to kill Matt, are you?"

Her father's lips twitched with amusement. "Not yet. Can I talk to you alone, though?"

Matt gave a nod and slid from the bed. "I'll go get us some breakfast. You want anything, Mr. Davies?"

"Sure, grab me whatever you're getting."

Riley was pretty sure she had died and was now living in an alternate universe. "Not yet?" she asked as Matt left.

"Nah. He's good enough to date you. Now, marriage is something else."

Riley tried to hide the tears threatening to spill and took a deep breath. "Tell me about that night."

Her father moved to hold her hand and started at the beginning. By the time he was through, she had lost her battle with her tears, but a weight she hadn't even known she was carrying was lifted. The bogeyman wasn't out to get her anymore. Well, someone else was out to get her, but she knew how to get them. She needed to get back to Frankfort and shake things up.

***

"Are you sure you want to be here?" Matt asked once again as he parked the car at the Capitol building.

"More than anything. Dad told me they couldn't determine whether the snakes were planted in my house or not, since they found what appeared to be an entrance point. Either way, I'm going for a little payback," Riley said with a grin that worried Matt.

"What do you have planned?"

"Want to help me release snakes into the House chambers?"

"You didn't."

Riley laughed and shook her head. Ever since her talk with Matt and then her father that morning, she seemed lighter. Nothing was holding her back now. She had agreed to see a therapist . . . well, she agreed to talk to Sydney Ashton Parker. Sydney was a sports psychologist and was Riley's cousin by marriage, but Sydney had all the certifications and was taking a crash course in an advanced class this week to be ready for their first appointment.

"No, but I thought about it. I just intend to make a very public speech."

Riley opened the door and with a bounce in her step

left him hurrying after her. At the door, DeAndre gave her a hug and shook his hand. "Damn, it's good to hear you're okay."

"How did you know I wasn't?"

"I know everything that goes on in and out of Frankfort."

"Are you sure your last name isn't Wolfe?"

DeAndre smiled. "I'm sure."

"Do aliens speak to you?" Matt asked.

"Nah, man. Just no one pays attention to the rent-a-guard. I hear all kinds of things."

"So, where did you hear about my hand?" Riley pressed.

"Everyone has heard about your snake incident. Too many people, if you ask me. Someone wanted to make sure everyone was talking about it. I can't pin down who said what first. There are two stories going around. One, it was an accident. Two, it was payback for being a pain in the ass."

"How's the split?" Riley asked.

"Pretty even. And I hear both of them being debated all the time, so it's hard to know which people think which theory is the correct one. The House has already started, so you'll make quite an entrance. Oh, and there's a camera crew in your office. Tell my baby 'hi' for me. She's loving her job so far. I think you created a monster when you told her she had free rein of the office," DeAndre joked.

Matt followed Riley and heard Aniyah before he was even halfway down the hallway. "And I told you, I don't give a fig who you work for. I work for Miss Davies, and I promised her I'd keep her office cleared of bullshit. And sugar, you reek of it."

A perky blonde stormed out of the office in such a huff she didn't even see Riley and Matt walking toward her with huge smiles on their faces. "I knew Aniyah would be perfect for my office," said Riley.

Matt just shook his head as Riley walked through her door and stopped. "I see you've done some rearranging."

"Oh! Bless me. I didn't expect you in today. I hope it's okay, Miss Davies. I didn't want anyone sneaking in on me," Aniyah said a she stood up from the desk positioned right in front of the door. There was barely enough room to close the office door without hitting it and Aniyah had the door propped in such a way that it connected with the end of her desk, leaving only one way to get past her and into the office.

"It's brilliant," Riley smiled. "And call me Riley."

Matt stood behind Riley and peered over her shoulder. There wasn't any room for him to stand anywhere else. Aniyah had her cross necklace draped nicely over cleavage pushing up from her one-too-many-unbuttoned blouse, but it worked. On anyone else, the tight pencil skirt and display of boobs would be ridiculed, but not on Aniyah. She was an interesting combination of classy and sassy. "Looking very professional. It also seems your desk is already working."

Aniyah preened under Matt's praise. "Thank you. This is my business attire. I thought since I was working in such a fancy place, I better dress for it." Matt looked down to her five-inch stilettos that made walking in stilts look easy and grinned. Aniyah's confidence is what pulled her outfit together. She was rocking it, and she knew it.

"What did Peel's assistant want?" Riley asked as she moved around the desk, and Aniyah closed and locked the door behind them.

"This shit is real. I mean, I thought those reality shows with them rich women, er, rich husbands — whatever they are — were messed up, but it ain't nothing compared to what's going on here. First of all, what happened to you? It's all everyone is talking about, and they are circling your door like vultures," Aniyah asked as they went to sit on the couch and chairs set back in a private corner.

"We don't know for sure. It could be really bad luck or someone planted a den of poisonous snakes in my closet," Riley told her.

Aniyah made the sign of the cross. "Lord, that is some messed-up stuff. It makes you miss the days people just shot each other."

Matt struggled not to smile, and Riley just nodded. "I hate to agree with that, but I would like to know who is behind this or if it really is just bad luck."

"The camera crew you wanted is hiding in your office. I made sure none of these spies saw them. What's going on?" Aniyah asked.

"Ever heard of Harvey Luttrell or LeeRoy Hager?" Riley asked, and Aniyah just shook her head. "See what you can find out. All these people visiting you want information, and now I want information. I want to know who is in Luttrell's and Hager's pockets."

"What information about you should I give them in return?" Aniyah wanted to know.

"Tell them I am thinking of changing my vote to support the highway if we get an exit into downtown

Keeneston. But I need this information immediately. I'm going to walk into the House chambers before the vote. Then, soon enough, they'll all know I'm not changing my vote."

"You got it, Miss R. I'll have them eating out of my hand in no time." Aniyah got up and hurried from the room. It was actually close to a sprint, and Matt just shook his head.

"How can she run so fast in those shoes?" Matt wondered out loud.

Riley laughed. "I was thinking the same thing. Now, let's go have a chat with the news crew."

Riley opened her office door and found none other than Dan from Channel 14 News sitting on her couch, having makeup applied. Riley had never seen so much bronzer being used before, or so much eyebrow dye on such bushy brows.

"Ah, Representative Davies. Dan Kentner, 14 News head anchor." Dan stood up with the napkins still stuffed in his collar making him look like an over-bronzed, furry-eyed pilgrim.

"I'm honored," Riley said seriously even though she was struggling not to laugh. She needed Dan on her side. He was the most prominent local news anchor in central Kentucky.

"What's so important that you called the station manager, who woke me up early to come here? I know it's the budget vote today, but that's not sexy. That's standard six o'clock news." Dan sat back down and was instantly attacked by the makeup lady.

"How about an alleged attempted murder by pit vipers over the proposed highway?" Riley asked sweetly.

Dan slapped away the woman putting on blush. "Now that's sexy. Someone get Representative Davies into hair and makeup. I have an exclusive interview to do."

Forty-five minutes later, the interview was given, and Aniyah was pacing back and forth while Dan finished taping his segment. Riley didn't even have time to ask Aniyah what she found before Dan did. "You're the assistant and you look like you know something."

"It's okay, Aniyah. Dan has an exclusive on this story," Riley said to calm Aniyah's ruffled feathers. Aniyah didn't like Dan at first glance. When she saw his eyebrows, she made the sign of the cross.

"Well, I heard that Luttrell and Hager go way back. Rumor has it they were middle school buddies in some small Podunk town here in Kentucky, but no one could remember the name of it. Luttrell's father was a farmer, and Luttrell went off to college in New York City to study business. That's where he got his idea to industrialize farming. He brought in investors, and then bam, the model exploded and no more local farms. Hager has a similar story. Worked construction on roads out of high school for years. Then his good buddy Luttrell talked a bank into giving Hager a loan to start his own road construction company. The rest is history," Aniyah said as she sat down on the couch and looked at Dan. "You need to tweeze your eyebrows. There's some crazy hair there, and it just ain't right."

Before Dan could explode, the makeup lady was

already attacking the eyebrows with her tweezers.

"So who is in bed with whom?" Riley asked, drawing Aniyah's attention away from the crazy eyebrow hair.

"That's hard to say. I know who all is voting for the highway, but besides Peel and Stanley, there's no one overly vocal about it. Now, Peel's bimbo . . . Did I say that out loud? Bless her heart, I shouldn't say something that cruel. Peel's personal assistant who assists in all things personal did say that Hager is building a road in Lumpur and that Senator Hump-her . . . Lord help me, my mouth is just running away today. She said Senator Peel and Hager have quite a few connections back home. Oh, and Luttrell regularly donates to Marge Stanley's charities. Besides that, there are plenty of people those two donate to, including yourself. Here's a list."

Riley nodded as she took the list of people who received donations from one or both of the men, and who were voting in favor of the highway. She and Dan had talked about that. The rest of the media outlets were having a field day saying Riley was a bought vote and she wanted to set the record straight. "Matt, do you think you can find anything out? Ask our sources back home."

Dan snorted. "Him? He's a journalist for a small town paper. What could he find out that I couldn't?"

Riley just shook her head, and Matt rolled his eyes. "How about we all work on digging up information. I don't think it will be as simple as a campaign donation. We need to go deeper. Who has a personal or professional relationship with Luttrell and Hager? And Dan, can you get your reporters to ambush them both as soon as my speech is over in the House?"

"I don't ambush. I question. And I have many questions for these two."

"Well, I think it's time for me to place my vote." Riley smiled and stood up. "Shall we, Dan?"

Riley linked her hand through Dan's arm, and they walked out of her office. "I'm not missing this. You coming, sugar?" Aniyah asked Matt. Matt sent her a wink, offered her his arm, and escorted her down the hall.

"I can't wait to see what she does," Aniyah whispered. "Miss Riley has just enough crazy in her to make politics fun."

Matt chuckled. "She's always interesting, that's for sure."

Matt watched as Riley pulled her hand from Dan's arm and the camera filmed her walking toward the doors the chamber. The two guards opened them at the same time and Riley walked through them and into the House.

"I'm sorry, am I late to the vote?" Riley said loud enough for it to echo off the granite walls and cause instant silence.

Chapter Seventeen

Riley felt devilish as she saw the look of surprise on the faces around her. The Speaker of the House rapped his gavel. "We've begun the vote, Miss Davies, and you are interrupting."

Riley put on an innocently shocked expression. "Oh, I'm so sorry. You see, I'm running late since someone tried to kill me to prevent me from voting here today."

Riley hid her worry that she was wrong. If she was wrong and the snakes naturally got into her house, then she would never live it down. However, she didn't think this was the case. The timing was off and the weather was too good for snakes to be seeking warmth in her closet. She had decided she was going to risk it all on her gut feeling that this had been an attack.

The room erupted in whispers and the Speaker rapped his gavel again. "Order!"

"I know that we're voting, but I think you'll allow me one minute to speak, since I was so horrifically detained." Riley held up her hand and the room gasped. She didn't wait for the Speaker to give her permission. She didn't need to when the camera crew stepped into the area reserved for press. Everyone started preening, and it gave

Riley the opening she needed.

"I've always been against the highway. Am I against progress? No. What I am against is bullying, and that is what this is about. Some people think because their food company or their road company donated to your campaign, they get to tell you how to vote. That's not how you envisioned being a politician, is it? You probably dreamed of doing what's best for your town, your neighbors, and your constituents. Not being forced to do something you know is wrong just to make sure you have the money to get reelected. Well, I don't care if I'm reelected. And I'm not going to be bullied or threatened," Riley held up her hand again, "into voting for something I know is wrong. Something that serves no point — we already have a highway connecting Frankfort and Lexington — and something that will destroy my historic town. And why? Why are people like Harvey Luttrell and LeeRoy Hager so determined to see this highway completed? If you know the answer, and I can guarantee you it's not to better our state, then you'd better vote against this highway. Because next, they'll come for your district."

The House went quiet and the Speaker cleared his throat. "May we finish our vote now?"

Riley smiled sweetly. "Yes, please."

She took her seat and watched, palms sweating and heart pounding, as the highway funding was narrowly shot down. She had won the first battle.

~

Matt was so proud of Riley. She was radiant with the

excitement from her win. They both knew it was going to be short-lived, though. The Senate was meeting over the weekend to review their budget. A vote was scheduled for Monday, and she fully expected Peel and Stanley to get the highway funded in the Senate budget. That meant next week, the final week in the session, both bodies of Congress would hash out those parts of the budget that only passed either the Senate or the House. But for this weekend, they were going to celebrate.

"Where are we going?" Riley asked as he turned off the road leading to her farm.

"My house," Matt said with a grin. "Remember, we're having dinner at your parents' house tonight, and I thought you'd want to change. I know you said panty hose were invented by the devil, so I figured you'd be dying for your jeans."

"Yeah, but aren't they at my house?" Riley asked confused.

"Not any more. I had them moved after the snake attack. You shot your floor to hell, and it's being fixed."

"You would have too, if tons of snakes were slithering out of your closet right toward you," Riley mumbled before shivering at the memory.

Matt reached over and gave her thigh a squeeze. "I know. That's why I moved your clothes over to my house. I thought you might want some time to recover before opening your closet door again. And this isn't permanent, unless you want it to be."

Matt held his breath as he pulled to a stop in front of his brick ranch house in the small, middle-class subdivision on the outskirts of Keeneston. He looked at the minimal landscaping and the basketball hoop in the driveway. Maybe it wasn't as nice as Riley's flower-filled country cottage, but it was all his. Besides, with all of the undercover work, he hadn't been home enough to appreciate it.

"It's strange. We've only spent one night together, yet I can't imagine ever spending another night apart." Riley leaned over the seat, careful of her still-sensitive hand, and kissed his lips.

"I love you, Riley. Before I left, I found out there were ten acres for sale behind your farm. I thought about buying it, but I don't know if it's still for sale. It made me think of you—of us. But anyway, I don't care where we are so long as we're together."

"Well, come on. We don't want to be late for dinner, and I'm eager to be shown the house. Especially the bedroom."

Matt shot up the driveway and into the garage. Before the garage door was all the way closed, he had Riley in his arms and his mouth to hers. He picked her up into his arms and closed the door. "Mudroom," he murmured against her lips as he walked through the house. "Kitchen, living room, our room."

He set her on the bed and kept his eyes on her as he stripped off his clothes. He held out his hand, and she put her healthy one in it. Helping her to her feet, he unbuttoned her blouse and unzipped her skirt. He hung them in the closet next to the clothes he had her cousin, Sydney Davies McKnight, bring over before sliding his hands around her ribs to unhook her bra. He let it fall to the floor and placed his lips on her neck. Riley moaned softly as he trailed his lips down the column of her neck, over her collarbone, and down to her breast.

Matt went to his knees, trailing his lips down her stomach. He pushed her panties to the floor and let his lips follow her curves. With his hand splayed across Riley's stomach, he pushed backward and she fell laughingly onto the bed. Matt started his kisses with her ankle and sucked, nibbled, and kissed his way up to the sweet spot between her legs.

Hearing Riley's moans of pleasure and feeling her spear her fingers into his hair had him struggling to move slowly. When he felt her orgasm near, he moved up her body and surged inside of her. The feel of her tightening around him, the sounds she made, and the way her hand grasped his arm, rocked him to the core. Love just didn't seem to be a strong enough word to convey the feelings he felt for Riley.

Riley didn't want to move for the rest of the night unless it was to make love to Matt again. She had her body wrapped around his, her injured hand resting on his muscled chest. "You're gaining your weight back," she said absently as she traced the contours of his abdominal muscles.

"I'll be glad when my pants don't sag anymore. Another week of eating all this food the town brought over, and I'll have to lose weight. Speaking of food . . ."

"Noooo," Riley whined. "Don't say it."

She felt Matt's chest rumble with laughter. "It's your family. Don't make me have to explain why we are late. I still don't know how I escaped with my life after your father heard about us having sex."

Riley smiled as she absently ran her fingers through the light smattering of light brown hair on his chest and let her fingers follow the nice little path that led straight to his . . . "Riley," Matt warned, "if your fingers continue on that path, we will be late and I'll be forced to tell your father it was your fault."

"Fine," Riley huffed as she sat up, giving him a good view of her breasts.

"I could be quick," Matt said before sucking a nipple into his mouth. His tongue swirled around it, and Riley thought being late wouldn't be too bad.

"Oh no," Riley complained as she pulled away. "My brothers are in town. I totally forgot they're here for the night before leaving on spring break."

Matt shrugged as he watched her leap from the bed. "So? If your dad likes me, your brothers shouldn't be a problem. They already like me."

"That was before you started sleeping with me," Riley cried as she pulled on a pair of jeans. "Do you have your body armor in the car?"

Matt laughed at her and Riley just shook his head. Moron, didn't he know her younger twin brothers were the hellions of Keeneston? It didn't matter that they were now twenty-one and about to graduate college in a few months. They were still beyond mischievous.

"I'll be fine. I've known your brothers since they were in high school. Stop worrying," Matt said as he tried to calm her.

"At lease promise me you'll pack your gun."

"I'm not going to shoot your brothers for no reason,"

Matt chastised.

"It would be in self-defense," Riley warned.

Matt buttoned his jeans and attached his service weapon to his waistband. "There. Happy?"

"I'd feel better if you put on your body armor," Riley muttered as she pulled on a University of Kentucky sweatshirt.

Matt buttoned up his lightweight navy flannel shirt and grinned at her. "You'll see. Tonight will be fun. I'm practically part of the family already."

Chapter Eighteen

He'd been wrong. Matt was ambushed before he even entered the Davies house. He had opened the door for Riley, who had gone inside. But before he could step foot over the threshold, her brothers, Porter and Parker, had appeared out of nowhere to block him. They still had a youthful appearance in their faces, but their bodies were not those of little boys. They stood at almost the same height at Matt's six-feet-two inches, with muscled arms crossed over their wide chests.

Unlike the newly married Zain and his identical twin bachelor brother, Gabe, Porter and Parker didn't look alike. They were fraternal twins. While they were approximately the same height, their hazel eyes were on the opposite ends of the spectrum. Porter had more green color to his eyes compared to the darker brown of Parker. They both had brown hair, but again, there were differences. Porter's hair was highlighted with blond while Parker had a touch of deep red highlighting his darker hair.

"Hey, guys," Matt smiled. They didn't smile back. "Where are you going on spring break?"

"We're riding in a rodeo tournament in Miami. Beach, babes, bulls — is there anything better?" Parker asked while he kept his face serious.

"Good luck." Matt smiled and then tried to step into the house. He would have to shove his way between them if he wanted to get through.

"Let's go for a walk," Porter suggested without any real alternative. It was a command.

"What about dinner?" Matt asked, suddenly wondering if he should have put on his bulletproof vest after all.

"We have a couple of minutes," Parker said as each brother took an arm and pulled Matt from the porch.

"When we were younger, we used to come out here and shoot before dinner. You know, have competitions to decide who got the biggest piece of dessert and whatnot," Porter explained as they walked farther from the house to where the shooting range was. It wasn't elaborate. Just a couple of targets set up with a mound of dirt behind each one to catch the bullets. There was a small open-air building with a table and some chairs along with lights. Farther out was basically a high school football field light that allowed them to shoot at night.

"We thought it would be fun to have a little chat while we took some shots." Parker grinned as he and Porter pulled out the guns concealed by their long-sleeved T-shirts.

Matt shrugged. He would have been more worried if one of the elderly Rose sisters pulled out a gun, which they had before. Their cataracts had caused their aim to go all out of whack. Everyone in Keeneston had a gun, though. Miss Lily had told him it came from their history of being a frontier town and just never went away. Until recently, there was never a state trooper in the area, and the sheriff's office was half the size it is now. You had to depend upon yourself and your neighbors if anything went wrong. Even though parts of Keeneston were modernizing, that mindset hadn't changed over the centuries.

"Well, I'm glad I brought my gun then," Matt smiled as he pulled out his gun and saw a brief flash of disappointment in the twins' eyes before Porter flipped on the lights.

"I'll go first." Parker stepped up to the line and aimed. "Are you sleeping with our sister?"

Bang.

"Yes," Matt answered as he waited patiently for his turn.

"Do you love her?" Porter asked as he stepped up to the line next.

Bang.

"Yes." Matt stepped up to the line and looked at the target. There were two holes near dead center.

"You know we'll kill you if you hurt Riley, right?" Parker asked as Matt took aim.

"Yes."

Bang.

Matt smiled as his bullet split the difference between the brothers' bullets.

"You going to marry her?" Porter asked while waiting for Parker to take his shot.

Matt paused a bit. Marry her? He knew the idea had been floating around in his mind, but he hadn't taken it too seriously since he and Riley had taken so long to get together. But they already knew they didn't want to be apart. They would be moving in with each other, even if it was unofficial.

Bang.

Parker's question was like a blow to the heart. It was so obvious. Matt wanted to marry Riley. He wanted to love her, to share his life with her. He wanted to fix things when they broke around the house, to kill spiders and snakes for her. He wanted to have her show him up in hand-to-hand combat, to make love whenever and wherever they wanted. He really wanted to see Riley glow with pregnancy and to share that moment at three in the morning standing over a crib watching a newborn sleep.

"Well, are you going to marry Riley?" Porter asked once more before taking his own shot.

Bang.

"Yes," Matt just answered as he lined up his shot, almost giddy with excitement. He knew down to his toes that marrying Riley was what he wanted. It felt comfortable and adventurous at the same time. There was no one else he'd rather share the adventure of life with than her.

Bang.

Matt clicked the safety on and put the gun back in his holster. "Good talk, boys." Matt clapped his future brothers-in-law on their shoulders and left them staring at his bullseye as he headed back to the house.

Riley slammed the meatloaf onto the table. "Where did the twins take Matt?" she asked her mother for the tenth time.

"They just said they wanted to hang out with your boyfriend for a moment," Gemma smiled and handed Cy a bowl of rice.

"Your mother wouldn't let me go," her father complained.

"They're young men, Cy. They need to bond," her mother said for what Riley guessed was not the first time.

"The last time they told you they were going to 'bond' with the guys, they set fire to a bale of hay and shot Pam Gilbert's garden gnome for ratting them out to Uncle Marshall." Marshall, the sheriff of Keeneston, had taken them to jail. It had happened the previous summer when they had turned twenty-one.

"How did I forget that?" her mother asked as she almost dropped the bottle of wine and pulled out her phone.

"Honey, what are you doing?" her father asked, shaking his head. "You know boys will be boys."

"That's so unfair!" Riley accused. "You didn't say girls will be girls when Reagan, Layne, and I were busted for breaking into the high school to prank our principal."

"Cyland," her mother snapped, "rascals are rascals no matter their gender, and our children are rascals. We just let two of them take a state trooper out into the woods. Alone. I'm calling 9-1-1."

"Why are you calling 9-1-1? Is everything okay?"

Riley spun toward the door and let out a sigh of relief. "You're alive!"

Matt looked confused. "Of course I am."

"The twins . . ." Gemma hedged.

"Lost to Matt at target shooting," Parker complained as he strode in with his brother.

Riley stared at them. There was no blood. No bruises

forming. What had they done? "What did y'all do?"

"Bonded," the three of them said at once as they took a seat at the table.

"Is anything on fire?" Cy asked.

"Nope," Porter responded.

"Did you shoot anything besides the target? Say, a gnome?" Gemma asked as Riley took a seat next to Matt at the table.

"No, Ma," Parker said with a roll of his eyes. "It happened *one* time. You're never going to let me live that down. I tell you, I did us all a favor. That was the creepiest thing I've ever seen."

"Are you sure you're all right?" Riley whispered to Matt as he took a slab of meatloaf.

"I'm great. I told you there was nothing to worry about," he smiled.

What the hell happened? Matt looked elated, the boys looked satisfied, and nothing was destroyed. Something wasn't right. Riley let it go, though, as the table quickly filled with news of the day. She told them about her plans for Frankfort, the defeat of the highway bill, and that the real battle was coming in a couple days. The twins talked about the rodeo and who was going to be there. The hotel they were staying at was apparently a favorite of celebrities, so Gabe, the bachelor prince of Keeneston, had hooked them up with VIP access to all the clubs. Riley saw her mother down her glass of wine. Keeneston could barely contain Porter and Parker—heaven only knows what they'd do to Miami.

Finally dinner was over and Riley tried to usher Matt out the door as fast as she could. So far so good, but she wasn't going to press her luck with hanging around any longer.

"Your house will be ready for you to return to tomorrow night," her father told her as she tried to escape.

"I'm staying at Matt's tonight," Riley called out as she dragged Matt down the porch. As she got into the car, she heard her mother soothing her father and the familiar low growl of his displeasure.

"What really happened when you were with my brothers?" Riley asked as they pulled out of the farm.

"Nothing. Just did some shooting. I'm glad you told me to bring my gun," Matt said as he kept his eyes on the road. He was lying.

"Did they threaten you?"

"Riley, relax. It's all good. There're so many more pleasurable things we could be talking about."

"Like what?"

Matt looked at her then and she didn't need him to answer. The way his dark blue eyes traveled over her body told her what he was thinking. Riley reached over and rubbed her hand along his upper thigh. She enjoyed the ability to make him squirm in the seat as his erection grew.

"See, I told you there were more pleasurable things to talk about," Matt said, his voice graveled with arousal.

"We're not talking, though," Riley said with a quirk of her lips.

Matt floored the gas pedal and shot through the sleepy streets until his house came into sight. Riley moved her hand to rub his erection through his pants and the car jerked to a stop as Matt let out a low hiss. Tonight she felt powerful. She had not backed down from the political bullies. She had shot a den of snakes. She had survived the boyfriend dinner at her parents' and could make the man she loved fall to his knees in passion.

Tonight she was in control, and by the noises Matt was making as they stumbled into the bedroom, tearing off their clothes, he didn't mind. She pushed him onto the bed and straddled him. Looking down, she saw passion, lust, love, and respect in his eyes. And when she took him inside her and they moved together as one, she knew this wasn't just another boyfriend, but someone she wanted to spend the rest of her life with.

Chapter Nineteen

Riley hummed as she showered the next morning. It was Saturday, and she was determined to take a full day off. She could worry about what the Senate was doing with the budget, but there was nothing she could do even if she went to Frankfort. The senators were locked in session hashing out the final details for the vote on Monday. They would be unreachable. Instead, she was going to take her first day off in months. Well, unless you counted her hospital stay as time off.

Matt had left a set of towels hanging for her next to the toiletries her cousin Sydney had brought over. Riley turned off the shower and toweled off. She was wrapping her towel around her head like a turban when Matt came in holding her ringing phone.

"It's Angela Cobb. I figured you'd want to take it," Matt told her as he looked over her nude body. "On second thought, you can always call her back."

Riley rolled her eyes. Together they were insatiable. Sex had been something she did with her previous boyfriends, but now she craved it with Matt. He could ignite her body with one touch. She took the phone and smacked his hand away as Matt cupped her bare breast and ran his thumb over her now taut nipple.

"Hi, Angela. What's going on?" Riley asked, shooing Matt from the bathroom and locking the door. If he were in the room with her, she wouldn't be able to concentrate on anything Angela was saying.

"The Senate is locked away, but I've heard from sources they have already included funding for the highway. I'm sorry. It looks like it may come down to the final vote on this one. Who are your staunchest allies? I can contact them to see if you have the support to make an amendment on the floor if it comes down to the final budget vote."

Riley rattled off her supporters and paced the small bathroom, brainstorming strategy with Angela until her hair was practically dry. "Let's meet tomorrow. I'll see what I can find out. How about brunch?" Angela asked.

"Sounds good. I'm moving back to my house tonight since the floors have been fixed, and the house is now completely snakeproof," Riley joked.

"Oh, I didn't know you weren't at home."

"I kind of shot my floor up. My dad got everything fixed, though. He didn't want me or my sister susceptible to snakes ever again."

"I forgot you live with your sister," Angela said absently as if trying to remember their past conversations.

"I do. But she's out of town this week for work. Hey, I know it's not the fancy places we normally go for brunch, but why don't you come here to eat. We can go to the Blossom Café. It's good home-cooked Southern food. Your hips may not like it, but your stomach will thank you," Riley laughed.

"Sounds good. I'll see you tomorrow at ten-thirty."

Riley hung up with Angela and sniffed the air. Breakfast. She hurried to get dressed and brushed out her hair before following the smells of coffee and pancakes. Matt stood in a pair of jeans and an old trooper 10K run shirt as he flipped the pancakes.

"I thought you'd be hungry after last night," Matt winked.

"Famished. And I'm more excited to have you all to myself today. Spring is in full force. Why don't we go for a horseback ride?"

"Sounds great," Matt began but was interrupted by a knock on the front door. By the curious expression on his face, Riley assumed people just dropping by didn't happen often.

Matt went to open the door, and Riley's cousin Layne rushed in. "I'm going to kill him."

"I probably shouldn't hear this," Matt said sarcastically as he moved to make more pancakes.

Riley just shook her head. Welcome to the Davies family. Aunts, uncles, cousins—they were always around. "What did your dad do now?"

"I found bugs in my office. My *office*!"

"How did you find them?" Riley asked. The Davies cousins were used to finding bugs on their things. Their fathers were just a smidge overprotective. But they had never looked in their work places before. They were usually just GPS devices on their cars, phones, etc. Sure they got mad, but deep down they knew it was because their fathers loved them so much. Plus they were all Daddy's girls so they couldn't stay mad long.

"Sophie paid me a surprise visit this morning after I finished with my volunteer patients." Sophie was Cade and Annie's daughter and one of the Davies cousins. She was in biometrics and had to travel a lot. She'd been especially absent since Nash Dagher had left. Nash was the security specialist everyone thought would be taking over security for the Ali Rahman family in Keeneston. He had been called back to Rahmi on a special mission for the king almost two years ago. No one knew what, if anything, had happened between him and Sophie. It was assumed there had been something that no one knew about.

"Sophie's back in town?" Riley asked surprised.

"Yeah. She needed me to make an adjustment on her shoulder. It had gotten dislocated. Before she had even said hi to me, Soph had pulled out some new device and in under ten seconds found all the bugs."

"Are you sure they're your dad's?"

"His initials were on them," Layne replied dryly.

"Ah, of course. So we wouldn't freak out when we find them. Did Sophie say what happened to her shoulder or how long she'll be in town?"

"Nope. I asked, but she wouldn't say. Her shoulder was bruised, but she just shrugged."

Riley cut into her pancakes as Matt passed Layne a plate of his. "She hasn't been around much since Nash left town. I wonder how he is. No one has heard from him in so long."

Nash had been gone for almost two years and everyone still missed him. He had come to Keeneston as an eager twenty-one-year-old. He was just three years older than Riley, and he had become instant friends with the

Davies crew. He had been skinny and weak but full of enthusiasm as Ahmed and Nabi and the Blossom Café put weight and muscle on him. Over the nine years he was in Keeneston, he had turned into an elite soldier. Who wouldn't with Ahmed and Nabi training him in combat and counterterrorism? He was like a brother to Zain and Gabe, and then he was just gone. He left without saying goodbye. Vanished in the night on a secret mission. Zain had heard from him a year ago, and he'd asked him to tell Sophie he was sorry. Sorry for what, no one but Sophie knew, and she wasn't talking. It didn't matter that he was from Rahmi, the small island country in the Middle East that Zain and his family reigned over. Keeneston and all its citizens claimed him as one of their own, and Keeneston didn't let go of or forget their own.

"He's fine. I talked to him when you were in the shower," Matt said with a shrug as he dug into his own late breakfast.

"You what?"

Riley turned to the door to find her cousin Sophie in all her glory standing there shocked. Her strawberry-blond hair fell loose over her shoulders and the inherited Davies hazel eyes flashed in anger.

Matt froze with a forkful of pancakes halfway to his mouth. "Hey, Sophie. It's good to have you back in town," he said finally. "Pancakes?"

"Sophie!" Riley called as she hurried to hug her cousin and one of her best friends.

Sophie hugged her back but then zeroed in on Matt as he tried to pay attention to the pancakes he was frying up. "Excuse me. Did you say you talked to Nash? Nash

Dagher? The man who left in the middle of the night two years ago without even saying goodbye?"

"Um, yeah. We talk every six months or so," Matt said as he cleared his throat and kept his eyes on the pancakes.

"Really?" Riley asked, hurt that Matt hadn't told her. They all loved Nash and everyone wanted to know how he was. "Where is he? Is he okay? Why doesn't he call anyone else?"

"Um. I mean . . . I've only talked to him three or four times in two years. He just wants to be filled in on what's going on around here. He wanted me to keep an eye out on y'all."

"Where is he?" Sophie asked through clenched teeth.

"I don't know. He calls on a blocked number. All he says about himself is he misses Keeneston. Personally, I think he's undercover. I know something about that, and I know you must keep what you're doing secret."

"But why *you*?" Sophie asked, sounding more hurt than Riley had ever heard her.

"We were good friends. And he knew I'd keep an eye on you all. When he calls, he wants to know what everyone is up to and that you are safe. We talk no more than two or three minutes. I guess he knows I'll get right to the point. If I'm right, and he's undercover, then he can only get away for a few minutes every once in a while. He doesn't have time to shoot the shit. And Sophie, you're always the first person he asks about," Matt said softly before handing her a dish full of pancakes.

"Yeah, well, screw him," Sophie said with no force behind her words. "Now, what's all this stuff about you accidentally coming across a den of vipers?"

"I don't think it was an accident. I don't have any proof, just a gut feeling."

"Well, Mom always says to listen to your gut feelings," Sophie said before taking another bite of pancakes. "Hmm. You found a guy who doesn't run in fear of your family *and* who can cook breakfast. Matt, you're a keeper."

"I couldn't agree more," Riley said as Matt gave her a smile and reached across the island to hold her hand. He was a keeper. And Riley hoped she would be able to keep him beside her forever.

Chapter Twenty

Matt was sore. It had been six months since he had gone riding. They spent the late morning with her cousins and then went out on the trail. They packed a picnic basket and ate a late lunch on the top of a high hill overlooking the farm. That night, they made love and then fell fast asleep back at Riley's. It was now the middle of the night, and Matt's sore butt and pounding headache woke him.

Matt tried to blink his eyes open, but he was hit with a wave of nausea that made his head spin. He was so tired. It had been six long months, and all he wanted to do was sleep. He pressed his fingers to his temples in an effort to relieve his headache. Even though his mind was a fuzzy haze, something was urging him out of bed.

With herculean effort, Matt got out of bed but grabbed the wall for support or he would have fallen over. What was causing a trigger in his mind for him to move? He took a deep breath and felt lightheaded. He willed his ears to open and thought he might have heard something, but he couldn't figure out if he had or not.

"Riley, do you hear something?" Matt asked, collapsing back on the bed as his stomach rolled in protest of standing. "Riley?"

Matt reached out and gave her shoulder a shake. Nothing. "Riley?" he asked louder as he shook her harder. Panic filled him as Riley refused to respond. She wasn't moving and her breathing was shallow. Everything was in a haze. Matt shook his head. He was dreaming — surely he was dreaming. He pinched himself but it didn't wake him up.

"Riley!" he yelled as loud as he could. She made the slightest moan but that was enough for Matt to realize this wasn't a dream. Something was horribly wrong with her. Her face was pale, her breathing was erratic, and her head didn't move on her pillow.

Matt stood up and wavered. He opened the bedroom door intending to get a cool washcloth for her head when he heard that sound again. It had been in the background of his mind since he woke up but when he opened the door, he heard it clearly. It was a hissing noise.

Not more snakes! Matt stumbled to get his gun before following the sound through the house and into the kitchen. His headache worsened, and he didn't know if he had the energy to find the damn snakes. Instead he collapsed into a kitchen chair.

A couple of minutes in the brisk air would help him wake up. Matt hefted himself out of the chair and went to open the back door. The kitchen door had a large rectangular window in the top half of it. He wouldn't have paid attention to what was outside if it hadn't been for the spark.

Off. On. Off. On. In the distance a tiny orange light appeared and then disappeared. Matt forced his eyes to focus. On. Off. On. Off. It wasn't a light. It was someone dressed in black flicking a lighter on and off. Why would they . . . "Gas!"

Matt shoved aside the oven and discovered the cut gas line. The house was filling with natural gas and someone was just waiting to set it ablaze. Matt looked out the window and saw the light flicking on and off as the person moved closer to the house.

Adrenaline shot through his body as Matt raced back to the bedroom. He was unsteady on his feet and slammed his shoulders into the walls as he went, but he made it to Riley's side fast enough and still standing. Turning and looking around the room, he spotted the quickest escape: the window. Matt was about to walk over to open it when he heard the sound of one of the kitchen door's glass panes breaking. The man must have discovered that Matt had thrown the deadbolt. Matt and Riley were out of time.

Matt yanked the comforter off the bed and wrapped it around his shoulders before he scooped Riley into his arms. He pulled the comforter tight around them and jumped backward into the window. His shoulder hit the window first, followed by his back. The glass might have held strong but with Riley's added weight to his momentum, it gave way, and he was propelled backward out the window as glass shards rained around them.

Matt held Riley tightly in the comforter as they landed on the pebbled, glass-covered grass wet with early morning dew. He hit hard on his back and lost his breath when Riley's weight landed a split second after he did. He didn't have time to give into the panic of suddenly not breathing. He didn't have time to take a deep breath and fight to get air back into his lungs. Instead, as he gasped to draw in any breath, he rolled over and jumped up with Riley murmuring in his arms and ran. He had only made it a few steps when he heard a *whoosh* and knew time was up.

With the comforter pulled tight around them, Matt clung to Riley as the force of the explosion catapulted them forward. It seemed an eternity as they flew through the air. They slammed into the ground, and Matt moved to shield Riley's body with his as flaming debris fell from the sky, landing on and around them.

Matt gulped in fresh air as the haze cleared from his head with every breath of untainted air. Smoke billowed into the sky. The house was completely ablaze, like the sun tearing into the darkness of the night. Matt lifted his head and looked at the carnage of what had been a house. To the side of the house, lit by the flames, he saw a shadow dart into the woods.

Rage filled Matt as he ran barefoot to his car. Using his elbow, he broke the glass and yanked the rifle from where he left it a couple days ago for a target practice that never happened. Also in the back seat was his workout bag. He pulled out a pair of athletic shorts and stepped into them while cursing that his shoes had gone up in the fire. With his shorts on, the rifle slung over his back, he only waited long enough to see headlights coming from the direction of Cy and Gemma's before taking off after the shadow.

Riley moaned and pulled the covers over her head. Her head was killing her and she was both hot and cold at the same time. She just wanted to go to sleep, but there was so much noise. The sound of something heavy crashing to the ground had her groaning in frustration as she shoved the comforter from over her head.

What the hell? She wasn't in her bed, but on the wet ground twenty yards from the house, which was currently on fire. The loud noise she had heard was the roof collapsing.

"Matt!" she screamed as she looked frantically around. She saw him running into the woods at the same time she saw headlights from all the residents on the farm heading her way.

The more she breathed, even with the smoke in the air, the better Riley began to feel. What was going on? Why didn't she remember anything? And why was Matt running full speed with a rifle into the woods?

"Riley!" her mother screamed out the truck window as her father slammed on his brakes. "Oh my God, honey. Are you hurt? What happened? Where's Matt?"

Riley looked as some of the workers who lived on the farm immediately began trying to slow the fire, but it was hopeless. The house had blown to smithereens. And Matt was alive and hunting someone or something. It all clicked as Riley scrambled to her feet.

"He left you?" her father yelled over the roaring fire.

Riley shook her head. He would never have left her for nothing. "He's going after someone. Quick, Mom, give me your robe," Riley ordered as her mother rushed forward to wrap her in her knee-length, dark red silk robe. Riley was thankful neither her mother nor her father commented that she was naked under her comforter. Her mother moved to pull her into a hug, but Riley placed a quick kiss on her cheek instead before darting around her to retrieve the handgun her father kept strapped under the driver's seat.

"What do you think you're doing?" her father asked as he tried to stop her from taking off.

"Matt went into the woods alone to chase the person or people responsible. I can't leave him without backup, and I know these woods better than anyone," Riley called back to her parents. She was already running toward the woods as the sound of police sirens melded with the sound of her house breaking apart under the heat of the flames.

Riley saw the layout of the farm as if it were a topographical map in her head. Matt entered the woods on a small path that led to a stream and then followed around the hills to a pasture on the other side. The hills weren't mountains by any means, but they also weren't little knolls kids rolled down for fun. Limestone jutted up from the earth to form these mini-mountains. Water trickled down the rock face and into the stream, which then led to the Kentucky River a few miles away.

On the far side of the pasture, three miles away, was a road. Was it possible the arsonist Matt was chasing parked there and hoofed it in? Emergency vehicles from Lexington and Lipston—Keeneston didn't have its own fire department—wouldn't pass that road. He or she could make a clean getaway.

Riley ran full speed into the woods with the Glock in her right hand. She splashed through the creek and up the other side, ignoring the pain as twigs and thorn bushes tore at her skin and feet. The path Matt had most likely taken followed the stream around the base of the hill; however, if she wanted to make up time, she had to go up and over.

Riley came to a stop and put her hands on her hips as she looked up at the thirty-foot limestone rock face. She dragged in some deep breaths, finding the path she wanted to take. She had been climbing it since she was a kid, but that didn't mean it was easy, especially since she was still weak from whatever it was that had knocked her out. Taking a deep breath, Riley tied the gun to her robe with the belt and double-knotted it so it wouldn't fall off.

Then, one hand after another, she started to climb. The rock hurt her feet, but the old muscle memory was still there. She automatically reached for the strongholds she knew by heart as she scaled up the cold, damp rocks.

Matt's lungs burned as he followed the path next to the small stream. He just hoped Cy would call this in so he would get some backup from the Keeneston Sheriff's Department. He knew they would be busy with the fire temporarily since they moonlighted as volunteer firefighters when needed. Maybe after this, the town would vote to approve funds to have a small fire department. For now, they depended on Lipston and Lexington.

He knew the man had a three-minute head start, but Matt was pushing hard. His feet were numb from pounding the terrain, and his lungs burned from pushing himself so hard. If he collapsed, he wouldn't be able to protect Riley. That drove him forward as he sprinted through the darkness, lit only by occasional glimmers of moonlight through the leaves of the trees. He wouldn't stop. They'd have to kill him first.

Riley's arms shook with exertion as she pulled herself onto the grassy top of the hill. Her hands were scraped; her feet probably were, too. Her fingers were cramped in a clawlike grip. She had to forcefully stretch them out just so she could grab her gun.

She untied the belt to her robe and took hold of the Glock, then forced her legs to start running again. It wouldn't be far, less than half a mile, to the other side of the hilltop. She would then have a view of the pasture below. They kept cows there—around one hundred if she remembered correctly.

Her body was letting her down. She realized she wasn't moving as fast as she stumbled over a fallen tree limb. The sounds of mooing reached her ears. It wasn't the normal sound they made as they ate, but the agitated sound she remembered from branding. She wasn't too late! Knowing she still had a chance at catching the person responsible for trying to kill her and the man she loved spurred her on. She pumped her arms, hurtled over downed trees and limbs and pushed herself until she broke from the woods. She slid to a stop and looked over the pasture. The land was higher on this side, the hill less steep and grassier. There were some trees but not the thick woods or the rock from the other side.

She could see better without the trees blocking the moonlight. She made out shadowed forms of cows, shifting anxiously around. Riley looked to her left. Miles of wire fencing kept the cows contained in the large pasture, unable to roam into the woods. Near the path from the woods was a metal gate, which was now open. Damn, she had missed them!

Her eyes were drawn from the open gate by the mooing of an angry cow. It was hard to figure out which one it was, but there were five that seemed highly agitated. They were shifting restlessly, and their moos held a bit of panic to them. Riley squinted into the herd. Either there was a calf in the middle, or someone was trying to hide in the herd.

The sound of sirens had grown distant as Riley ran. She could still faintly hear them, but she was now far enough away that she could also hear nature. Birds suddenly flew from the trees near the gate to the darkness of the woods. Riley saw Matt's bare chest come into view. The shadow by the cows rose, and Riley didn't think as she took off at a dead sprint down the hill. She kept her knees bent as she ran with her feet turned sideways and leading with her right leg to prevent falling. When the shadow raised a gun, Riley slid to a stop. She lifted her pistol and fired without hesitation.

Chapter Twenty-One

Matt burst out of the woods into the moonlit pasture. He saw the open gate in front of him and scanned the cows for a human racing through the field. He took a deep breath and slowed to a walk, as he now took his time to examine the pasture.

The cows were restless as they mooed their displeasure over being disturbed. Matt was about to run into the field when he heard the sound of gunshots echoing off the land. The dirt near his feet kicked up as a bullet impaled itself in the ground. A second shot went off, and he dropped to a crouch, trying to locate the two shooters. He didn't have to look far. The cows had taken off in a stampede, and Riley raced down the hillside.

"He's in with the cows!" Riley screamed so loudly Matt was afraid her vocal chords would rupture. Although she had no choice if she wanted to be heard. It was the only way he could hear her over the noise of the stampede.

Matt closed the metal gate and climbed up on the rail to see where Riley was pointing. Brief glimpses of a man's shadow could be seen running with the cows. They were quickly outpacing him, and he had somehow managed to stay upright without being run over.

Matt didn't wait to see more. He kept his eyes on the target, leapt from the gate, and took off through the pasture. Pumping his arms, he sprinted toward the man. When the last cow passed him, Matt could finally get a good view of the perpetrator. By his build, it was definitely a man. Around six feet and average weight. That didn't help much, but he could rule out Harvey Luttrell. As if Harvey would do his own dirty work. However, his build did fit LeeRoy though Matt doubted LeeRoy was in such good shape. They must have hired someone.

Matt went down to one knee and pulled his rifle from his back. "Stop or I'll shoot!" he yelled quickly. The man was getting close to being out of range. Matt controlled his breath and put the scope to his eye. He scanned the field until he found his target that stopped, turned, and fired his own weapon. Matt took a slow breath, and right after he exhaled, squeezed the trigger as if he were caressing a lover.

Matt's shoulder absorbed the recoil from the rifle as he kept his eye on the target through the scope. The man stumbled backward as the shot to the arm flung him back. "Damn," Matt cursed. The man went down but was able to quickly get back up. Matt put him in his sight again, but the man was returning fire and hitting closer now that Matt was in clear view. He had to flatten himself to the ground as he heard Riley taking shots to cover him.

The man zigged and zagged toward the sound of an engine revving. A truck with no headlights burst through the angry mob of cows, taking advantage of the open gate at the far side of the pasture and pouring out of the enclosure. Riley fired at the truck even though she was too far away to hit it. Matt lay in the grass and held the rifle propped up by his elbows on the ground. He looked through the scope and fired at the truck. He heard the ping of bullets hitting metal but the truck didn't stop. The driver was in darkness, and Matt couldn't tell if it was a man or a woman.

As the truck bounced by the man, he leapt into its bed and returned fire, forcing Matt to roll out of the way and Riley to the ground. Without slowing down, the truck tore through the wire fencing. Sparks flew from the fencing dragging on the pavement of the main road before they quickly disappeared from view.

"Dammit!" Matt smacked the ground and pushed himself up.

"Matt! Are you okay?" Riley yelled to him as she rushed forward.

"I'm fine. Just pissed I couldn't catch him. How are you?" Matt ran his hands over her shoulders and down her arms as he tried to see every scratch and bruise in the moonlight. "I didn't think you'd recover so fast from the gas."

"I have a headache from hell, but the fresh air has helped. Plus, I took a shortcut. So I had a little more time at home before taking off." He could see Riley deflate. "A home I no longer have. All my stuff. My clothes, my pictures, my riding trophies. How am I going to tell Reagan all her things are gone as well?"

Matt pulled her into his arms and felt the shock of the night wrack her body. He felt the wetness of her tears on his bare chest as he slowly ran his hand up and down her spine in hopes of soothing her.

When he felt her relax against him, he cupped her face with his hands and forced her to look up at him. "We have each other. We can try to replace everything else. Some of the pictures may be hard, but we can take new ones."

"Thank you, Matt. If it weren't for you . . ." Riley didn't need to finish. Matt knew and the idea terrified him. The thought of losing her was too much. To banish it from his mind, he lowered his lips and claimed hers. He wasn't gentle this time. It was rough and frantic. They clung to each other, and the knowledge that they had been so close to death infused them more than ever with the desire to bask in life.

Riley hissed as she and Matt limped toward the road. She would rather hitchhike than walk back home through the woods. The inferno was no longer lighting the night sky so the fire department must have arrived. She felt sore and bruised, but she was alive. She could not believe she had lost her house. She was so beyond fury that she felt a crazy little smile steal over her face.

"Um, Riley. You're looking a little . . . off," Matt said slowly as he helped her limp along. He started helping her after she stepped in a cow patty, which, while disgusting, had soothed her feet for a minute. Riley had insisted she could walk on her own and she had—right into the cow patty—and then another.

"I'm just thinking of ways to torture the person behind this. I think I'm going to walk over to Luttrell's house tonight and pay him a little visit," Riley said as she quickly tried to figure out which way to go.

"While I applaud your tenacity, let's get you home and

cleaned up. You can take them all down on Monday when you surprisingly show up at work." Riley heard Matt sigh in relief and looked up. "A car."

A truck bounced off the road and into the field. Riley tensed but felt better seeing her cousin Sydney's husband behind the wheel. "There they are!" Sydney cried as she stuck her head out the window. "Are you all right? Are you hurt? Everyone is worried sick!"

"We're fine except for some scrapes and bruises."

Sydney jumped out of the truck and ran toward them. Her husband, Deacon, followed closely behind. "Boy, are we glad to see you. Cy and Gemma are fit to be tied. To prevent the fire from spreading, they had to stay and help contain it until the fire department arrived. By then, half the town was there helping. That is, until the cow situation," Deacon explained.

"What cow situation?" Riley asked as Syd engulfed her in a hug.

"What is that smell?" Sydney sniffed.

"I had a cow patty incident."

"Two," Matt hid under a fake cough.

"Well, I have Robyn's towel in the back of the truck that you can use to clean up a little," Sydney said as she carefully helped Riley to the truck bed. "Honey, can you text Uncle Cy and let him know they're safe."

"Already done," Deacon said in his smooth Georgian voice. The way he talked, you thought they were sipping mint juleps on the veranda instead of hoisting a cow-pattied cousin-in-law into the back of a truck after her house exploded.

"Let's get you home. Your mom said she has some

clothes, and I'll bring over all I have tomorrow," Sydney said through the sliding window separating the truck bed and the cab.

"Ugh," Riley groaned. Spending the night back at her parents' house was the last thing she wanted. *Smothered* wouldn't even begin to describe what would be in store for her.

Matt leaned over and pushed her hair from her face. "Don't worry. We'll get your clothes and then use my car to go to my house. Somehow, I don't think your dad will let me spend the night at his house and I have no intention of letting you out of my sight."

Riley closed her eyes and leaned against Matt's chest. Deacon drove the truck out of the field and turned toward Keeneston. Going in that direction, they were only a few miles from the farm entrance. They could turn onto Maple and wind their way past the old houses and the bed-and-breakfast, where they would then turn left onto Main Street and pass the Café before heading out of town to the farm. Basically, they were traveling in a circle since the cow pastures were cut off from the main farm by the large hills and woods.

The truck slowed and Riley felt Matt stiffen beneath her. "Holy shit," he muttered as he frantically started tapping her arm.

Riley opened her eyes and felt her mouth fall open.

"Get out of here, you beasts!" Miss Daisy yelled as she sprayed a hose at a cow. The cow seemed to enjoy it as she tried to lick the water. More cows lumbered closer to where Miss Daisy was standing on the porch with her sisters, their cousins Poppy and Zinnia, and the B&B guests staring as a hundred cows roamed down the street into downtown.

"Don't even think about eating that rose!" *Thwack*. Miss Lily smacked a cow on the head with her broom. The cow licked the broom and took a bite of the corn bristles.

"No, we have to scare them, not feed and water them," Miss Violet tried to explain.

"Well then, just take off your nightgown and say *Boo*," Miss Daisy snarked back as she turned the hose onto jet and blasted a cow right in the side. The cow mooed happily as another one tried to bite the stream of water.

"There's going to be a cow fight soon over who gets to play in the water," Riley laughed as they stared out of the bed of truck.

"I have a taser. You think that would get the cows moving?" Syd asked with a smile.

Deacon just shook his head. "Not anymore you don't. Remember, you traded your taser for your favorite red lipstick last week. But I'm sure the cows will appreciate a makeover."

"You better hurry and get me home. I'll grab my horse and help round up these ladies," Riley told Deacon, rapping on the roof of the cab.

Slowly Deacon made his way down the street and out of downtown. The lights of the fire trucks and emergency vehicles were still flashing as the sun began to rise. Riley saw her entire family and all her friends standing in a semicircle watching both the Lipston and Lexington fire departments hosing down what had been her house.

"Here they are!" Sienna Ashton Parker called loudly.

The entire semicircle spun around and swarmed the truck.

"What happened? Are you both all right?" Ryan, Sienna's FBI husband and Riley's cousin, asked.

"Nothing major. Just some cuts and bruises from not having the right clothes and shoes. But we have a bigger problem," Riley told them as Matt lifted her from the back of the truck.

"I'll get my gun," the entire group said in unison.

Riley laughed and felt that the cows and her family had saved her life. The emotional wreck she had been drifted away on the tendrils of her laughter. How could it not? Cows were moseying through Keeneston, her family were all in their night clothes, and everyone was prepared to go to battle in the early morning dawn while water sprayed on the smoking ashes of her home.

"We caught up with the man who blew up my house in the cow pasture," Riley explained.

Ahmed shrugged. "Then I'll get the shovel."

"I'm going to pretend I didn't hear that," Matt said with a roll of his eyes but a smile on his lips. If he was going to be part of the family, he had a feeling he was going to start sounding like Marshall Davies, always covering his ears and complaining about his family's enjoyment of the gray area of the law.

Riley shook her head. "I didn't catch him."

"Well, that's okay, dear. I'm sure you'll shoot him next time." Aunt Annie, who was former DEA and currently a sheriff's deputy, patted Riley's shoulder comfortingly.

"I shot him. Does that count?" Matt asked Annie.

"Did you kill him?" Cy asked him.

"No. Shoulder wound."

"Then no, it doesn't count."

"I think it should count," her mother said, giving Matt a kind smile.

"Me too. I mean, he did hit his target. Just not a bullseye," Uncle Pierce put in as his wife, Tammy, nodded her spiked blond hair in agreement.

"I'll bake you one of my famous apple pies to thank you for shooting that bastard," Marcy Davies, Riley's grandmother, told Matt fondly.

Riley put her fingers to her lips and blew. A piercing whistle had everyone silent in seconds. "As I was saying, we have a problem. The reason he got away was because he had help. Someone tore through the gate in a pickup to rescue him while taking a good part of the metal fence as they left. The cows have wandered into town. When we drove by, they were trying to eat Miss Lily's prize roses."

"Why didn't you say so?" Uncle Cade, a former Special Forces soldier turned high school biology teacher, asked as the family members scrambled into the back of pickup trucks and SUVs. "Get us to the barns, fast!"

Trucks sped away from the smoking pile of timber and over to her father's stables. After fighting with the Special Forces, Miles, Marshall, and Cade had all moved back to Keeneston and bought farms of their own. Her father, she had just learned last year, had been a spy when he met her mother in Los Angeles. Her mother had thought he was a stuntman, but it turned out he did a lot more than pretend to shoot a gun. When he met Gemma, they came back to Keeneston and never left. He retired from being a stuntman and a spy, and started a farm along with his other brothers. Pierce, the youngest of the Davies brothers, had made a lot of money inventing the next age of agricultural equipment now being used on farms all over the world. So, if there was one thing her uncles knew, it was how to ride, and Riley had never been so relieved for their country life when, in less than ten minutes, everyone was on horseback and riding toward town in their pajamas, ready to round up the rose-eating cows.

Chapter Twenty-Two

"I will say this, Marcy and Jake Davies sure know how to make babies." Riley heard Miss Lily sigh. Riley swung her horse around and looked at her father, uncles, a handful of cousins, and friends rounding up the last of the cows.

They were all riding in athletic shorts or pajama bottoms. She didn't think anything of it until Poppy similarly sighed. "I think your roses were worth the sacrifice so we could see this. It's like the *Magic Mike* movie if they were all real-life cowboys."

It was then that it registered for Riley what they were talking about. None of them had shirts on. Riley had been so focused on watching Matt shirtless on a horse as he worked his way through downtown, rounding up cows, that she didn't think of anyone else. Besides, that was her family and just—*eww*.

"Maybe I should swoon. Do you think Carter would catch me?" Zinnia said with a giggle as Riley cut off a cow trying to head back to Miss Lily's rosebush, now missing a couple blooms.

"Or Wyatt. Look at those muscles," Poppy said with wonder.

Miss Violet sighed longingly. "And I've had them all in my bosom. I miss those days. But I promised my dear Anton no more flirting after we tied the knot." Anton stood behind her and shook his head with a smirk on his lips.

Riley snorted. Miss Violet hadn't given up her famous smothering hugs. She just made sure she did it when no one was looking. Ryan had told them he was afraid he'd pass out from lack of oxygen the last time Miss Violet grabbed him for a hug — a hug that just happened to bring his head right into her pillowy bosom.

"You're so lucky," Poppy and Zinnia said as the men rode by.

It was the first time Riley had heard Poppy or Zinnia talk about men. It hadn't really dawned on her that neither of them had dated during their time in Keeneston. They were both in the mid to late twenties, yet Riley had never seen either one with a man. Though, come to think of it, she really didn't know much about their past except that they had come from a small town in Alabama six years before to help out their cousins — cousins they never knew existed until Miss Lily tracked them down. They fit into Keeneston perfectly, but something told Riley there was more to their story.

"Riley! That's the last cow. We have room for one more in the trailer. Bring her over here," her father called to her. Riley shook off her thoughts. She was becoming paranoid, thinking there were secrets everywhere when there was probably nothing to the sisters' story at all.

All her aunts had driven to their farms and retrieved trailers to fill with cows rather than trying to herd them all back through town. People were already at work repairing the fence in the pasture.

"Nolan Flynn just called," Riley's mom yelled from the cab of the truck. "He said he has the new gate from the feed and farm store up, and his crew should have the fence repair complete in the next half hour."

Riley ushered the last cow down Miss Lily's driveway and into the waiting trailer. Nolan was a hard worker. He was a couple of years younger than she was and had dated Abby Mueez when they were in high school. It was short lived, but the friendship remained intact. He had gone to college and returned with a business plan to keep Flynn's Feed and Farm on the map. Part of that was working with her Uncle Pierce to make sure Flynn's had access to the latest inventions from Pierce's company. It included a beta program in which farmers would sign up to test products ranging from new seeds to new machines.

Riley shifted in the saddle and hoped that Sydney had dropped off some more clothes at Matt's house. She was in old jeans from her freshman year of college and the top button wouldn't close. She was also pretty sure she had split the pants along her bottom.

Matt rode up to her and the thought crossed her mind that torn clothes may be easier to get out of faster. What was it about a man on a horse that sent a *zing* straight to her hoo-ha?

"Hey. Don't you have that meeting with Angela Cobb soon? I don't know if the café's going to be open," Matt called as he sent a wink to Poppy and Zinnia, who were startled out of a trance from gazing at all of the men sitting on their horses.

"Oh, right!" Poppy gasped.

"Free pancake brunch at the café for all the cow wranglers!" Zinnia called out. "Anything to keep them from putting shirts back on," Zinnia winked to Riley before taking off at a jog toward the café.

Riley saw her mother smile and roll her eyes as the men whooped. "I'll bring the guys back from the farm and pay for their meals to thank them for their hard work, too. I'll see you all shortly."

The diesel truck roared to life and slowly chugged its way toward the farm. Riley followed the group toward the café as everyone eagerly talked about this morning's happenings. She also didn't miss the fact that Poppy was busy taking bets left and right after it quickly spread that, at the time of the explosion, Riley and Matt had been in bed. Together. Naked.

"I don't even know how to explain this," Riley said as she looked down from her horse to where Angela stood, looking splendid in a fitted pants suit. She looked around at the shirtless men swinging their legs over the saddles and tying their horses to the street lamps.

"It's like *Magic Mike*, but real," Angela said with wide appreciative eyes.

"That's what I said," Poppy giggled as she rushed by to help open the café.

"If I had known Keeneston was like this, I would have moved here instead of Cairo," Angela muttered as the men nodded to her, making their way inside. "Hello, Mr. Davies, it's nice to see you again."

"Ah, Mrs. Cobb. You too. You're in for a treat. Zinnia is whipping up her famous pancakes," Cy smiled before headed inside.

"I don't think it's the pancakes that are the treats," Angela softly said before starting to go inside after Cy.

"Eww, that's my dad," Riley groaned.

"Face it. Your dad's a DILF."

Riley felt her face flush. "How do you know what a DILF is?"

"I may be old, but I'm not dead. You may have competition for reelection because I am seriously thinking of relocating. Now, do you want to tell me why you're in a T-shirt and jeans that are two sizes too small? Or why the men in town are half-dressed? Not that I'm complaining about that one, mind you," Angela said as they headed inside the café.

Riley found a small table in the back and told Angela what had happened. By the end of the story, Angela blinked, then stared at Riley. "I don't know whether to be horrified or to laugh hysterically. At least the people after you have been unable to succeed. I worry for you, though. You could have been killed and all over this stupid highway." Angela shook her head and reached across the table to take Riley's hand in hers.

"Riley, I hate to say this, but I think you should drop your fight against the highway. It's just not worth your life."

Riley looked around at her friends and family and townspeople filling the café. There was laughter, teasing, love, and support flowing as freely as the iced tea. "No. I won't give up. This place is worth it."

Angela let out a frustrated breath and leaned back in her chair. She nodded her understanding, and Riley knew her mentor didn't agree but was going to support her anyway. "I apologize for even more bad news, but I think it's going to be an uphill battle. The budget the governor and the Senate are set on includes funding for the highway. I've talked to everyone who you said were supporters. You don't have the votes. Most have seen the writing on the wall and switched their votes. The Senate is voting tomorrow morning and it will pass. We'll be locked in debate thereafter. The end of session is this week and we have to pass a budget. My sources tell me the Speaker is going to bring the budget to the floor everyday until one passes. I'm sorry, but I think it could possibly pass on Tuesday."

Riley felt the news like a punch to the gut. No, it couldn't pass. Good couldn't lose to evil. Wrong should never trump right. "No," Riley said shaking her head. "What can I do to stop it?"

"I'm sorry, honey, but I don't think you can. If the Senate sways enough Reps, there is nothing you can do. And they have."

"I can filibuster," Riley said decisively. "That can buy me more time."

"A day, maybe two. But Riley, you need to be realistic. I'm sorry, but it looks like the highway is a reality."

"Tell me what I can do, Angela. There has to be something," Riley said desperately.

Angela let out a long slow breath. "You could vote for it."

"No way!"

Angela held up her hand to calm Riley. "Let me explain. Everyone is in a bargaining mode. They would do practically anything to get your vote. Why not agree to vote for it with conditions, conditions that could minimize the harm to Keeneston."

"Like making sure we have an exit or finding a way for them to build the highway around downtown," Riley said with defeat.

"Exactly. They'll give you anything to get the publicity of your support."

"Everything except for doing the right thing by not dividing Keeneston in half." Riley felt her throat tightening. She was going to lose. "I just don't understand it."

"Understand what?" Angela asked.

"Why the highway? Why Keeneston? It's as if someone is out to destroy my town."

"That's ridiculous, Riley. No one has a grudge against a town. It's just business."

"That seems even worse somehow," Riley said sadly. "I'm sorry, but I just can't do it. Not until I've tried absolutely everything."

"What else is left for you to try?" Angela asked.

"I don't know, but I'm not a quitter. I'll think of something."

"You'd better think fast. I think Tuesday is your deadline. I'll let you know if anything changes, or if I can think of anything that may help."

Angela stood up from the table and placed a twenty beside her plate. She gave Riley a tight smile, and suddenly Riley felt the weight of the town on her shoulders as Angela left. Was she doing the right thing by not giving up, or would her stubbornness be the downfall of Keeneston?

Chapter Twenty-Three

"What do you need?" Matt asked as soon as Angela left. He didn't need to know how the conversation went. He saw the look on Riley's face and that said it all.

"I don't even know," Riley said with a hint of defeat in her voice.

"Tell me everything Angela told you," Matt said, sitting down in the seat Angela just vacated. The jovial feel of the café had shifted. They had all picked up on Riley's unease.

Riley told him about her conversation. "She said it was just business, but why Keeneston? That's still bugging me."

"Maybe it is business," Matt murmured as his mind raced.

"You sound just like Angela."

"No, think about it. What do you do?"

"What do you mean?"

"What's your job?" Matt asked her.

"I run a farm."

"Exactly. You are a farm manager. Marge Stanley is a community volunteer. Gregory Peel is a lawyer. Maybe this has nothing to do with politics and everything to do with business."

Matt saw Riley sit up straight in her seat. The fire was back in her eyes as she looked at him. "It's good business to build a new highway," she repeated as his point hit home.

"Exactly. Whose business would benefit from this? Not donations, think money in their own pockets."

Riley shot to her feet. "Where are you going?" Matt asked.

"I need to be in Frankfort. I need to know everything that's going on."

"I have a better idea." Matt pulled out his phone and placed a call. "DeAndre, I need your and Aniyah's help."

Two hours later, Matt had moved Riley's campaign headquarters to Desert Farm. Mo and Dani's horse farm also had a state-of-the-art security building since they were royalty. Mo and Dani's second son, Gabe, stood next to him as Riley paced the meeting room while on the phone with Aniyah.

Nabi, the head of security for the royal family, was known for his ability to ferret out information. He was armed with a list of names of all the congressmen who supported the highway. His daughter, Faith, sat in the chair next to him.

She had her father's dark hair and her mother's curls. "I'll take this one," Faith said in her childlike voice. By the way she worked a computer, you forgot she was only nine. Her fingers flew over the keyboard as images and documents started appearing on the big television screens that covered the entire wall.

"Good job on remembering to find and then search under his wife's maiden name, sweetie," Nabi praised as he worked his own computer.

Riley burst into the room waving a piece of paper. "Aniyah said everyone is tight-lipped. But, she got a few more names from eavesdropping in the women's restroom."

She handed the paper to Nabi. "It's going to take time to go through all these names. And Faith has school tomorrow, so I'll be short-handed."

"I'll see if I can get Uncle Cade to help after school tomorrow," Riley offered, already sending a text to Cade. "Oh good, he's on his way over now. Maybe we can find the people behind this before the Senate votes in the morning."

"I can try the president," Gabe offered. "She said she'd do anything she could to help."

Riley unconsciously worked her lower lip, and Matt knew she had an idea. "Can she make sure no federal funds are used?"

Gabe nodded. "I'll see what I can do. Zain and Mila are in DC visiting Abby. I'll send them to the Hill to have a little chat with the congressmen to make sure they don't fund it either. If Zain's winning smile doesn't work, then maybe Abby's *Abbyness* will sway them," he winked before heading out of the room.

Nabi printed off some documents and passed them to Matt who looked them over, then hung them on the wallboard under the picture of the senator in question. They had stuck up pictures of every supporter of the highway and were currently learning what their family businesses were. They were looking for anything that led back to Luttrell Foods or Hager Construction. Direct links were in green. Secondary connections were in yellow. No connections to Luttrell or Hager were marked in red.

Before Matt knew it, the wall was a quarter filled as Nabi, Faith, and Cade worked the computers. They hacked into private documents, government files, and cloud storage accounts. Nothing would be admissible and Matt just refused to observe the activity. It was a lame attempt at plausible deniability, but he was sticking to it.

His phone rang and Matt answered it immediately. "DeAndre, what's the news?"

Matt hung up and tried not to show the stress he was feeling. "The Senate has reached an agreement. They vote tomorrow morning, and it will pass with the highway funding in it. They've all left for the night."

"Night?" Riley said surprised.

"It's ten o'clock at night, Ri," Cade said softly.

"But we're not even close," Riley whispered before straightening up. "I won't give up. We'll just work through the night."

"I know one person who won't be," the soft voice said from the door. Matt turned and saw Faith's mother, Grace, standing there. "I'm sorry, Riley, but it's time for me to take Faith home."

Nabi stood and crossed the room to his wife. He placed a sweet kiss on her lips, and she looked sadly at his drawn lips. "It'll be all right. You'll figure it out, dear," she told her husband so softly Matt almost didn't hear her.

"Do I have to, Mom? I was just breaking into the

juvenile records for this representative who had a hit-and-run while drinking when he was seventeen," Faith whined.

Grace smiled patiently at her as Riley made her way over to the little girl who was no longer quite to so little. "You've been such a big help, Faith, but we've got it from here. You certainly have a talent."

"You sure do, sweets," Nabi said and kissed the top of his daughter's head.

"Kale taught me over Christmas break," Faith said about Ahmed's and Bridget's youngest son who was at MIT before she hugged her dad goodnight. "I hope you find out who's behind this, Miss Davies."

"Thanks, Faith." Riley hugged her. Grace smiled worriedly at them all as she put her arm around her daughter and took her home.

Matt watched as they left for the night. Annie arrived shortly after with a late night snack for them, and he and Riley worked side-by-side reading through all the documents Nabi and Cade could find that could be relevant.

The shadows in the parking garage crept across the floor as the moon rose in the night sky. The cars pulled to a stop and the lights were cut. Doors opened and footfalls echoed against the concrete walls.

"You idiot. How did you fail?"

"The man I hired barely escaped with his life. I'll get her tomorrow. You can count on it. It was a damn good thing I was there, or we'd all have been caught."

"I'm tired of doing it your way. I'm sending my man in

to help."

"You just have to do everything your way."

"We all know who the brain is here—me. Now shut up. It's my time to take over. Riley Davies is a dead woman."

"It's not just Riley. It's that reporter, too."

"Matt Walsh? Can't you just spin him a story?"

In the dark, a head shook. "She's sleeping with him. He knows too much. He went after my man, shot him in the shoulder. For a reporter, he seemed very confident with a gun."

"Damn," they cursed in the dark as reality settled in.

"If he's not a reporter, then who is he?"

"Doesn't matter if he's dead."

"I agree. We need your man too. The lovebirds can die together in a car accident. Whatever it takes to make it look like an accident. It can't relate back to us. He hasn't left her side. It shouldn't be that hard to kill them both at the same time."

They all agreed and parted ways. Like smoke in the night, they disappeared into the shadows.

The central computer room had no windows. Only walls filled with television screens and now paper trails on supporters of the highway. It was why Matt was surprised when his phone rang at the same time Riley's did.

"DeAndre, what are you doing up so late?" Matt asked into the phone at the same time he heard Riley greet Aniyah. It wasn't late. It was early, very early on Monday morning, and the Senate had just passed the budget.

"Shit!" Riley cursed as she hung up. "They're bringing it to a vote in House today. I have to go."

"Today?" Cade asked in surprise and got up and stretched. He was going to be late for his class.

"It's just a prelim vote. It won't pass, but it will give the House a chance to respond to the parts of the Senate bill they have issue with. It tells us where we have to start the bargaining. They're pushing this hard and fast. I need to get to Frankfort. Aniyah said people have been stopping by my office since six this morning."

"She was there that early?" Matt asked.

"She never left, bless her heart. She slept on the sofa. She said she wasn't going to leave until this den of vipers was killed. Her words, not mine." Riley shivered.

Matt stood up. "Okay, let's go."

"You can't go," Riley said suddenly.

"Why not?"

"I need you here to help with all this," Riley said as she waved to the papers sitting on the desk, including the ones Nabi just handed to Matt.

"Someone needs to go with you."

"I'll go with her," Gabe said as he walked in, looking devastating in a tailor-cut suit. "It might be good to have a member of a royal family who brings a lot of revenue to the state by your side, especially one armed with a letter from the president of the United States saying she hopes Congress will not authorize any federal funding to be used for this project. Abby and Zain also have the assurances of the Speaker of the House and the Majority Leader."

Riley squealed before leaping into Gabe's arms and hugging him. "They were counting on five million in federal funds. This could kill the bill."

"I just hope it's not too late. The president wouldn't put anything in writing until it was a reality, not just a debate. And my mom sent me with this," he pulled out a bag and handed it to Riley. "I guess it's a good thing I came back to Keeneston for a short layover before heading to Paris," he winked as Riley hugged him.

"A suit. Thank goodness. I'll be ready in five minutes." Riley rushed into the bathroom and slammed the door.

"Have you found anything out?" Gabe asked quietly.

"Not really. We have a lot of potentials but no definite suspects," Matt told him as Gabe went to look over the wall of suspects.

"Could this have anything to do with us?"

"Us?" Matt asked.

"The Ali Rahman family. We'll lose a good chunk of land if this goes into law. We honestly didn't think it would. Today, Father and I will be meeting with the governor to try to stop this. If she changes her tune, then maybe the legislature will, too. I'm hoping with the pressure from the president, she'll see it as a blemish to her record. We have international news outlets picking up the story. Also, we have the best attorneys fighting the legality of the proposed highway and they'll be presenting their arguments as well."

"Why didn't you do that sooner?"

"It gives the opposition time to mount a defense. In politics, it's all about appearance, not facts. Towns who have fought this in the courts have lost due to the Supreme Court's ruling. We don't want to fight it in court. We want to fight it in the media. A small town in Indiana just did that and won. They didn't give the opposition time to come up with their own spin. Camera crews are arriving in Keeneston within the hour to start filming the town. The story will be live by eleven this morning and calls from across the country will pour in right in time for us to meet with the governor," Gabe explained.

Matt shook his head. "Politicians," he said with a curse.

Gabe just grinned. "I would take offense, but I'm a diplomat. Completely different," he laughed.

"Okay, I'm ready," Riley called as she rushed out of the bathroom. "What did I miss?'

"That Gabe's a diplomatic badass and Frankfort will have no idea how to handle that."

"Great, because I'm ready to kick some ass." Riley grinned as she put on her lip gloss and pearls.

"We're going into political war, not a Southern society event," Gabe told her.

"You're right. I need more lipstick," Riley said as she dug into her purse.

Matt shook his head. "I've been to some of these society events. She's right. It's all pearls and sweet tea as they sharpen their claws on each other. So, you'll need this." Matt held out a knife to Riley. "DeAndre will be at the main door. Make sure you use that entrance."

Riley looked down at the switchblade. It looked harmless tucked away in the matte black rectangular grip. But Matt knew it wasn't. If she flipped it out, the six-inch blade could do some serious damage. Riley went to put it in her purse and Matt stopped her. "Keep it on you. You may not always have your purse with you."

Riley gave him a nod and slid it into the inside pocket of her suit coat. "I'll walk you out," Matt said as he slipped his arm around her waist. He didn't want to tell her what he was feeling. He had to trust in Gabe, and he had to trust in Riley. "I'll come up when we finish here. Whenever Gabe isn't with you, stay with Aniyah and DeAndre."

They stopped at Gabe's waiting black SUV with diplomatic flags on the front. He was really going all out. Matt turned her toward him, looked down into her eyes, and swallowed hard. His whole life was in his arms, and he didn't want to let her go.

"Promise me you'll be careful," he whispered and brushed back a stray piece of hair from her face.

"I will. After all, I have you to come home to." Riley rose up on her toes and placed a soft kiss on his lips. "Don't wait up."

Matt let her pull away from him and watched as she walked to the SUV. "I love you," he called after her.

"I love you, too," Riley smiled before the driver closed the door.

Chapter Twenty-Four

"Praise the Lord! You're back!" Aniyah kissed her cross and then offered it up as thanks to the heavens. "There are things going down that reality television couldn't even think up."

Riley paused at the door to her office and fought the laughter as Aniyah jumped up from behind her desk so fast the "girls" partially bounced out of her shirt.

Gabe looked down at his feet and cleared his throat as Aniyah stuffed her boobs back into her too-tight top before sending him a panty-melting grin. It wasn't a nip slip, but it was close. "And this must be Gabe. You could have told me to prepare for every news station in the country and some outside of it to be calling. I just got off the phone with the news in the UK, and I'm not talking about our basketball team."

"I brought Veronica, she's my brother's right hand, and she'll help you handle all the calls and interviews." Gabe stepped aside and the blonde bombshell stepped forward with a smile for Aniyah.

"Hi, Aniyah. I've heard such great things about you. I look forward to working together. I have a lot of information for you," Veronica smiled.

"You look like Malibu Barbie in a suit. A little thing like you couldn't scare a fly. But I'm sure you're good at your job, bless your heart." Aniyah looked to Gabe's pants and back to Veronica, making it very clear what she thought Veronica's job was.

Gabe opened his mouth but Veronica held up a perfectly manicured finger. She took a step closer to Aniyah and towered over her. Aniyah wasn't the only one who liked five-inch heels. "First, these pearls were earned by kicking the ass of every debutante who thought she could walk over me. Second, he's not my type. I like my partners strong, sexy, and curvy — more like you," Veronica winked and stood back up. Aniyah turned five shades of red as what Veronica had told her sank in.

"Well," Aniyah said as she ran her hands over her hips, "thank you. I mean, if you have such excellent taste, you can't be that bad after all."

Veronica sent a winning smile to the group. "Perfect. Now, here's my PR plan."

Riley left Veronica and Aniyah to handle the door and phones, and she took the list of messages to her office with Gabe. Normally the halls of the annex were quiet, but today they echoed with nonstop chatter.

Riley looked down at her phone. "I got an email with the latest suspects from Matt." She pulled up the file and smiled as she looked over it. "They also sent convincing arguments for some they deemed on the fence. Well, Prince Gabe, are you ready to play politics?"

There was a knock on the door a second before Aniyah opened it. Her hair was now in a fancy chignon. A beautiful shade of pink lip gloss coated her lips, and Riley recognized one of Gabe's dress shirts tied over her tight black shirt as if done on purpose. It was still Aniya, but tamer. "Representative Davis, Your Highness — BBN, the nation's largest news outlet, is here to speak with you. I've already given them a summary of the events and Veronica has given them the press kit."

Riley blinked. What happened to Aniyah?

"I look all fancy and shit, don't I?" Aniyah winked. Ah, there she was.

"Now I'm ready to play," Gabe smiled. He held the door for Riley who took a deep breath and wished she'd been Veronica-ized.

Riley stepped out into the lobby to find Veronica blocking the door as staffers not so subtly tried to see inside. The game plan was to put pressure on them with the presence of America's biggest news station, so Veronica didn't close the door. Instead, she smiled at each of them and asked which member of Congress they worked for. If they answered with one of the names on Riley's list, Veronica would just smile and sadly say, "Well, bless your heart." The staffer's eyes would go big and they would rush off to inform their boss that something was up.

It only took five minutes for the first senator to arrive. He was up for reelection and faced strong competition. "Oh, I'm so sorry to interrupt. I didn't know Representative Davies had company. I wanted to discuss the upcoming budget vote, but I can come back."

Riley turned from where she and Gabe were answering questions for the reporter and smiled. The cameraman swung to take in the scene. "It's no problem at all, Stephan. Why don't we talk in my office? Prince Gabe was just telling the BBN here why he and the President of the United States don't support this highway."

Stephan swallowed so hard his bow tie bobbled. Riley stood up, but it was Aniyah who smiled and said, "Right this way, Senator." Aniyah showed him to the chair across from Riley's desk and dropped her smile. "Pucker up, big boy. It's time for you to do some ass kissing."

Stephan inhaled sharply as Riley turned her head so he wouldn't see her laughing. "What can I do for you, Stephan?"

"So it's true. You got the President of the United States to publicly side on a local matter. How the hell did you manage that?"

Riley shrugged. "Don't forget the Speaker of the House and the Majority Leader of the U.S. Senate. Although I think the better question is how are you going to manage to win reelection when you received illegal campaign donations from your wife's father's company? About $58,000, if my math is correct."

Stephan turned white. "I don't know what you're talking about," he sputtered as his bow tie bobbed.

"Oh, I think you do. Now, tell me, Stephan, why do you support this highway? What's in it for you?" Riley asked.

"N . . . n . . . nothing," he stammered.

"Okay, well, I need to go have a little chat with BBN." Riley stood up, but Stephan was already begging her to sit back down.

"Fine. It was Luttrell. He made a very large donation to my campaign and told me to vote for the highway as a favor. I'm guessing you already knew that, though."

Riley nodded. "The question is what are you going to do about it?"

"I need something to change to my vote. I can't just change it, or Luttrell will come after me and tell my constituents I'm a lame duck."

"You need a quid pro quo. Got it. What is it that your district needs?"

"There's a vote tomorrow for a state-funded vocational school in my district. I need your vote on it," Stephan asked quietly.

"Send the information to Aniyah. If it checks out as clean, you have my support."

"And the campaign donations?"

"All I can say is if I found it, then others could too. If I were in your place, I would pay the money back and admit to an accounting error that has now been corrected. I won't turn you in. Unless you force me to."

And that was how her day went. Subtle hints of blackmail and bargaining, though she was proud to say her blackmail was at a minimum. When pushed, most politicians wanted to do good. They simply got too caught up in the game to remember that's why they wanted to be politicians in the first place.

The camera crew followed her to the House vote on the Senate's budget, which failed by only eighteen votes, and then BBN went with Gabe to the governor's office for a little chat. Meanwhile, Riley met with politician after politician who suddenly had a change of heart.

At six that night, Angela came in and took an exhausted seat. "You've been busy."

"I have. The vote was too close this morning. Only

eighteen people and it will pass, especially since some of them have gotten their amendments tacked on to the budget. However, I've gotten thirteen to agree to change and vote against the highway, but I don't know how many Peel and Stanley have gotten to flip to their side. Have you heard anything?"

Angela shook her head. "Everyone is walking on eggshells. No one is saying anything. I did hear the governor caved to the prince and has sent a memo out requesting the highway not be funded. That's a big win for you. Another vote is scheduled for tomorrow morning at nine."

Angela stretched and hid a yawn behind her hand. "Well, I'm done in. I'll be here bright and early, though. Are you staying late?"

Riley nodded. "Gabe had to go back to Keeneston, but Aniyah and I are going to work late. My crew is sending someone up to stay with me later."

"How did the story for your paper turn out?" Angela asked as she stood up.

"The story?" Riley blinked. "Oh, for *The Keeneston Journal*. It's not done yet," Riley said with a smile as she thought of Matt.

Angela chuckled softly. "So, that's how it is. Good for you. If I were an undisclosed number of years younger, then I would be smiling at the thought of that reporter, too. Be careful; reporters can't be trusted. You know that."

Riley nodded. She wanted to say more but she couldn't. Instead she just gave Angela a hug and walked her to the office door. Aniyah and Veronica stood quickly as Aniyah hurried to open the main door to the office for

Angela.

"Phew," Aniyah said as she kicked off her shoes after shutting and locking the door. "This day has been crazy. And so much fun. I loved being able to say whatever I wanted. I mean, I got to tell a man you weren't voting for cock-fighting, even if it wasn't roosters he was talking about."

Veronica snickered and Riley collapsed on the couch next to her. Yeah, the weirdest request of the day had come from an amendment asking for money to be earmarked for a particularly specific kind of adult entertainment. "Any idea on where we will end up on the vote tomorrow?"

Veronica pulled out a chart. "It's so close. It all comes down to the group of undecided voters. Have Matt and Nabi found anything yet that could put an end to the vote one way or another?"

Riley shook her head. "I just got all the normal blackmail information. I was also pleased to see a lot of people are just trying their best. Upon talking to them, I found out they were open to hearing both sides of the argument. Sadly, no nail in the coffin."

There was another knock on the door and Aniyah got up to answer it.

"Sugar! Is that pizza?" Riley and Veronica shot up with wide eyes at Aniyah's exclamation as DeAndre came in carrying two pizza boxes. They moaned in pleasure and then attacked the boxes.

"You all don't have to stay. Matt said they're running a couple more backgrounds, and then he'll be up to stay the night with me at the office. I don't think I can leave. I'm too nervous about the vote in . . ." Riley looked at her watch. It was eleven at night. "Ten hours."

Veronica stood up and yawned. "I need to get a new suit for tomorrow. Even more camera crews will be here by seven for interviews. BBN's coverage has the nation weighing in on this issue. If I hurry, I can get back to Keeneston, raid Sydney's closet, and send some clothes with Matt. If not, I'll bring everything up and meet you here at six for hair and makeup."

Aniyah looked down at herself. "I don't want to leave Miss R. Sugar, can you go home and bring back all my dress clothes?" Aniyah asked DeAndre.

"Anything for you, baby. I'll be back in a while. There's no one here, so lock the doors," DeAndre told them as he stood up with the empty pizza boxes. "I'll walk you out, Veronica."

Aniyah went up on her tiptoes and kissed DeAndre. "Love you, sugar."

"Love you, too."

Riley stood up from the couch and groaned. She was exhausted, but she still had the latest emails from Matt to look over. "Why don't you take a nap?" Riley suggested as Aniyah yawned.

"What are you going to be doing?" Aniyah asked as she slipped an oversized University of Kentucky basketball sweatshirt on.

"Probably the same thing. I have a couple of reports to read, and then I'm going to sleep until Matt gets here."

"Are the doors locked?" Aniyah asked as she double-checked the main office door and then followed Riley into her office and checked the private door to the hallway.

"Okay. We're all locked in so I guess a little shuteye won't hurt. It'll take DeAndre a couple hours to get everything together. He'll open my closet and freeze at all the choices and end up packing the whole thing, bless his heart. I'm a light sleeper so call me if you need anything."

Riley smiled sleepily as she took the paper off the printer and kicked off her shoes. She left the connecting door open while she read the reports on the rest of the supporters of the highway. Nothing.

Suddenly all hell broke loose. The couch shook and Riley felt the vibrations from Aniyah's snores shaking her body. Riley tried not to laugh, but it sounded as if a water buffalo were snorting in anger in the next room. Standing up, Riley closed the connecting door and sent a text to Matt. A second later her phone pinged. He was waiting on one last search and would be at her office between midnight and one.

Riley lay down on the couch and pulled her grandmother's crocheted blanket over her. In seconds, even Aniyah's earth-rattling snores couldn't keep her awake.

Chapter Twenty-Five

Matt ran his hand over his face as he stared at the giant color-coded wall. Nothing. He'd been at this for over twenty-four hours and nothing. He was running on coffee and adrenaline. Both were beginning to wear off. If he looked half as bad as Nabi, he wasn't sure he'd be able to make the drive up to Frankfort.

"I don't get it," Nabi muttered as he looked at the wall covered with all the facts, details, and documents of the congressmen and women who were voting in favor of the highway. "There's no connection besides campaign contributions to Luttrell and Hager. Nothing sticks out at all."

"Maybe if we find out more about Luttrell and Hager, we'll find a third person who could be the liaison between them and congress?" Matt suggested as his fingers flew through his notebook to where he had information on the two men. "Rumor on the Hill is Luttrell and Hager were best friends growing up, and Luttrell got the bank to give Hager his first loan."

"Okay." Nabi nodded as Matt could see his mind starting to process all the possible outcomes. "That should be easy enough to track. Give me a minute."

Matt stared over the list of names and all of their occupations. There were a couple of bankers on there. In fact, Matt shoved the papers around and pulled out the research on Marge Stanley. "Marge's husband owns a bank. Do you think that's our connection?"

Nabi's fingers flew over the keyboard as document after document flashed across the two large television screens hanging on the wall. "They grew up in Lumpur," Nabi said suddenly as he pulled up a yearbook for Lumpur Elementary School. There were pictures of LeeRoy Hager and Harvey Luttrell as twelve-year-olds smiling back at them.

Matt stood up and looked closely at the yearbook pages as Nabi continued to work. "Damn," Nabi cursed, "the bank owner isn't a congressman. It is someone named Jonathan Painter."

"Find out more about him. How many loans did he approve? What's his relationship with these men now? Has he made any political donations?" Matt asked as he stepped around the computer desk and walked right up to the fifty-inch screen with the yearbook of the sixth-grade class on it. There, at the bottom, was a candid photograph of Luttrell and Hager with their arm around a third person. A third person he recognized.

"I found it!" Matt yelled at the same time Nabi did. Matt looked at the other screen and cursed. It wasn't just a coincidence. He should have known all along someone else was manipulating things on the Hill.

Matt leaped over the table and yanked his phone from the table, calling Riley as he ran for his car. Two headlights came into view right as her voicemail picked up. Thank goodness, she had arrived.

Matt didn't even let the car come to a stop before he pulled open the door. "Riley," he started to say, but it wasn't Riley. It was only Veronica smiling back at him.

"Sorry to take so long. I got the perfect suit for you to take to Riley to wear tomorrow," Veronica said as she got out of her car and shoved the suit at him.

"Where's Riley?"

"She's at her office waiting for one of you all to come stay with her. She said she wasn't coming home tonight. Is everything all right?" Veronica asked worriedly.

"Is she alone?"

"No. She's with Aniyah. And DeAndre was just running an errand and was coming back to stay with them. What is it?"

"I know who's behind it."

"Matt!" Nabi called out as he ran down the steps with a duffle bag. "Take these with you."

"Thank you." Matt grabbed the bag and leapt into his truck. He couldn't shake the feeling he was too late. "Hold on, sweetheart," he whispered to himself as he tore out of Desert Farm.

Riley slowly became conscious of a second sound in the office. Aniyah was still snoring so loudly a painting had fallen off the wall, but it was a soft clicking sound that had awoken her. Someone was typing. Riley blinked her eyes and looked toward her desk.

"Ah, you're awake. I swear, I don't know how you can sleep with that racket going on out there."

Riley felt her brow crease in confusion. "What are you

doing here?"

"I had something I had to type up real quick. I need to talk to you anyway so I thought I would do it here."

Riley sat up when she saw the latex gloves on the typist's hands. She gasped as realization hit her. "It's you."

The cold smile confirmed it. The dark eyes glanced next to Riley, and it was then Riley realized there was someone else in the room with them. She went to scream but six million volts of electricity shot through her as the man pressed the stun gun to her neck.

Matt slid to a stop at the annex door closest to Riley's office. He saw another car behind him in the distance and hoped it was Jacob Tandy. He'd asked his friend to increase his patrol of the Capitol that week. Grabbing the goodie bag Nabi gave him, Matt ran from the truck, leaving the door open and the engine on.

Matt used the key DeAndre had given him to get in through the door and paused. He couldn't rush head first into danger. He needed to creep up behind it so he could slit its throat. Matt opened the bag and pulled out a Glock. Treading quietly up the stairs, he made it to Riley's floor. The nightlights cast a soft glow down the hall of offices. A rumbling sound echoed softly as Matt raised his gun and walked on silent footfalls down the hall.

The noise was coming from Riley's office. The closer he got, the louder it was. Matt reached down with his left hand while keeping his gun trained on the door. The door was locked. He swallowed as he calmed himself and slowly slid the key into the lock. The rumbling noise stopped, and he froze. It sounded mechanical as it chugged back to life. Matt turned the key and felt the lock tumble. Slowly, he turned the knob and silently opened the door to the office.

The overhead lights were off and a single lamp from Aniyah's desk illuminated the office. Riley's office door was closed, but the noise was coming from the couch. Matt held tight to his gun as he worked his way into the room. He stopped when he looked down at Aniyah, lying on the couch. Her hair was sticking straight up and her mouth was wide open as she shook the room with every breath she took.

Matt knelt down as he kept his gun trained on Riley's door. He reached out and gently shook Aniyah's shoulder. "Wake up, Aniyah," he whispered. Nothing. Maybe they'd drugged her. Matt knew she was alive so he decided to leave her. He headed for the connecting door and paused to listen behind it. When he didn't hear any strange noises, he slowly turned the knob. The lights were off except for the glowing computer screen. Matt cleared the room. Nothing. No Riley. Matt paused at the couch and looked down. The pillow was indented and Riley's grandmother's blanket was on the floor.

Matt was about to turn when he heard Aniyah's snores pause again. He slipped against the wall and listened. Her snores started up again, but he had heard it anyway. The sound of the door opening. Matt tuned out the snores and closed his eyes. He heard the scuff of a shoe on the carpet. The sound of a gun being cocked and Matt made his move.

Matt ran straight at him. He slammed into the back of the man standing over Aniyah with his gun leveled at her head. Both of their guns dropped, one hitting Aniyah on the head the other falling to the floor.

"What the . . . Lord help me!" Aniyah grabbed the gun and blindly fired off a shot that whizzed by Matt's head and lodged in the floor inches away. He would have cursed, but he was too busy grappling with the man on the ground and praying he wouldn't be shot.

"Where's Riley?" Matt asked the man as he managed to get a hit in before they both leaped up.

"She's in her office," Aniyah told him. "You want me to shoot him? I can do better now that I'm aiming."

"She's not in her office. They took her," the man responded.

Aniyah leapt from the couch and ran into the office, not bothering to give Matt the gun. Matt and his adversary circled each other. "Whose man are you?"

"Whoever pays me," he responded.

He was about six feet and looked as if he spent more time in the gym than any sane person should. When Aniyah let out a shriek, he made his move. Matt saw him coming and lashed out with a kick to the knee. The man went down. Matt spun around him so he could slide his forearm against the man's neck, pinning the man's back to his own chest. Matt pulled tighter, and the man gasped for air.

"Riley's killed herself!" Aniyah cried as she rushed from the office with Riley's laptop in her hands.

Matt froze and the man tried to reach for the gun on the floor but Matt dragged him away as he choked the man. "Where did they take her? How many people are there?"

"But it says . . ." Aniyah stopped talking as Matt shook

his head and squeezed the man's throat as the man scratched frantically at Matt's arm.

"Read it," Matt said, his voice tight with fear and anger.

"I've let my family, friends, and town down. I was never meant to be a politician, and find I can no longer tell right from wrong. I can't live with myself and the pressure to do what is right. I took bribes to fight the highway and then I . . . I can't even say what I did to such a lovely person as Aniyah whose only crime was discovering mine. I can't embarrass my friends and family with a trial. I feel there are no more options except for me to take my life so we can all move forward. I love you all. I'm so sorry. Riley Davies." Aniyah wiped a tear and couldn't look at Matt.

Matt felt his heart slam into his chest. There's no way Riley committed suicide. "No," Matt said so forcefully Aniyah jumped. "They're behind this. They're going to kill her if they haven't already. They sent this man to clean up the loose ends, didn't they?"

The man grunted and Aniyah looked questioningly at them. Matt narrowed his eyes at the gun in her hand. "The gun, look at the grip. Now!" Matt ordered.

Aniyah set down the laptop and turned the gun over in her hand. "RMD."

"It's Riley's gun from home—a home that blew up. How did you get this gun?" Matt demanded as he saw the pieces clicking together for Aniyah, and suddenly the gun was aimed right at him.

"You! What did you do with my friend?" Aniyah yelled. Matt jumped back as Aniyah fired. The bullet ripped into the man's shoulder, and he cried out.

"Not again, motherfu—" the man groaned through clenched teeth.

Matt shoved the man to the ground and ripped the sleeve from his shirt. Right next to the bleeding bullet wound courtesy of Aniyah was a freshly stitched graze. Matt pulled back his fist and slammed it into the man's injured shoulder. "You're the one who blew up her house. Where is she?" Matt screamed over the man's wails.

The door to the office was kicked in suddenly, "Freeze!" DeAndre shouted. Matt looked up as DeAndre took in Matt's bloodied knuckles, the man shot on the floor, and Aniyah holding a gun. "What the hell? Can someone fill me in?" DeAndre asked while turning his gun to the man on the floor.

"He blew up Riley's house, and they have her now. They left a phony suicide note, and this man was coming to clean up all the loose ends. Those loose ends include almost shooting your girlfriend."

"You were going to kill my baby?" DeAndre asked menacingly as he pressed the gun barrel to the man's head.

Matt nodded silently to DeAndre as Matt dug his thumb into the man's shoulder wound. "You want the pain to stop? You tell us where Riley is."

The man screamed as Matt dug in. Sweat covered the man's face as his body shook in pain. "Lord forgive me," Aniyah said as she crossed herself one second before slowly pressing the heel of her stiletto into the man's crotch. The man's screams went up five octaves. "You tell me where my friend is or you'll spend your time in jail as a eunuch."

Matt sat back and stared along with DeAndre as

Aniyah pressed a little more and the man hit Mariah Carey-level notes. He looked frantically to DeAndre and Matt. Matt just shrugged. "I'm not going to stop her. The only way this stops is if you start talking."

"Fine!"

Aniyah froze and DeAndre put the gun back against the man's head.

"Where is she?" Matt asked.

"The House chambers."

Matt slammed his fist into the man's chin. His eyes rolled back into his head and Matt ran for the bag of goodies he'd left in the office. He grabbed two guns and a knife from the bag. As he shoved the weapons in his waistband, he called over his shoulder for DeAndre to call Tandy, along with an ambulance, and to keep the man in custody.

"I'll come with you!" DeAndre called out. "You need backup."

Matt shook his head. "I need you to keep this man secure. Trust me, he's going to try to get away."

Matt took off running for the tunnels beneath the annex and the Capitol. The dark tunnels lined with small square tiles on the walls and cafeteria type flooring seemed to stretch on for miles. "Hang on, Riley, I'm coming."

Chapter Twenty-Six

Riley felt as if she were in college all over again during that one horrible night. Her mind was hazy. It was hard to think of one thing long enough to make a complete thought. Her muscles were tired, too. She felt someone carrying her, and she forced herself to open an eye. She had to show herself this wasn't that night so long ago. She wasn't in that car about to be attacked. She was alive. It seemed like a colossal effort, but she finally managed to crack one eye open. She took in the carpet that reminded her of something and a shoe that reminded her of something else.

"Set her down here."

That voice. Then like a flood it all came back to her. The people in her office. The stun gun to the neck. She was going to be killed. Riley kept her eyes closed and let her body stay dead weight. The man who was carrying her set her down roughly in a chair. She was at her desk in the House chambers.

She listened carefully as she flexed her toes in her shoes. She had feeling back in her feet and her legs, thankfully. She couldn't risk testing her hands, but they were no longer tingling. There were two of them. One she knew was the brains and the other the brawn. She had to go after the brawn first. If she could take him down she might have a chance to live.

Matt's face flashed before her, and she knew she would never go down without a fight. And boy, did they pick the wrong woman to start a fight with. Riley let the man push her back against the chair and then she slid to the side as if she couldn't support herself. It was hard not to tense as she hit the floor, but instead she managed to free her legs from under the desk.

"Just like her to be difficult. Do you have the gun?"

"Yes."

"Good. Get her back up in the seat and then we'll put it in her hand and let her shoot herself in the head. With a little help, of course."

Riley swallowed back bile as she felt the man lean over to pick her up. Riley waited until the shadow behind her eyelids darkened and then slammed her head forward with all the strength she had.

Her head cracked into the man's nose. Riley felt the warm blood cover her face as she landed punch after punch to his stomach. There was screaming, and Riley wasn't sure if it was the man, the other person, or herself.

The man howled in pain and lashed out at her. His hand connected with her cheek and pain exploded as her face throbbed but it didn't stop her. All the lessons her father had taught her and all the hours sparring with Annie and Bridget came roaring back to her as muscle memory kicked in.

Riley pulled her hand back and arched her fist into the side of the man's neck. He froze in place and blinked as oxygen was temporarily cut off from one side of his brain. She only had seconds, but it was enough to get out from under him. Her effort was halted when a hand fisted itself in her hair and pulled. Riley clamped her hands on top of the hand and let herself be dragged away from the man.

"I didn't take you as someone to hire out your dirty work."

"You don't get to where I am by getting your hands dirty."

"That would ruin your manicure, wouldn't it, Angela?"

Her mentor smiled. "I see I've taught you well. Too bad it was for naught."

Riley kept her eye on the man with blood dripping over his lips and off his chin. He wasn't happy. Angela stopped pulling on her hair, and Riley made sure her feet were under her.

"Why would you do this?" Riley asked as the man stalked toward her.

"Why else? Money, power, and just to be a good friend."

"Friend?" Riley asked as the man stopped in front of her and smiled a bloody smile at her.

"Oh, you didn't know? I guess I forgot to mention I grew up with Harvey Luttrell and LeeRoy Hager. We've been best friends ever since. It was my husband's bank that gave LeeRoy the business loan for his road construction company, a company my husband happens to own a share in."

"So your husband is the one getting rich. Hope he doesn't leave you," Riley grunted as Angela pulled on her hair again. Riley felt some of the hair tearing away from her scalp and winced.

"You don't have to worry about me. I know why they want the highway through Keeneston. And when it happens, I'll become a very rich woman in my own right. When you're a real estate investor, it pays to know when there's going to be a good deal on land. See, when that highway comes through, that land is going to lose a lot of value. Harvey is going to come in and have the government go ahead and take all that beautiful, expensive land around his new headquarters through eminent domain so Luttrell Food Industries can build a new corporate headquarters. He'll say he needs housing, shopping, and so on for his headquarters and buy up almost all of that open land just waiting for someone with my vision to take it. We'll develop an adequate headquarters, and then he'll sell all the unused land to my company at a fraction of its value. I'll be turning it into strip malls, condos, and over-priced neighborhoods. I'll make a fortune," Angela said gleefully. "Now, enough talking. We have a suicide to commit."

Angela let go of Riley's hair and shoved her backward onto the floor. Riley landed on her back, and when the man came near enough, she kicked her foot up and connected with his balls. The man bent at the waist, cupping his damaged testicles as Riley arched her lower back using momentum to kick both legs up so only her shoulders still touched the ground. She wrapped her legs around the man's throat, dragging him back down to the floor with her. His face rested in her crotch as she hooked her left foot behind her right knee and squeezed him into a triangle hold.

Angela shrieked as Riley's assassin gasped for air. Riley didn't say anything. She just hung on. She had to wait for him to pass out before reaching for the gun.

"You're ruining everything!" Angela screamed as she kicked Riley in the side. Riley took the hit and breathed out the pain as Angela kicked again and again.

Riley knew the moment Angela remembered the gun. She halted mid-kick and stared at the man's waistline. Angela lunged and Riley twisted. She squeezed her legs so tightly she felt the man fall limp against her. Riley tried to reach for his gun, but Angela was already there, pulling the gun from his waist.

"That's my gun!" Riley looked in amazement at one of the two handguns from her mirrored set. They were made to fit her and monogrammed with her initials. Her father had given those to her for graduation.

"That's right. And your other gun is being used to kill that loud-mouthed secretary, that nosy guard, and that hot reporter. And this one is going to be used to kill yourself after your breakdown. I'll have to go back and work up a better suicide note to account for the others, but that will be a pleasure. A murder-suicide always plays well in the news."

Riley stared up as Angela held the barrel of her gun to her forehead. She was out of options. No matter how fast Riley was, she wasn't faster than a bullet at close range.

"I'm so going to enjoy your funeral," Angela smiled as she moved her finger onto the trigger.

Riley closed her eyes as all the what-might-have-beens ran through her head: marriage to Matt, holding their children, seeing her parents again, laughing with her sister, teasing her brothers . . . A tear ran down her cheek. "I love you, Matt," Riley whispered as the sound of gunfire exploded through the chambers.

Matt raced down the underground hallway as if the hounds of hell were after him. Instead he realized he was racing straight toward them—straight toward the woman who wanted to use the latest Supreme Court ruling that allowed corporations to be given land taken for the "betterment" of the town's economy. She would kill Riley over her highway vote, because without the highway, the land would never be considered blighted or devalued enough for her to push the state to take it by eminent domain. And without that highway, whatever development she planned wouldn't have a main road to it. Angela, LeeRoy, and Harvey had found a way to have the state pay for their real estate scheme.

They had tried to kill Riley twice before and they weren't going to fail a third time. They were already sending out a cleaner. Too bad for them, Matt was better at his job than the man they had sent. Not to mention Aniyah's love for very pointy stilettos.

Matt burst out of the tunnel and heard the sounds of sirens in the distance but didn't have time to wait for backup. He just prayed he wasn't too late. He sprinted up the gray marble stairs and ran past the decorative balusters lining the length of the building toward the doors to the House of Representatives.

He heard voices and slowed his approached. The doors had frosted glass in them, and he didn't want to be seen. Matt pressed himself to the clay-colored wall and slid toward the doors.

"I'm so going to enjoy your funeral," Matt heard in a voice that had to be Angela's.

Matt's gun was already in his hand as he kicked open the door.

Angela stood over Riley with a gun pointed at her head. The sound of a gun firing echoed through the chamber.

Chapter Twenty-Seven

"Riley!" Matt yelled with his heart in his throat.

Angela's surprised look would forever be etched on her face as she fell to the ground with a bullet lodged in her forehead.

With tears streaking her cheeks, Riley turned and gasped. "You're alive!"

Matt was on his knees beside her in a heartbeat. He wrapped his arms around her and pulled her tight against him. He buried his face in her hair as she clung to him. "Shh, it's over now. You're safe," Matt whispered, even though he knew it wasn't true. They had a few loose ends of their own to clean up.

The clatter of boots running up the marble stairs sounded impossibly loud along with a second gun shot echoing in the empty building, but it was the sound of stilettos pinging on the stone that reached them first.

"Who else can I shoot?" Aniyah huffed as she ran into the room on her five-inch heels. The man Riley had choked groaned as he started to come to, and Aniyah pulled the trigger. Matt flung himself over Riley to protect her from Aniyah's bad aim.

The man yelped. "The bitch shot me in the toe!"

"Whoops. That's a real sensitive trigger. I mean, the gun is beautiful, but with my salon nails, I'm just shooting up everything. I just took out a chunk of the Abraham Lincoln statue in the rotunda, and that man's a national treasure. I don't so feel so bad about taking a toe from this man, though." Aniyah waved the gun toward the figure writhing in pain, and Matt flung himself over Riley again.

"State police!" Tandy yelled as he rushed into the room with his gun drawn and backup flanking him. He looked around and holstered his gun before he stepped over to Aniyah and held out his hand palm up. "Hand it over," he said as gestured with his fingers for Aniyah to give him the gun.

"But—"

Tandy shook his head. "No buts. I don't know how you beat us over here in those heels. And while I respect the hell out of that, you can't shoot worth a damn."

Aniyah rolled her eyes and placed the gun in Tandy's hand. "It's the nails," she said stubbornly as she flashed the long, pointed fake nails that spelled out KENTUCKY on her fingers with a galloping horse on one thumb and a University of Kentucky Wildcat on the other thumb.

"Are you two hurt?" Tandy asked as Aniyah went over and looked down at Angela.

Aniyah clucked and shook her head. "She's not having an open casket, that's for sure."

Tandy looked as if he couldn't decide if he wanted to roll his eyes or bust out laughing. In the end, he just shook his head and turned to Matt. "I'll call in the coroner for Ms. Cobb. I have an ambulance arriving soon for the man in Riley's office. I guess I need two," he said, looking down at the man cursing Aniyah, who just smiled back and blessed his cold heart.

"Riley, are you injured? There's so much blood..." Matt ended on a whisper as he pushed back her hair and studied her face. He felt as if he had been punched in the gut as he looked for injuries.

"I'm okay," she said softly as she covered his hand with hers. "I broke his nose for knocking me out with a stun gun."

Matt brought her to his chest again. *She's safe. She's safe,* he repeated to himself as he held her in his arms. He never wanted to let her go again. Matt just clung to Riley, trying to bring his feelings back under control. He opened his eyes when he heard the unexpected sounds coming from the state police officers securing the scene.

"Commissioner Elton," Matt said with surprise as the Kentucky state police commissioner strode into the room. His white-streaked red hair was sticking up at all angles as if he'd just rolled out of bed, which he probably had done at this late hour.

Commissioner Elton was one of the few people who knew about Matt's undercover work. The old policeman had started out in patrol, and over the course of thirty years, worked his way up to commissioner. He was a tough country boy who didn't give a fig about saying or doing the politically correct thing.

"What in the Sam Hill is going on here? Walz, you bastard, you were supposed to be on leave for the month. And somebody please tell me there is a good reason for a ranking member of the House to have a freaking bullet in her head!" Elton put his hands on his hips as he looked down at the man cursing up a storm about police brutality. "And who shot this pansy in the foot? Stop your whining, it's just a toe. It's not even your big one."

Matt helped Riley stand up as Aniyah snorted and more than happily told Elton she was the one who shot off the toe.

"Baby!" DeAndre said with fear in his voice. "You shot another one?" He smiled as she wrapped her in a hug.

"Another one? Who the hell are you?" Commissioner Elton bellowed.

DeAndre froze as he sputtered his name.

Matt walked over with one arm around Riley and slapped DeAndre on his shoulder. "Elton, this young man will be your next top trooper," Matt smiled. "Now, let's go to Riley's office so we can explain what's going on. And call your wife. You'll need her to bring your uniform. The fancy one with all the medals so you look real nice on national news telling how you took down a corruption ring intent on murdering a public official over her vote, with the help of an undercover officer and a Capitol guard, of course. But first we have two more people we need to visit. Want to have your wife bring your SWAT gear and have some fun for old time's sake?" Matt winked as a giant grin spread across Elton's face.

He pulled out his phone and called his wife. "Meet me in the annex. Yup, both outfits and don't forget the bulletproof vest." Elton hung up and nodded at the group. "Now, I want to hear what you've been up to on your time off, Walz."

Riley let Matt explain the situation in a very concise, fact-based timeline. She sat on her couch in her office urgently texting the entire town of Keeneston that she was safe, that things would be over soon, and please don't come up to Frankfort. And yes, a pie would be nice.

"And that's how I discovered the connection between Angela, her husband, Luttrell, and Hager. In the meantime, Riley was here and learned it as well. Sweetheart, can you tell the commissioner what happened?"

Riley nodded and took a deep breath. She told the commissioner about the note, the stun gun, Angela's confession to the attempts on Riley's life, and the reasons behind it all.

Elton reached out his hand and patted her knee. "You did real good, Miss Davies. And so did you, Walz. I take it you'll be sponsoring Mr. Drews here for the academy. Let me know when you send in your application, son. But maybe you should keep guns away from your girlfriend. I noticed Lincoln is also missing a toe. I'd watch your feet if you ever get in an argument with her."

"Dear?" a soft voice called from the doorway. "I'm sorry to interrupt, but I brought your *I'm a badass* outfit along with your *I'm important* outfit." A woman, who couldn't be more than five-feet-two inches tall with gray hair cut in a cute bob and a teasing smile, spoke so politely it was as if she were letting him know meatloaf was for dinner.

Riley struggled not to laugh as Elton looked at his wife with love and adoration. "Thanks, dear. I appreciate you bringing these down here in the middle of the night."

Elton stood up and took the clothes from her and kissed her cheek. His wife reached to the side of the door and brought out a 12-gauge pump-action shotgun. She pumped it in one hand and smiled. "And I brought Big Bertha. I know you've missed her."

Elton grabbed the shotgun and smiled before kissing his wife on the lips. "You're the greatest." Then he turned to Walz. "Come on, Walz. I need you to liaise with the Lexington and Keeneston police so we can plan the simultaneous arrests of Luttrell and Hager."

Riley held up her hand. "I can do that for you. My uncle's the sheriff of Keeneston, and my cousin's the head of the Lexington FBI field office. Will that do?"

Elton smiled. "If you can get me warrants in the next twenty minutes, I'll let you have a couple of minutes alone with Luttrell"

"Promise?" Riley smirked as she typed into her phone. A minute later her phone pinged. "Marshall will meet you a mile from Luttrell's home in Keeneston and Ryan will meet whichever group you send to Lexington."

Elton's phone beeped. "And that's your warrant for Luttrell. Ryan will have the one for Hager in a couple minutes," Riley smiled. "Oh, and the Rose sisters want to know if you'd like a vanilla cake or brownies?"

"No wonder you love Keeneston so much," Elton said with a shake of his head while his wife mouthed *brownies* to Riley.

"And you need to get out of my way!" Riley heard a raised voice say from the hallway.

"Veronica?" Riley questioned as she stood up and hurried to the hall in time to see a perfectly put-together Veronica tongue-whipping a uniformed officer.

"Oh, thank goodness. If my calculations are correct, the

police will be raiding the houses in one hour, and the news reporters will be here at the Capitol in two hours for live morning news coverage. I need to get you ready." Veronica looked over at the clothes Elton was holding and nodded. "Stay in the SWAT outfit. Very hands-on for a commissioner." Then she looked at Matt as Elton went to get changed. "Are you going to wear that?"

Riley hid her laugh behind a cough as Matt looked down at his jeans and Country Boy Brewery T-shirt. "What's wrong with this?"

"It's great beer, but the word POLICE doesn't show up anywhere," Veronica stated as she looked around at the officers filling the office. "You," Veronica snapped at the officer holding a M4 rifle. "Give me your jacket."

The man didn't think twice about responding to Veronica's command. "Yes, ma'am," he snapped and tugged off his windbreaker with a Kentucky State Police star embroidered on the front and the word POLICE in big letters across the back. She handed it to Matt and smiled. "There. Now you can keep your T-shirt and look official. Have you ever thought of using hairspray?" Matt narrowed his eyes and Veronica held up her hands. "You're right. The rugged look is really in right now. Besides, your face will be blurred."

Elton walked in a minute later all suited up. "Ready or do we need a mani/pedi before we bust the bad guys?"

Riley lost her control and a laugh slipped out when Veronica looked at Elton's nails. "Well—" Veronica started before she swung around and cringed at Riley. "I don't think I'll have time for that. But you could always stop at the Fluff and Buff in Keeneston when you're driving through. Now, gentlemen, do your thing and we'll meet you back here in ninety minutes for the press conference. I'll also have a speech prepared for you if you'd like to use it." The way she stated it, it didn't seem to be an option.

"Who is she?" Riley heard Elton ask Matt as they left.

"PR genius and right hand to the Prince of Rahmi," Matt answered before turning back and striding across the office.

Riley's breath caught at the look of desire and love in his eyes a moment before his lips met hers. It was hard and quick, but when he drew back he was grinning. "Couldn't leave without a good luck kiss."

Matt gave her a wink and strode out of the room with a canvas bag over his shoulder and a smile on his face. Riley shook her head as Veronica started dictating a speech for Aniyah to type while she moved Riley to a chair and got to work cleaning her up.

Chapter Twenty-Eight

Matt felt the adrenaline pumping through his body as an officer used a battering ram to break down Harvey Luttrell's mansion door. The men hired by Angela, Luttrell, and Hager had seen the writing on the wall and spilled everything they knew about their employers, including their directions to kill Riley and Matt so it looked like an accident.

"Breaching the front door," Matt heard Ryan Parker say into the coms. The Lexington arrest was running simultaneously so neither party could alert the other that they'd been caught.

Matt swept up the stairs with his gun drawn and Elton behind him. The door at the end of the hall opened, and Luttrell stumbled out as he was tying his robe.

"What the—?"

Matt didn't let him finish. He had Luttrell pinned to the ground and in cuffs before he could finish his question. "Harvey Luttrell, you're under arrest for conspiracy to commit murder," Matt said before he listed off all the charges and read him his rights.

"We have Hager," Ryan said over the coms.

Matt didn't listen to Luttrell's denials. He simply

escorted him down the stairs with a satisfied smile on his lips. "I'm sorry, don't you know? We have your henchmen in custody. We can't get them to shut up," Matt said with a shake of his head.

Elton looked down on his phone. "Smile, boys," he muttered as he read the text from an unknown number. "Who's this from?" Elton asked as he opened the door.

Cameras flashed and reporters began yelling out questions. Elton's phone beeped again. "I thought I told you to smile. Tell them you'll have an update for them at the Capitol in thirty minutes. Looking hot in those SWAT getups, guys."

"Son of a bitch. It's that blond nightmare," Elton said between clenched teeth as he let go of Luttrell's right arm and headed for the press. Matt kept his face serious and his head down, put on a baseball cap, and pulled it low over his eyes, but those eyes showed his amusement. Veronica was a force of nature.

Riley stood between Ryan and Elton as Elton gave his press conference. He hadn't argued when Veronica had handed him a speech, just shook his head and offered her a job — a job that she politely turned down.

Before she was ready, Elton was stepping back and allowing Riley to step forward. She spoke from her heart as she described the events, the corruption, and the attempts on her life. "I am saddened and disheartened by the events that have unfolded since I took office, but I want to send out my sincere appreciation to the state police, my assistant, Aniyah, and the best Capitol guard around, DeAndre Drews. Thank you."

"Are you going to seek reelection?"

"Will you be completing your term?"

Questions were shouted, but Riley quickly tackled them. "It's too early to even think about reelection. And yes, I will be finishing my term. There are many important votes still ahead of me in this last week of session. I have a job to do for my district, and I won't disappoint them."

"What does this mean for the highway project?"

Riley looked straight into the camera. "Well, I hope it means it's as dead as Angela Cobb."

Matt chuckled from where he stood off to the side, the reporters gasped, and Veronica buried her face in her hands as Riley stepped back and let Elton end the now fever-pitched conference.

"Nice," Ryan laughed as he and Matt escorted her back to her office.

"There's my firecracker," Matt said, kissing her temple.

"I'm tired of mincing words. Hell, I'm just plain tired," Riley mumbled as Aniyah and DeAndre hurried after her.

"Now, that was a 'Real Politicians of Frankfort' confessional right there. You just said what we all thought, bless her cold dead heart," Aniyah said as she made the sign of the cross.

Riley took a seat on her couch while a cleaning crew got the blood out of the carpet in the main waiting room. Veronica rushed in and headed straight for Riley's desk and started pulling out drawers.

"What are you looking for?"

"This." Veronica popped the top to a bottle of bourbon open and put it to her ruby-red lips. "Dead as Angela Cobb? Are you trying to ruin me?"

Aniyah starting shaking her head as she looked at her phone. "Turn on the news," she said to Veronica, who grabbed the remote and turned on the television.

"Straight shooter Riley Davies has set the new bar in politics," Dan from 14 News said into the camera from outside the Capitol. "Willing to die for what is right and showing no remorse for sticking up for her constituents. She is leaving the rest of the state wondering why their representatives aren't doing the same for them." Dan looked off screen and yelled out. "Senator Peel! Would you like to comment?"

Senator Peel froze as he was trying to sneak in through a side door. "Not at this time. What Representative Davies has gone through is quite remarkable, and you'll be sure I'll be talking to her about it soon and how we can better work together in the future. Thank you."

The room leaned forward as Ryan stepped forward with three other FBI agents. "Senator Peel, you need to come with us." The camera zoomed in as Peel was escorted to a waiting car.

Veronica turned off the television. "Well, I guess it wasn't a total disaster. My job is done here. Let me know if you need anything else." She tossed back another shot of bourbon and sashayed out the door.

"No wonder she's a lesbian," Aniyah smiled. "No man could handle that."

Riley spent the rest of the day casting votes in a very crammed Senate chambers since the House chambers were off limits as a crime scene. Peel and Stanley had talked to her, along with the governor. For the first time in history, a section of the budget had been unanimously voted down. After a little wheeling and dealing, the rest of the budget passed, giving the governor something besides corruption to talk about at her own press conference.

By the end of the day, Riley was ready to fall over where she stood leaning against the wall, listening to the last measure. She looked behind her and saw Matt leaning against the back wall with his arms crossed over his Country Boy Brewery shirt and a gun at his hip. His eyes never left hers. She smiled softly at him, and after she cast her final vote of the day, she moved through the crowd to his side.

"Ready to go home, sweetheart?"

"With you, always," Riley rested her head on his chest as he put his arm over her shoulder. She let the sounds of people calling out her name and the flashes of cameras disappear as Matt guided her out of the Capitol.

"I love you," Matt whispered against her ear as they snuck around the wall of television reporters lobbing questions at Senator Stanley for her involvement with Peel and why the FBI asked to meet with her.

"I love you, too." Riley stopped walking and looked up at the man she loved. "I don't ever want to be apart from you again. I shouldn't have denied my feelings for you. We've lost so much time."

"It'll remind us to make the most of what we do have, which is a lifetime, after all," Matt grinned down at her before.

Matt opened the door for her, and she climbed into his car. They were quiet as they drove home. She didn't mind. She had a lot to think about and it appeared Matt did, too.

He kept his hand on her thigh and the way his thumb gently traced circles caused her body to relax. Before she knew it, he was carrying her into his house.

"I'm sorry, I didn't mean to fall asleep," Riley said as she rubbed her eyes.

"It's okay, sweetheart. Let's get you into bed." Matt helped her undress, and they slid under the covers together. Matt pulled her to him and Riley fell asleep with her head on his arm and her leg thrown over his.

For one month, Matt had enjoyed every second with Riley. He'd used his leave to write the story for *The Keeneston Journal* before asking her father for a job on the farm. He had baled hay, helped birth foals, and mended fences. Did he need to do it? No. But it was a good part of his healing process. He didn't have to pretend to be someone else, and it gave him time to come to grips with his fears of moving forward with Riley.

They had spent every moment they could together after she had finished her session and had gotten back to work on the farm. Every night, he held her in his arms and every night he felt more and more sure he could never let her go. They went to Lexington to try new restaurants. They went hiking through the Red River Gorge. They played poker with their friends. She was the woman of his dreams, and he loved her more than he had ever known was possible.

There was only one thing stopping him from asking her to marry him — his past. Matt hammered in a nail and stood up to wipe the sweat from his forehead. The fence he was mending was almost complete. As he bent to place the last few nails into the board, he saw a car in the distance. The dust cloud behind it showed it was coming up the seldom-used dirt road to the pasture where Matt was working.

Matt hammered the last of the nails in place and tested the board before standing back up. He slipped the hammer into his tool belt and pulled off his work gloves. He watched as the SUV came to a stop, and he smiled at the man who got out. He was in his early seventies. His dark blond hair had turned lighter with age, but it was still in the same buzz cut it had been since Matt moved in with him as an angry teenager.

Simon Walz had grown softer over the years — his stomach more jolly than hard and his face more relaxed — but he always had a ready smile for the closest thing to a son he'd ever had.

"Dad," Matt smiled as he hopped over the fence. "What are you doing here?"

Simon smiled at the name. Matt had started calling him that after his second year of college and had never stopped. After all, he was more a father to him than his own had ever been.

"Your mother told me she had a feeling I should come see you. Apparently, she heard something in your voice when she talked to you yesterday," Simon told him as he slapped Matt on the back. "And you know how she is about her feelings."

Matt nodded. Simon's wife hadn't been able to have children. When Simon had shown up with a malnourished, neglected, angry seventeen-year-old boy, she hadn't blinked an eye. Instead, she had wrapped her arms around him and welcomed him to his new home.

"So, you want to tell me what's worrying you, or do I have to send in the big guns? Your mother did send your favorite cookies to bribe you," Simon said as he reached into the car and pulled out a storage container filled with cookies and a note attached saying *I love you ~ Mom*.

Matt turned and took a breath. What was wrong with him? It was all this time outdoors working with nothing but his thoughts to keep him company. He was getting so emotional. He took a deep breath and decided to embrace it for that day only and then he swore he'd stay cool afterward.

"It's Riley," Matt said softly as he leaned back against the black four-board fence.

"Is something the matter? Your mother and I got the impression when you were both over for dinner that everything was going quite well. Your mom even mentioned the *G* word."

"*G* word?" Matt asked.

"Grandbabies."

Matt laughed and shook his head. "Ironic, isn't it? That's the one thing stopping me from asking Riley to marry me."

He could see his father's eyebrows rise, but he didn't say anything. Instead, he waited for Matt to explain.

"I love her so much. I want nothing more than to have a family with her, but what if I turn out like them?" Matt didn't have to explain *them* to the man standing before him.

"You're not your father, Matt," Simon said softly.

Matt went rigid. "Do not call him that. You're my father. He doesn't deserve that title."

"You know firsthand what it feels like to be on the receiving end of that rage. You've never acted out. You've never been overtaken with it before. And from what you've told me about some of the situations you've been in, it would have manifested itself by now if you were anything like him. You're your own man, Matt. One your mother and I are very proud of," Simon told him, knowing now wasn't the time to touch him.

Matt let out a breath. "It's not him. It's my mother's legacy I worry about the most. This past job, I had to take drugs. They still call to me occasionally. Riley got me into NA, and I've been good since, but what if . . . ?"

Simon grabbed Matt then. Matt was so startled he almost jumped back. "You can't let what-if dictate your future. What if you die tonight? What if you fall out of love? What if, what if, what if. They'll paralyze you, son. What do you want to do right now? Your heart, your mind — what do they want?"

"Riley," Matt answered instantly.

Simon let go of Matt and gave him a caring smile. "Then I think you have your answer on what to do. You have love and support all around you. If you ever fall, we'll be here to catch you. But never stop living for fear of the what-could-happen."

Matt felt dazed. Was it really that simple? God knows he loved her with all his heart and wanted to spend the rest of his life with her. "Oh, crap," Matt whispered as he closed his eyes and let his head fall back.

"What is it?" Simon asked with concern.

"I have to go ask her father for permission to marry his daughter."

Simon just laughed. "How hard can that be? I'm sure he's already expecting it."

Matt shook his head. "You don't know her father."

Chapter Twenty-Nine

An hour later, Matt was showered and standing at Cy and Gemma's front door. He stared at it for a full minute before ringing the doorbell. The door opened instantly and Cy looked down at his watch. "One minute and seven seconds. I was wondering how long you were going to stand there staring at the door like an idiot."

Matt waited for Cy to step back so he could come inside, except Cy never moved. Instead, he stepped outside, forcing Matt to step back. "I assume you're here to talk to me, so let's sit outside."

Matt looked down to the military sniper rifle Cy had in his hands. "Spring cleaning?"

Cy just grinned and Matt relaxed. He had Cy's support. If he didn't, Matt would already be in trouble. "There're too many prying ears inside," Cy said softly as he took a seat on the porch and laid the rifle across the wicker table. "You'll learn this. Wives say one thing, and it means the complete opposite."

Cy raised his voice in imitation of his wife. "I'm *fine*. I'm not mad. I just want to *talk*. Don't worry about taking the boys to the doctor, I'll take them so I don't interrupt you enjoying that beer and watching TV — it's *no problem*.

Don't even think about bugging our kids' phones. *Don't shoot Matt* . . . you get the point. Always saying one thing and meaning the other." Cy picked up the gun and clicked a magazine into place. "So, what did you want to talk about?"

Matt cleared his throat as Cy raised the rifle to check its sight. "I know I'm not the perfect man for Riley . . ."

"Is this because of the whole NA thing? Or is it about your biological parents?" Cy asked as he gently squeezed the trigger, and the top of a bright red daisy exploded six hundred yards away near a storage barn.

"Cyland Davies, are you shooting my flowers again?" Gemma yelled from inside the house.

"No, honey, that was Matt," Cy yelled back. Matt blinked. Great. He was now being blamed for killing a flower, and his whole past he had hoped to stay secret was now laid out there as a reason not to marry Riley.

"So, which is it?" Cy asked as he calmly shot the stem of the now bloomless flower.

"Oh no, your cable sports package just went out," Gemma called from inside the house. "So sad. No playoffs."

Matt didn't think Gemma sounded sad at all as Cy chuckled. "See, always saying one thing and meaning another," he whispered to Matt before calling out. "I love you, sweetheart."

"I love you, too. You're still not getting your sports package back."

"Don't worry, I can think of other ways to occupy myself at night," Cy said with a grin.

"Will you stop hitting on me and let the poor boy get

your permission to marry Riley?" Gemma called back with amusement—amusement Matt wasn't feeling.

"So, are you going to answer the question?" Cy asked him again.

Matt cleared his throat and lowered his voice. He now knew Gemma had her ear pressed to the door. In fact, it had silently opened about an inch a second before Cy had shot the daisy.

"How did you know about that? NA and my birth parents?" Matt asked.

Cy set down his gun and shook his head. "I was a spy." At least he was nice enough to not call him an idiot again.

"Both," Matt simply said. "As I was saying, I know I'm not the perfect man for Riley, but I love her, and I'll do whatever I can to make her happy. And it's not because you'll shoot me if I don't. I'm going to ask her to marry me next week."

Cy grunted. "I don't care about your past. You rose above it, and I respect that. You're a good man, Matt, but you'd better not be having any children."

The front door was flung open as Gemma rushed out. "Oh, this is wonderful! I've got to call the girls. And yes, children. Lots and lots of children! Of course you will, since the whole twin thing runs in the family. Oh, this is so exciting!"

Cy groaned and yanked his wife into his lap. His lips covered hers in a kiss that left Matt both impressed and embarrassed for witnessing. When Cy looked back up, he shrugged. "Works every time," he said as Gemma had a happy, dazed look on her face. "You were saying?"

"Um, that I just thought you should know I'm going to propose. I hope you'll approve, and I kinda need Mrs. Davies to help."

Gemma blinked out of her daze. "See, I told you I liked him. And of course we approve. And call me Gemma, please. How can I help?"

Riley collapsed with a sated sigh onto Matt's bare chest. She had never known it was possible to be so close to a person and not in just a physical way. Over the past month that Matt had worked on the farm, he'd put back on the muscle he'd lost during his six-month undercover stint. Plus he seemed at peace now.

His rich laugh was more readily heard, and he never let them fall asleep without kissing her goodnight and telling her he loved her. That night, he'd made love to her with such surety and emotion that Riley felt he'd shared his soul with her.

Matt stroked her hair as they lay in each other's arms. It was at night after making love they talked about their hopes and dreams. Riley told him she was thinking of running for a second term after next year's session. Peel and Stanley had resigned and were cutting a deal for their involvement in paying Karen to spy. Nabi had turned over information to the FBI showing the two had paid for Karen's children's private school tuition. That night, though, she was worried about his future. While Matt was happier than Riley had ever seen him, she knew Monday brought the return to reality—a reality that Matt could be sent away at any time for another undercover operation.

"Do you know what you're doing on Monday?" Riley asked as she ran her fingers over the sculpted muscles of his chest.

"Business as usual. Since the news announced I was an undercover agent, my face was blurred in all the pictures and was never shown in the live shots. So I'm still cleared for undercover work. I guess I have Veronica to thank for that. Elton said when his office sent in the media request, there was one prefiled."

Riley nodded against his chest. She loved him, and she knew this was a big part of him. Just because she worried about it didn't mean she didn't support it. Matt was one of the best officers out there.

"But for now I'll just be patrolling around here and Lipston. Elton wants me to take some time off from undercover work, and I can't say I'm sad about it."

Riley raised her eyes and looked into his, so dark blue they almost couldn't be seen in the night. "You aren't?"

Matt stroked his hand down her back and nodded. "I'll do my job when I need to, but for now I find myself not wishing to leave you or our town. I much prefer sleeping in your bed than sharing a shoddy motel room with a couple of guys. Do you want me to show you why?" Matt asked as his voice dipped lower along with his hand.

"You may have to show me multiple times."

"My pleasure," Matt whispered as he took her with his body and heart.

Riley stretched early the next morning and sat up suddenly when she realized Matt wasn't in bed. A quick sniff of the air told her where he was. He was cooking breakfast. Riley admitted it—she was easy to please. Sex and breakfast were all it took to have her drooling. She slid into her robe and headed for the kitchen.

Matt was just putting bread into the toaster when she sat down at the island. She nibbled on the bacon as they talked about plans for the day. Riley's phone pinged and she looked down at her text. "Hey, have you read the paper yet?"

Matt shook his head. "Not yet. I just brought it inside before I made breakfast. Why?"

"Reagan just texted me and asked. I told her not yet." Another text came through and Riley picked up the paper. "She said it's the best edition yet."

"Read it to me," Matt said as he put the toast onto a plate.

Riley picked up the paper and scanned the headlines. "A cow from Hickman's Farm got loose and was almost hit by a car. I'm starting to think we have a cow problem like some towns have stray cats." Riley moved onto the next headline. "Judge Cooper is retiring, and Kenna has been placed on the ballot this month to replace him. She'll be good at that."

"Is anyone running against her?" Matt asked.

"No. It says Henry Rooney thought about it but decided against it. I'm sure it had to do with the robe hiding his shiny suits," Riley joked of the town's defense attorney slash pick-up artist extraordinaire, and not a in a good way. "Let's see, there's a Memorial Day Parade."

"Yup. Guess who gets to be on duty for that. To serve and protect from errant cows." Matt winked.

"Oh goodness. Nikki Canter of the Belles has been named the Belle of Keeneston and will be riding in the front car. There's something you can do. Find out how she rigged that vote. Oh, this is rich. Andy, Deputy Dinky's son, was voted Beau of Keeneston." Andy was the nicest, kindest man in Keeneston. He just wasn't the most handsome. His freckles, carrot-red hair, short stature, and the fact he had been the high school mascot had put him in Friendsville for any girl that grew up with him.

"Nikki's going to be beyond mad," Matt laughed. "I thought Gabe was the shoo-in."

Riley scanned the article. "He's going to be in Monaco that weekend and nominated Andy to take his place. Everyone agreed that sometimes good guys like Andy shouldn't finish last, and he won by a landslide."

"Poor Nikki won't nab her prince after all," Matt said, trying to sound sad about it. It was hard to, though. Nikki didn't put the B in *bitch*, she was definitely the *itc*h in it.

Riley moved onto the next article "Oh, Addison Rooney is graduating law school at the end of this month. She'll be taking the bar exam in July."

Riley turned the page and scanned the results and odds of the latest bets going on at the Café before reading the next article. "Here's one," Riley said out loud. "Local Girl Receives Marriage Proposal."

Matt turned around from the sink and came to read over her shoulder. "Who's getting married?"

Riley started to read the article her mother had written. "The proposal took place Saturday morning, shortly after the printing of this article." Riley looked up to Matt. "That's strange, right?" When Matt nodded, she went back to reading.

"When interviewed, the bride's mother said she couldn't be more thrilled to welcome such an honorable man to the family. The father of the bride is quoted as saying, *I didn't shoot him, did I?*" Riley snorted. "That sounds like my father."

"The man is said to have proposed by going down on one knee and asking, 'Riley Davies, will you marry me?'" Riley blinked and looked at it again. Nope, she hadn't read it wrong. That was her name. She turned to ask Matt about it and found him on one knee with a ring in between his fingertips.

It was a good thing she gasped in surprise, because after that she forgot how to breathe. Matt looked up at her with all the love he had for her in his eyes. "Riley, will you set off fireworks with me for the rest of our lives?"

Riley nodded her head. "Yes!" she said as Matt slid the diamond ring onto her finger. She remembered to breathe when Matt wrapped his arms around her waist, stood up, and lifted her into the air.

"I'll love you forever," he whispered before she brought her lips to his. The kiss was long and full of the future.

An hour later, Riley was back with her head on Matt's bare chest. She was exhausted, satisfied, and naked. Was there anything better? She laid her hand, now with a sparkling ring on it, on Matt's chest and felt his heart pumping. "How are you still alive? I mean, you obviously told my parents beforehand. I'm just surprised my dad didn't kill you."

She felt Matt chuckle. "He shot your mother's flowers instead. And I had to promise him we wouldn't have any children. I think in his mind that means we're not having sex."

Riley sat straight up in bed, the sheet pooling around her thighs. "You promised we wouldn't have children? But I want kids."

Matt just grinned at her in return. "I do too. I just figured by then, your dad might think twice about killing the father of your children. I took a calculated risk."

Riley swatted his arm as she laughed. "I'm surprised my mom and the entire town isn't here with casseroles and placing bets on when the wedding will be and when I'll be pregnant."

"Ah," Matt said with his grin widening. "That's because your mother and I have a side deal going on. See, I swore to her I *would* have children, but only if she kept everyone away until tonight when I promised we'd go to their farm for an engagement celebration. She's probably standing at the entrance of the neighborhood with your father's rifle right now."

Riley shifted so she was straddling him. She felt Matt's erection growing under her as she ground into him. "Then we better not waste anymore time. After all, we only have six more hours all to ourselves."

"Don't worry, sweetheart, we have the rest of our lives. But I sure would like to start with these six hours." Matt reached up and ran his hands over her breasts, down the curve of her side, and clasped her hips as they started enjoying every single second of the rest of their lives.

Epilogue

"This is the worst day of my life," Cy muttered as Riley slipped her hand through her father's tuxedoed arm.

"Dad!" Riley cried as she shot a glare up at him. "It's my wedding day."

"I know," Cy snarled.

"I thought you liked Matt."

"I do," Cy grudgingly admitted. "Marshall and Will told me today would be hard, but I thought if I didn't think about it, then it just wouldn't happen."

"Think about me getting married?" Riley asked as they waited at the doors to Saint Francis.

Her father turned his head away from her and nodded. "The day I lose my baby girl," he said softly.

"Oh, Daddy. You won't lose me. You'll just gain another son," Riley said softly, tears filling her eyes. She rose up on her toes and placed a kiss on her father's cheek as the doors opened.

Her father kissed her cheek, and the guests all rose to their feet. "I'm glad of that, honey. I'm so proud of you. And of Matt. Marshall told me he's retiring next month and that the board voted last week to hire Matt as the new sheriff. I really am happy for you both. I couldn't have asked for a better daughter or son-in-law. Just don't forget I'm here for you, even if you just need a flat tire changed or help unscrewing a lid."

"I love you, Dad," Riley smiled up to him.

"I love you, too, honey. Now, let's not keep your husband waiting."

On her father's arm, Riley started up the aisle. She smiled at her sister, her maid of honor, and at Sophie, Layne, Sydney, and Piper, her bridesmaids. But it was Matt who held her attention. He stood tall before her, looking devastatingly handsome in his tuxedo. The look in his eyes made her heart sing. Love, as pure and as true as she'd ever known.

Matt shook her father's hand before taking Riley's in his. As one, they turned to Father Ben, who cheerfully performed the service. Before Riley knew it, Matt was dipping her back with her long veil lying on the train of her satin gown as he kissed her. The church erupted in applause, and Father Ben announced them as Matt and Riley Walz.

※

Gemma watched her daughter dancing with her new husband and sighed happily.

"Come on, let's toast the happy couple," Paige said as she handed her a glass of champagne. Gemma took the glass from her sister-in-law and turned to her friends, all waiting for her.

"To Matt, Riley, and grandchildren!" Dani toasted.

Gemma clinked glasses and took a sip of champagne. She had done it. One down, three to go.

"Mrs. Davies. It good to see you again."

All her friends stared as Gemma turned and smiled.

"Officer Tandy. It is a pleasure to see you again, too."

The nice trooper who served as one of Matt's groomsmen smiled at her. "I never did get a chance to thank you for your help locating Matt. I never would have thought to call DEA dispatch without you telling me. And I see you have a new trooper assigned to your town since Matt was appointed sheriff."

Gemma looked to where DeAndre and Aniyah were dancing and smiled at the officer. He was set to start the next week. "Yes, we're very lucky to have those two in Keeneston." Gemma smiled.

"I hope you enjoy the rest of the reception. Save me a dance." He smiled before tipping his head to her friends and heading out onto the dance floor with Abby.

"See you *again*?" Kenna asked.

"Thanks for your *help*?" Morgan asked with a smile on her lips.

"You know," Katelyn tried to say seriously, "for knowing *exactly* where Matt was."

"And for contacting the *DEA*," Tammy said trying not to laugh. "I'm surprised you didn't call them yourself!"

Gemma shrugged. "A mother's gotta do what a mother's gotta do."

"Cheers to that!" Annie and Bridget called as they lifted their glasses once more.

Riley smiled at her husband as they cut the cake. Tonight had been perfect, though she could have gotten married in her jeans at the courthouse for all she cared. The most important part was she was now married to Matt.

"The bride and groom wish to dedicate this song to all the couples here tonight who have inspired them by their love and devotion to each other," the D.J. said as couples made their way to the dance floor. "Umm, also, a pair of women's panties have been found outside, hanging in the lower branch of a tree. If the owner of them would like them back, Miss Lily is holding them for you."

Sophie shook her head as her father, Cade, dipped her mother, Annie, on the dance floor. Married thirty-three years and you couldn't tell them apart from the newlyweds.

Sophie had to go, but before she left she wanted to give the happy couple her best wishes one more time. She loved seeing her cousin so in love. It gave her hope that her happily-ever-after was still out there, and he hadn't disappeared forever in the middle of the night two years before.

She had tried to get back into the dating game after Nash left, not that they were ever in the game together, but she just didn't have the heart for it. Instead, she'd poured herself into her work for a private company with the Department of Defense contract. Which was probably why she was standing alone at the wedding, watching everyone else dance.

Cody Gray, one of the sheriff's deputies had asked her to dance, but it had felt strange. Somehow he seemed to be a kid at twenty-four compared to her almost thirty-one years. Probably because he hadn't seen or done half the stuff she had. Sophie kept the smile on her face as the song finally ended. She made her way through the crowd to where Riley and Matt were laughing as they grabbed another drink.

"Hey, guys. I'm so sorry to cut out before you leave, but I have to catch the red-eye to London." Sophie gave her cousin a hug and kissed her radiant cheek before giving Matt a quick hug as well.

"I understand," Riley said with more truth than Sophie thought she should have. Sophie had been MIA for most of the last two years and felt like a horrible friend. However, with her job it was a must. At least, that's what she told herself. "Let me know when you get back to Keeneston. We'll have a girls' night at the café."

"Sounds like a plan. Congratulations again." Sophie smiled and tried not to run out the door. Her flight to New York City was leaving soon — too soon to even change out of her bridesmaid dress. She hoped the blush strapless dress with a satin sash under her bust and a slit up the flowing material on her leg would get someone to buy her a drink or two on the plane.

Too many hours later to count, Sophie was finally in London. Her flight from New York to Heathrow had been cancelled. After waiting most of the night and a good part of the morning to get on a new flight, her company finally hired a private jet. She normally flew in one of the company's jets, but the president and some of the board were using the fleet to get ready for the big launch.

So finally, at ten o'clock at night, British Summer Time, Sophie was riding the elevator to her suite at The Dorchester in Hyde Park. The chignon her strawberry-blonde hair had been in for the wedding almost twenty-four hours before had long since fallen. The only thing keeping her from looking like a psychotic prom queen was the fact that her hair had natural waves that were quite fashionable. Basically it meant instead of looking homicidal, which was how she felt, she had that freshly-tumbled-by-a-hot-man look. At least, that's how she saw her hair in her dreams.

Sophie reached down and pulled off her heels a second before the elevator stopped at her floor. She hoped no one would see her walking barefoot, but at this point she didn't care. She just wanted a hot shower, some food, and a bed. The order didn't really matter.

Sophie lucked out and didn't pass anyone in the hall. When she had picked up the special package her employer left her at the front desk, a special package containing a never-seen prototype gun she had helped develop, she had been told her bags were already in the room so she wouldn't be disturbed. Perfect, she thought as she unlocked the door. She opened it up to find the living area cast in shadows, but her skin prickled with awareness nonetheless. Always trusting her instinct, she had the gun in her hands and was aiming it at the dark figure sitting in the chair by the time her eyes adjusted to the darkness.

Sophie gasped, and she suddenly felt lightheaded when she could finally make out the man waiting for her.

"Hello, Soph," Nash said as he turned on the light.

The End

Other Books by Kathleen Brooks

The Forever Bluegrass Series is off to a great start and will continue for many more books. I will start a new series later in 2016, so stay connected with me for more information. If you haven't signed up for new release notification, then now is the time to do it:

www.kathleen-brooks.com/new-release-notifications/

If you are new to the writings of Kathleen Brooks, then you will want to try her Bluegrass Series set in the wonderful fictitious town of Keeneston, KY. Here is a list of links to the Bluegrass and Bluegrass Brothers books in order, as well as the separate New York Times Bestselling Women of Power series:

Bluegrass Series
Bluegrass State of Mind
Risky Shot
Dead Heat

Bluegrass Brothers Series
Bluegrass Undercover
Rising Storm
Secret Santa, A Bluegrass Novella
Acquiring Trouble
Relentless Pursuit
Secrets Collide
Final Vow

Bluegrass Singles
All Hung Up
Bluegrass Dawn
The Perfect Gift
The Keeneston Roses

Forever Bluegrass Series
Forever Entangled
Forever Hidden
Forever Betrayed
Forever Driven

Women of Power Series
Chosen for Power
Built for Power
Fashioned for Power
Destined for Power

About the Author

Kathleen Brooks is a New York Times, Wall Street Journal, and USA Today bestselling author. Kathleen's stories are romantic suspense featuring strong female heroines, humor, and happily-ever-afters. Her Bluegrass Series and follow-up Bluegrass Brothers Series feature small town charm with quirky characters that have captured the hearts of readers around the world.

Kathleen is an animal lover who supports rescue organizations and other non-profit organizations such as Friends and Vets Helping Pets whose goals are to protect and save our four-legged family members.

Email Notice of New Releases:
www.kathleen-brooks.com/new-release-notifications

Kathleen's Website:
www.kathleen-brooks.com

Facebook Page:
facebook.com/KathleenBrooksAuthor

Twitter:
twitter.com/BluegrassBrooks

Goodreads:
goodreads.com/author/show/5101707.Kathleen_Brooks

Printed in Great Britain
by Amazon